Anne Glenconner

MURDER ON MUSTIQUE

HODDER

First published in Great Britain in 2020 by Hodder & Stoughton
An Hachette UK company

This paperback edition published in 2021

3

A CIP catalogue record for this title is available from the British Library

B format ISBN 978 1 529 33638 2
eBook ISBN 978 1 529 33636 8

Typeset in Celeste by Palimpsest Book Production Ltd, Falkirk, Stirlingshire

Printed and bound in Great Britain by Clays Ltd, Elcograf S.p.A.

Hodder & Stoughton policy is to use papers that are natural, renewable
and recyclable products and made from wood grown in sustainable forests.
The logging and manufacturing processes are expected to conform
to the environmental regulations of the country of origin.

Hodder & Stoughton Ltd
Carmelite House
50 Victoria Embankment
London EC4Y 0DZ

www.hodder.co.uk

For Colin who made Mustique a household name.

'We must go on, because we can't turn back.'

Robert Louis Stevenson, *Treasure Island*

PART ONE

Tropical Weather Outlook

National Hurricane Center, Miami FL

Friday, 13 September 2002

For the North Atlantic and Caribbean Sea

The National Hurricane Center is issuing advisories on Tropical Storm Cristobal, located one hundred miles east of the South Carolina coast.

Cyclone tracking south-east, current risk rating: mild

Friday, 13th September 2002

IT'S 5A.M. WHEN Amanda Fortini strolls through the palm trees in a red bikini to Britannia Bay. She's barefoot, still slightly drunk after last night's party. Her skin is tanned from diving on the island's coral reef, and lazing by friends' swimming pools, her blond hair two shades lighter than when she arrived in Mustique six weeks ago. She pauses for a moment, inhaling the island's smell of wild vines, hibiscus flowers and adventure. The scent lifts her spirits higher as she follows the track through shoulder-high ferns. She's twenty-three years old and feels in charge of her life for the first time ever. She has made mistakes and picked the wrong men, even though her life as a New York socialite has introduced her to many eligible bachelors – but no more. Certainty fills her mind as the ocean comes into view, a glitter of turquoise filling the horizon.

The young woman smiles as she surveys the beach, its pink-tinged sand unfolding in a wide crescent. The heat is increasing already, even though she's on the western side of the island, the newly risen sun warming her back. It's still so early there's no one in sight. The ocean beckons her closer, tempting her to sprint into the waves like an over-excited child. She can do just as she likes here. No journalists are hiding among the trees, waiting to ambush her like they do in Manhattan, making her permanently self-conscious. Celebrity is the price she pays for belonging to a wealthy family, but its demands are constant. Every detail of her life is pored over on the pages of the glossy magazines. Mustique is the one place she can relax, without witnesses. That heady sense of freedom makes her spin in a pirouette, taking in the jungle's depths, a pristine white villa on the hilltop, and the sun dropping coins of light onto the water's surface. The Caribbean is as calm as a basin of mercury, waiting to welcome her.

Amanda walks into the sea, slowly at first, letting it erase last night's heat from her skin, when she danced by a fire on the beach. A huge yacht hovers on the horizon ahead, its decks glinting in the sunlight. She allows the next tall wave to lift her off her feet. Her muscles feel loose and relaxed as she sets out from shore, arms and legs cutting through the water in a rapid crawl.

She turns only once to catch her breath. Mustique looks like an advert for tropical holidays as she treads water: its hills rise above her, circled by acres of tall trees and deserted beaches. Amanda floats on her back, content to drift for a while, turning her face to the sun.

A faint noise starts up while she admires the island's lush profile. She can hear the ugly mechanical whirr of a speed-boat, growing louder all the time. It could be a local fisherman or the yacht's owner, but why is it going so fast? Everyone knows that there are swimmers in the water all day long. When she spins round, a motorboat is racing straight towards her. Instinct makes her dive below the water's surface, until her lungs burn. The boat's propeller misses her face by inches. Didn't the driver see her waving frantically to make it change course? The boat spins in a tight circle, panic flooding her system as she dives again. When it speeds towards her for a third time her reactions are too slow.

The boat's prow tosses her into the air like a rag doll, until she plummets back down into the water. Faces of people she loves flicker past her eyes: her mother, her best friends. Amanda is barely conscious when she surfaces, the waves' tumult ringing in her ears. Her gaze lands on the island again, like a camera lens, taking a last shot of paradise.

1

Saturday, 14th September 2002

MY HANDS HOVER over a cardboard box with the words 'Princess Margaret' scrawled on its lid. I'm at home in my Norfolk farmhouse this morning, completing a task I've delayed for months. I already know what the box contains: every present the princess gave me, during my four decades as her lady-in-waiting. I've let it stand in my attic since her funeral seven months ago.

Princess Margaret's letters lie in neat bundles, bearing my full title, Lady Blake, in her flamboyant handwriting. The sight of them brings a lump to my throat. She always wrote to me if we were parted by illness, or family duties, but I can't bear to reread them yet. I only need to choose an item for my goddaughter Lily Calder's twenty-first birthday, because the glamorous world the princess occupied has always fascinated her. The sight of so many presents makes time slip backwards. Delicate white china eggcups traced with gold, a turquoise silk scarf and a soap dish carved from ebony. The princess loved to give items with a practical value, taking great care selecting each one. They trigger memories of royal tours and the glitter of flashbulbs that surrounded her, flattering at first, then cruel, in the months before her death. I pick up the silk scarf to admire it again. It's the first present the princess gave me after Jasper bought Mustique on a whim in 1955, long before the island had electricity or running water. It will make an ideal present for Lily, especially when she hears about its origin. I know the princess wouldn't object to it being passed on; she always loved possessions being put to good use.

It's a relief when the telephone rings at 9.30a.m., before the past can swallow me whole. I feel certain it will be my husband, offloading his worries, but the voice at the end of the line belongs to my goddaughter. I've looked after Lily for the past sixteen years, ever since her mother died. She lives in our villa on Mustique, but I wasn't expecting her to call home; the island is five hours behind the UK, so she must have risen before dawn. Her voice sounds breathless, yet she doesn't explain what's wrong. I listen to her describe how she's been spending her time, running the conservation project her mother started so many years ago, to save the reef that protects the island. She's worked like a trooper on it every summer since she hit her teens, and full-time since completing her marine biology degree in July. Volunteers have been helping her replant live coral onto areas bleached white by pollutants and the sea's rising temperature. Anyone with a less well-tuned ear would miss the anxiety in her voice.

'There's nothing else to report, Vee. I just wanted to touch base.'

'You're up terribly early, darling. Is everything okay?'

She hesitates for a beat too long. 'Fine. I'm looking forward to seeing you, that's all. You and Jasper will be here for my birthday, won't you?'

'We wouldn't miss it for the world. I'm flying over next weekend, so we'll have a week to decide what you'd like to do, and Jasper's promised to join us.' I hear her take a long breath, like she's trying not to cry. 'Something's wrong, isn't it?'

I wait for her reply; silence is always the best way to break down Lily's reticence. The girl has a sunny disposition, but the anniversary of her mother's death is looming, which always knocks her off balance.

'Amanda was meant to come over last night, but she never arrived.'

'Maybe she forgot. Why not pop round later today?'

'It's been a strange week. I heard footsteps on my way home from Basil's Bar, a few nights ago. I think someone followed me.'

'Are you sure? It could have been someone staggering back to their villa after too many cocktails.'

'You may be right,' she says, her voice steadying. 'Let me know when you're arriving, once you have details. I'll collect you.'

'Spend the day with friends, Lily. I hate the idea of you alone in that great big house.'

'I'm okay, honestly. There's plenty of work to do on my boat.'

'You're allowed to relax occasionally, darling. I shall distract you with picnics and gossip, the minute I touch down.'

She gives a quiet laugh. 'That's what I need, I've been missing you.'

'Me too, but we'll be together soon.'

I end our conversation by telling Lily I love her, then say goodbye. The tension in her voice stays with me after our conversation ends; she never makes a fuss unless there's a genuine emergency. She must have been working too hard if she's worried about being followed, in one of the safest places in the world. The girl is more inclined to fret about the needs of others than her own, which is why I'm planning a huge surprise party to honour her birthday. I want her to know how much she means to Jasper and me, and our grown-up children. Raising her has been a pleasure, yet she never seems fully confident about her place in our family.

My thoughts remain with Lily as I peer into the box again. The next item I select is a rope of citrine beads, which trigger happier memories. Princess Margaret gave them to me because they would look perfect with my favourite dress. I'm about to put the box back in the attic when my phone rings for a second time. I can tell it's my husband from the angry silence at the end of the line. The man's temper is so mercurial he can shift from charm to abject fury in moments.

'Jasper, is that you?'

'Who else would it be?' he snaps.

'A friend perhaps, or one of the children.'

'Oh Vee, for God's sake, everything's falling apart out here. I should ditch the whole project.'

'What do you mean?'

'The bloody architect's an imbecile. The villas are a disaster, and the casuarina trees I wanted saved have all

8

been felled. I might as well throw in the towel.' His voice is rising in pitch, warning me that he's set to explode.

'You'll get things back on track,' I say calmly. 'Listen to me, Jasper, please. I'm flying to Mustique next Saturday, to prepare for Lily's birthday party. Promise me you'll collect the costumes and bring them over in good time. It's not just a family affair; people are flying in from all over the world.'

'It's a fortnight away, for goodness' sake. You've spoken of nothing else for months.'

'Remember it's a surprise. You mustn't breathe a word to anyone, especially Lily.'

'I can keep a secret, Vee, you know that. Oh, I wish you could see the Caribbean, it's crystal clear today, not a cloud in the sky. It's like the days when we slept in a tent on Mustique. Weren't they marvellous?'

'Apart from the wretched mosquitoes.'

Jasper laughs. 'Poor thing, one bite and the whole swarm descended on you.'

'Don't remind me.'

'Phillip's over here, cheering me up. Don't you miss us all?'

'Yes, of course.'

'Do you remember how it began, on Mustique? We fished for lobsters in the lagoon with our bare hands, then basked in the sun all day. It was my idea of paradise.'

The stress in Jasper's voice has been replaced by yearning, his gentle side coming to the fore. My husband has been in St Lucia for the past fortnight, overseeing his latest project: creating a beachside community of villas to rival the cachet of Mustique. I won't let myself ask how much it's costing, because it's already consumed a huge amount of his fortune. I've spent my life observing his mood swings, delighting in the highs and weathering the lows. It's better to forget the money that flows so easily through his fingers and concentrate on the future.

When I put down the phone the apple trees outside my window are shedding their leaves. It's the start of autumn's slow decline, my least favourite time of the year, because it reminds me that I'm seventy years old. But my parents were inspired by a particularly stalwart heroine in a novel by H.G. Wells, choosing to give me her middle name, Veronica. I always try to follow her example. Instinct tells me to change my plans and fly to Mustique this afternoon, to be with Lily. I shall book my ticket and go, without delay.

2

DS Solomon Nile is in his office, wondering how to fill his day. He's only been in post three months, his role as Mustique's only fully trained police officer resting uneasily on his shoulders. He flew home from the UK in June, and summer has passed without a single incident, giving him no excuse to request a deputy to safeguard the island's territory. The police chief on St Vincent would laugh out loud if he claimed that Mustique needed another officer. The island of his birth is just three miles long, by one and a half miles wide, with no record of crime. Any wrong-doing would result in a spell in St Vincent's jail, twenty-five miles away, and permanent exclusion from the privately owned island.

Nile needs to impress his senior officers during his probation period; his father is sick, and at thirty, he's the oldest of two sons. A large part of his wage is spent on the old man's medicines. This police job isn't the one he dreamed of, but loyalty, and a need to make decisions about his future, made him accept it. He's helped his father raise his younger brother Lyron, ever since his mother died when he was seven years old. The job gives him breathing space, even though his workspace is only large enough to accommodate a battered desk and two plastic chairs, the air-conditioning unit grinding noisily all day long, but failing to lower the temperature. The starched white shirt and black trousers of his uniform may look smart, but they're not fit for purpose when the temperature outside is touching eighty degrees.

The detective glances through the half-open door at his colleagues playing cards, Winston and Charlie Layton. The brothers are a decade older than him, out of shape from sitting down ninety per cent of the time, the word 'security' emblazoned on their yellow T-shirts. Nile wouldn't trust either man in a crisis.

Nile does a double take when the phone on his desk rings for the first time in weeks. He listens to Lily Calder in silence, her voice low and compelling, already on his feet by the time she says that someone is missing. Her friend Amanda Fortini was meant to visit her last night, but she never arrived, and she's not answering her phone. The young woman should be easy to trace; only a few dozen villa owners have remained on the island at the end of the season. The majority have flown home to avoid the tropical storm that's making slow but inexorable progress across the Atlantic, their time on Mustique just a temporary break from reality.

The Layton brothers are too immersed in their poker game to say goodbye when Nile takes his leave. He glances back at the police building and feels another stab of disappointment. Nile won a place to study history at Oxford University at eighteen, certain that the world was his oyster, but his view has changed since he returned home. His office has badly fitted windows, two makeshift holding cells built from breeze blocks, and a corrugated-iron roof that's sure to leak when autumn's tropical rainstorms arrive. He plans to ask the police chief on St Vincent to modernise the place once he completes his probation in six months' time.

The detective's mood improves as he mounts the off-road dune buggy that comes with his role. It's the quickest way to cover the island's mixed terrain and the best perk of his job, even though it takes three attempts to start the motor. He could walk to the Fortinis' villa, but the trade winds have stopped blowing, breathless heat surrounding him as the buggy sets off. The police station lies in a section of the island that few holidaymakers visit. Most simply check into their villas and remain there, only emerging for cocktails at Basil's Bar, Firefly or the Cotton House, before jetting home.

Nile scans the dense thickets that lie beyond the stone-paved path. The island has changed a great deal since his childhood, but the developers have retained the illusion of a tropical jungle, even though almost a hundred villas lie hidden among the trees. When he was a boy, turtles still crawled onto the beaches to lay their eggs, and red-footed tortoises roamed the jungles. The island's wildlife still includes plenty of birds. A green-tailed parakeet flits overhead as he passes Britannia Bay, where a few holidaymakers are taking a dip, their beach towels the only spots of colour on the pale sand.

The detective's curiosity rises as he parks his buggy outside the Fortinis' holiday home. It looks more like a fairy-tale palace than a villa, with huge terraces built into the side of the hill. It's one of the most impressive properties on Mustique, which isn't surprising. The Fortini coffee empire is the largest in the world. Nile has always wondered what the place looks like inside, and today he'll finally see for himself.

One of his neighbours from Lovell is sweeping the porch when Nile climbs the steps to the entrance. He's known the middle-aged woman all his life, yet suddenly she's unwilling to meet his eye. It's not the first time his police badge has drawn a cool reception. When he asks if Amanda Fortini is at home, she tells him to speak to the housekeeper.

'She'll be fussing in the kitchen by now.'

The cleaner shoos him inside with a waft of her hand, returning to her job of sweeping invisible dust from the terrace before he's even said goodbye.

When Nile catches his reflection in a window, he's suddenly reminded of the mismatch between his stature and his self-image. He's six feet five, almost as tall as Usain Bolt, his shoulders thick with muscles earned from swimming all year round, but that's where the similarity ends. Nile has the sprinter's physique, but none of his swagger. His brown eyes are shielded by circular glasses with thin gold frames, which make him look studious rather than athletic. His gaze contains curiosity, but little confidence. The policeman stifles a whistle of admiration when he enters the hallway. It's more like a cathedral than a private home. Marble stairs spiral through the building's core, edged by gold handrails, with light pouring down from windows overhead. When he calls out a greeting to the housekeeper, there's no reply, except his own voice echoing from the walls.

The grandeur of the place increases with each step. The sitting room is bigger than his entire home, and even though the views from his back porch are just as good, they look better framed by perfectly designed arched windows. There's an infinity pool with tiles that mirror the bleached-out sky, strings of fairy lights hung between palm trees, and a confetti of bougainvillea petals on the lawn. He's never been particularly interested in art, but the paintings strewn around the place look valuable. The only style he recognises is a seascape by Mama Toulaine, his father's closest neighbour in Lovell Village. He pauses by her watercolour of Gelliceaux Bay, which catches the sunset perfectly, the sea turning oyster-shell pink.

It's only when he's surveyed the entire ground floor that Nile spots an open doorway, leading down to the cellar. It's the one place in the Fortinis' villa that carries no polish or glitter, with a bare concrete floor and hundreds of wine bottles lying on racks that line the walls. He spots a woman clutching a duster in each hand as he reaches the bottom of the stairs.

The housekeeper attends his father's church. She's around sixty years old, her round form wrapped in a housecoat, busy polishing dust from the bottles. She gives him a far warmer greeting than the cleaner upstairs.

'Solomon Nile,' the woman says, beaming. 'Don't you look fine in that uniform? Come by my house next Sunday afternoon; both my daughters need a decent husband. You can take your pick.'

'I'd love to, Mrs Jackson, but it wouldn't be fair. I'd sooner take a walk on the beach with you, any time.'

'That's a great big lie.' She puts back her head, releasing a loud belly laugh.

Nile falls into the pattern of teasing and laughter that he remembers from childhood. He misses the ease of being universally accepted. He has struggled to fit in since his return after years in the UK.

'I'm looking for Miss Fortini,' he tells the housekeeper. 'Lily Calder's been trying to contact her.'

'Is that right?' The housekeeper's relaxed manner suddenly cools. 'That young lady doesn't listen to anyone. She makes her own rules.'

'How do you mean?'

'Miss Amanda's from a good family, but she plays around. When her parents fly home she's in the bars every night. I can't say a word, even though I was her nanny, once upon a time. If she was my daughter I'd lock her in her room.'

'When's the last time you saw her?'

'Thursday, two p.m. She wanted crayfish and saffron rice for her lunch, with no dessert, and no wine thank you, just ice-cold *eau naturelle*. I'll bet she had a hangover, that's why.'

'Not since then?'

The woman looks thoughtful. 'I made breakfast for her yesterday, but she never appeared, her bed wasn't slept in either. You can draw your own conclusions.'

'Is it okay to search her room?'

'Go ahead, Mr Policeman. It's on the top floor, last door off the landing, on your right.'

Nile thanks her before saying goodbye. Something about the property unsettles him as he climbs the stairs; it feels ghostly, even though the interior sparkles with light. The place is sterile too, every inch of the floor buffed to a high shine. The bedrooms are all decorated with modern furniture, just a few antiques thrown in, to give the place style. His curiosity peaks as he enters Amanda Fortini's room. The bed is freshly made, shrouded by mosquito nets that drop down from the ceiling, to protect her as she sleeps. When he looks inside her wardrobe, there's a pile of flip-flops and espadrilles, flimsy skirts and a dress covered in sequins. Photos pinned to a board on the wall show the young woman circled by friends, her blond hair and smile neon bright. It looks like she's never felt a moment's doubt in her whole life, but Nile knows from experience that appearances can be deceiving. He scans the room again for anything personal. There's a box full of jewellery beside a make-up tray on her dressing table, no sign of a mobile phone.

The detective finds a leaflet on the girl's bedside table. It carries information about Lily Calder's Reef Revival project, which the whole island's talking about. The fishermen have been trying not to damage the coral atoll for years, but it's a losing battle. Soon there will be no breeding grounds for the snapper, lobsters and crayfish that appear on every menu in the Windward Islands. If the coral dies, their livelihoods will perish too. Most of them are grateful that the young woman is putting her energy behind a good cause.

Amanda Fortini's personality is hard to pinpoint when Nile scans her room again. The young American has left her purse behind, full of credit cards, yet it looks like she's getting her hands dirty, helping the conservation project. It's only when he draws back the mosquito net that Nile spots something odd. A large piece of coral rests on her freshly made bed, a foot wide, scattering sand across the sheets. It's pure white, and feels brittle in his hand, delicate tendrils starting to fragment. Its saline smell is completely distinct. Someone has used a knife to carve two crossed arrows into its surface. But why would Amanda Fortini dirty her sheets with sand-encrusted coral? She could have left it on her dressing table instead. Nile is still holding the coral when he checks her en-suite bathroom. There's nothing personal there except a faint whiff of citrus perfume, already beginning to fade.

The detective's head is so crammed with questions as he leaves the villa, he forgets to say goodbye to the cleaner who's still sweeping the terrace, but she notices the slight. A stream of Creole curses follows him as he walks away.

3

I CATCH THE afternoon flight from Gatwick to St Lucia by the skin of my teeth. I know for a fact that my timing will upset Jasper. He would prefer me to visit his building project instead of jumping on the last connection to Mustique, but my first priority is to support Lily, and make sure that my plans for her party are coming together. Once I've reassured myself that details are in place, I can swim and sunbathe to my heart's content, until Jasper arrives to help out.

England looks grey and gloomy as we take off, but I can feel myself relaxing already. Princess Margaret treated every flight she took as a rest from royal duties and being on show, and I intend to do the same. I listen to an audio reading of *Sense and Sensibility* and let myself drift, but after a few hours my concentration is wearing thin, the past crying out for attention.

I remember the lead-up to Lily entering our lives like it was yesterday. Her mother, Dr Emily Calder, was a close friend until sixteen years ago, newly divorced and renting a villa near ours. She was in her thirties, with a doctorate from Harvard and a growing reputation as a ground-breaking marine conservationist. Emily spent each summer on Mustique, working on the reef. Everyone adored her company, because she was fun, charismatic, and clever. I was glad to become godmother to five-year-old Lily. The child was so good-natured, happy to splash around in the shallow end of our pool, while Emily and I chatted, after her long days in the sea. She barely mentioned her divorce, but I still regret missing the danger signs. Emily must have drunk her last sundowner with me, gone back to her villa then walked into the sea while Lily slept, leaving nothing behind to explain her suicide. No trace of her was found, apart from her sarong, folded in a neat pile on Macaroni Beach. I've never been able to make sense of it. Emily was young and beautiful, with many friends to listen to her woes, yet she threw it all away, abandoning Lily to her fate. I can only assume that she had been battling with depression but keeping it secret. If she left a suicide note, it was never found, leaving no words of comfort for her daughter.

Jasper was quick to agree that we should raise Emily's child. The juvenile streak in his personality helps him to enjoy children's company, and our own brood had already flown the nest. They accepted Lily's presence without question, but her childhood was overshadowed by her mother's death, then her father's disinterest. Henry Calder is an oil magnate, who seems to believe that setting up a small trust fund is his only paternal responsibility, rarely bothering to contact his daughter. The girl has sufficient money to live, but she'll never be rich, and she has no one to rely on except myself and Jasper, yet she's an eternal optimist. She's intent on saving the reef, and I have a feeling that nothing will get in her way.

I fall into a fitful sleep, and when I wake up, the captain is announcing that St Lucia is just half an hour away, but our approach could be bumpy, as we pass through turbulence. The plane reels and judders as time rearranges itself. It's just after 5p.m., the island lagging five hours behind the UK.

It crosses my mind to call Jasper, but the flight has sapped my energy. I decide to postpone it until a night's sleep has refreshed me. The small airport is heaving with relatives eager to greet family members from the plane, taxi drivers and porters, offering to carry my bag for a small fee. I'm about to check in for my next flight when I spot someone familiar in the crowd. It's Simon Pakefield, the British locum who stands in for our beloved Dr Bunbury while he visits relatives in the UK. The entire island misses Bunbury while he's away, because he's taken care of our ailments so well for decades. Pakefield doesn't acknowledge my wave even though we've met half a dozen times. The man has an odd manner, pale and poker-faced, with a shock of jet-black hair. It seems odd that his bedside manner is gentle, yet he lacks social graces, always happier to deal with people as patients instead of friends.

Pakefield has receded into the crowd when another voice calls my name. My old friend Phillip Everard rushes towards me, his hand raised in greeting. The Canadian actor must be well into his sixties, but you'd never guess it. His features look much as they did when he starred in half a dozen stylish comedies that took the world by storm in the late eighties. He's the kind of man who draws attention from men and women of all ages, his open bisexuality only adding to his charisma. Phillip is wearing a blue linen shirt that highlights his tan, grey hair cropped close to his skull, his clean-cut features more distinguished than ever.

'You're still so dashing, Phil, the perfect lead man.'

'Not half as gorgeous as you.' He grins before wrapping me in a hug. 'How do you keep your skin so smooth?'

'Lucky genes and Harrods face cream. What on earth are you doing here?'

'Lily told me you were coming, so I delayed my flight home, after helping Jasper deal with his nasty French architect.'

'You absolute sweetheart. Is Jasper okay? I've never heard him so despondent.'

'He needs you to mop his fevered brow and he's inclined to throw tantrums, so it's business as usual.' He looks amused. 'I've spent the afternoon hunting for a birthday present for Lily.'

'What did you get?'

'Freshwater pearl earrings and a matching bracelet. Is that too boring?'

'She'll love them.'

'Thank God you're coming straight to Mustique, not going to that hell hole Jasper's created.' Phillip's voice carries a soft French lilt, from his childhood in Quebec.

'Don't tell me, darling. I need vodka in my system first.'

'Drinks must wait. There are delays and we are on the last flight out; they're shutting the airport after we take off. There's a tropical storm heading this way, apparently. God knows why they're so worried, the damn thing's nowhere near us.'

Phillip leads me through the airport at a rapid march, his hand grasping mine. We've been friends for thirty years, ever since he bought one of Mustique's smallest villas, despite having enough Hollywood dollars to build himself a palace. He wanted a bolthole, to escape the paparazzi, but his modesty has never allowed him to decorate it in grand style. Phillip was the life and soul of every party and carnival, but recently his pace has slowed. I can't remember the last time he worked. When I watch him arranging our transfer, all business-like and serious, I can picture him playing a high-minded human rights lawyer, or an American president with old-school values. There's a sudden change in his mood as we approach the minute plane that's waiting on the runway.

'Did I tell you Jose's been acting strangely? He's looking after our gardens fine, but he's been following me around, morning, noon and night.'

'That doesn't sound good.'

'What should we do?'

'I'll talk to him, if you like.'

'Let's not terrify the poor boy, I just want him to stop behaving like my bodyguard.'

Jose Gomez has worked for Phillip and me for the past five years, dividing his time between our two gardens. The young man is blessed with green fingers, but mute since birth. I hear him whistling as he tends the lawn sometimes, but he's never uttered a word. Phillip seems relieved to get the matter off his chest, grabbing my hand again as the island hopper prepares for take-off.

23

'I've been longing to tell Lily about the party, but keeping my lips sealed. She's fascinated by the old days, isn't she? Mustique's gatherings are legendary in her eyes.'

'This one needs to trump them all; she deserves an ego boost, and it's only two weeks away. Jasper and I have got designers on St Lucia making dozens of gorgeous costumes for our guests, including you.'

'Is there a theme?'

'We're calling it the moon ball, because it should be full that night, and I'm praying for clear skies. I want the island to shine in Lily's honour.'

'No one takes party planning as seriously as you and Jasper. I remember you making trips to Kerala to buy costumes and props for a party years ago. You even hired a yacht so guests could dress at sea, then arrive on the beach looking perfect. It took weeks to build that palace on the lawn, didn't it?'

'Lily's tastes are simpler than ours, but I don't care. Everyone's coming: royalty, supermodels, rock stars, and you, of course.' I smile at him again.

'It's never too late to marry me.'

'Jasper would never give me a divorce, and you'd leave me for the first pretty boy or girl who crossed your path.'

Dr Pakefield is sitting three seats ahead while Phillip teases me. The medic is gazing out of the window, lost in thought, while the plane's engines roar. Taking off in the ten-seater aircraft is like being catapulted into the sky, but Mustique is waiting for me at the end of our journey, which makes any discomfort bearable. Dusk is already falling and the captain must be eager to reach the island, because landing in darkness is forbidden. The artificial lights of St Lucia fade as we head south, miles of ocean rippling below us. I don't know why a chill travels across my shoulders when the island drifts into sight; it's still so thick with trees and undergrowth it looks like an emerald, afloat on a skein of dark blue velvet. The island's original wildness still lingers in my memory, when feral cows and goats ran through the jungle, the air teeming with mosquitoes. Our plane skims over Mustique's highest peak, then Phillip's hand grips mine again as we drop like a stone to the tiny runway.

4

DARKNESS FALLS MINUTES after we touch down. I can just make out the plain that lies at Mustique's heart, once part of an old cotton plantation, still rimmed by two-hundred-year-old palms. My heart lifts once we step off the plane, to be greeted by warm air and the scent of orchids. Staff are waiting outside the small terminus to welcome us, and the building speaks volumes about the island's relaxed atmosphere. Mustique's glamorous guests arrive and leave every day in high season, yet the building remains simple. Palm leaves cover its peaked roof, the words 'arrivals' and 'departures' daubed on hand-painted signs above two small doorways. The airport manager gives me a bow, not bothering to check my passport, as if I still owned the island. He enquires after Lord Blake with great courtesy and even though I love the kindness I'm shown on Mustique, it takes so long to exchange pleasantries I'm relieved to get outside.

My butler has delivered my dune buggy to the car park, which has space for only a few cars to accommodate the island's tiny fleet of vehicles. I enjoy walking everywhere in Mustique under normal circumstances, but tonight I'm glad of the transport when Phillip and I set off for his villa, with my suitcase on the back seat. The island's smells fill my lungs as we drive: the sweetness of decaying leaves, sea salt, and paprika drifting from someone's kitchens. I can feel my shoulders relaxing already, but Mustique has changed in the six months since my last visit. The paths through the casuarinas and lush undergrowth have been paved, and soon the whole island will be criss-crossed with formal walkways, instead of the sandy tracks I love. Many of my friends' holiday homes stand empty. There are no lights on in Mick Jagger's property, so there will be less excitement on the island, and none of the impromptu cricket matches he organises. David Bowie's house lies in darkness too, so trips to Basil's Bar will be less fun than usual, until both men fly in for Lily's party.

Phillip's villa lies due west from mine, overlooking Plantain Bay. It's one of the few homes on Mustique with no fences protecting it from the winds that thrash the island in hurricane season. It's named after the jacaranda trees that surround it, still heavy with purple blossoms. Jacaranda is just a simple cottage, clad in bleached timber, and topped with a slate roof. It speaks volumes about Phillip that he adores the simplicity of the place, and employs only two staff – an elderly maid, and Jose to tend his garden. He invites me inside for a drink, but I'm keen to see Lily, so I invite him over for a late lunch tomorrow instead. He promises to bring fresh papayas from his tree, before saying good night.

I slow down to listen to the peace on the last stage of my journey through thick stands of trees. There's no evidence of human activity, just the mosquitoes the island is named after, and cicadas chirruping like a round of applause. It's the sound I imagine when I'm in England, that quiet hum lulling me to sleep. Then I hear a new noise: footsteps, slow and regular on the path behind me, but when I look back, all I can see is a dark mass of palms, and the stars gleaming overhead. The footsteps pause for a moment, then draw closer.

'Come and join me, whoever you are,' I call out.

Simon Pakefield blunders out from the undergrowth. I can read his discomfort from twenty yards, shoulders hunched like a schoolboy awaiting punishment.

'How are you, Simon? I tried to catch your eye on the plane, to say hello, but you seemed in your own world.'

'Sorry about that, Lady Vee.' The man gives an awkward smile. 'I didn't see you.'

'Never mind, let me give you a lift home.'

The doctor appears to relax as he steps into the buggy. We're heading in the same direction, because he always stays in Dr Bunbury's villa while he's away. Pakefield talks about his plans to continue our doctor's work during his two months on the island, raising funds for new X-ray equipment, and to upgrade the medical centre's small ward with new beds and furniture.

'That sounds marvellous, I'll organise a fundraiser. Is your wife over with you this time?'

'Chloe stayed with the children; we didn't want to uproot them again.'

'That's a pity. You must come to dinner soon; it doesn't pay to spend too much time alone.'

'That's very kind, but my patients keep me busy. I'm fine, honestly.'

'Let me arrange a date anyway, we'd love to see you.'

When we come to a fork in the path, the doctor says good night and heads back to his borrowed villa, leaving me full of sympathy. Simon Pakefield relies on his wife's social confidence; he'll need extra support during his stay, to avoid isolation. The encounter has reassured me that Lily probably imagined being followed home this week. I'm still surprised she chose to return to Mustique, after returning from California this summer. The island must hold many painful memories, yet she's determined to use the boat her mother left behind for her conservation work, and build up the Reef Revival charity. I would never dream of wrenching her away but sometimes wish she could forget the past.

My heart lifts when I catch sight of Eden House, through the dense tangle of branches. Jasper christened our villa before the first brick was laid, and it felt like heaven to live in luxury, after the tents we camped in at first. The three-storey house looks striking from a distance, particularly at night, dozens of tall windows glittering in its facade. It was designed by Oliver Messel, an architect famed for his sense of drama and gingerbread style. The pure white building has his trademark blend of modern and classical features, ornate woodwork adorning the roof, and the delicate balconies on the top floor. It looks romantic enough to be a film set for Romeo and Juliet, the marble terrace on the ground floor sweeping out to greet me. The gardens look glorious too, with outdoor lights glancing across the pool that lies on the far side of the lawn, our wooden pool house freshly painted.

I call out Lily's name once I'm inside, but no one replies, which isn't surprising. My staff have left for the day and my flight here was delayed. I feel an odd sense of discomfort, even though the quiet elegance of the place is always welcoming. Maybe it's because I've rarely been alone in the house Jasper and I have adored for so many years. There's no reason to be on edge apart from my long journey. I push the feeling aside, then walk through the ground floor. I chose the décor myself, with a little help from my friend Nicky Haslam, whose taste is impeccable. The rooms have tall ceilings, and white walls, celebrating the light that floods inside every day. The corners of each room are filled with pieces I've collected on my travels with Jasper and Princess Margaret, in India and the Caribbean. Tall mirrors hang from the walls, their silver frames engraved with mythical figures by skilled craftsmen in Jaipur a hundred years ago. My spirits are reviving by the time I go upstairs. My wardrobe contains the clothes I left here last time, and our collection of paintings still gives me pleasure. The vivid landscape I bought from a local artist fizzes with colour above the bed, and the delicate vase I found in Japan remains on the dressing table, waiting to be filled with flowers.

I could walk down to Britannia Bay, to look for Lily in Basil's Bar, but combing my hair and putting on a fresh dress feels like too much effort. I take my time walking down the corridor, picking up objects I haven't seen for months. When I look through the open doorway Lily's room is less chaotic than usual. An old pair of sandals lie on the floor with some crumpled beach towels, but everything else looks tidy. She hasn't changed the décor since she was a child, evidence of her passion for the oceans visible in every corner. A great white shark launches itself at me from the poster above her bed, and a chart showing different species of tropical fish is pinned to the wall, beside an underwater photo of a flourishing bed of coral.

Once I'm downstairs I switch off the swimming pool lights, then relax in a deckchair. Starlight is always the best form of illumination; the universe glitters overhead, a million stars like chips of diamante scattered across a giant blackboard, the moon drawing a path across the ocean's surface. The only sounds are old-fashioned calypso music drifting from someone's villa, faint laughter, and snakebirds singing their night-time chorus. It feels wonderful to bask in tropical air instead of Norfolk's autumn cold. My memories of this place are already helping me unwind. Princess Margaret and I often sat here, watching the sunset with our eyes trained on the horizon, hoping to see the fabled green flash in the sea that's meant to appear when the sun vanishes. We never did witness it, but had plenty of fun chatting as we kept watch.

When I hear footsteps on the path, I know immediately that something's wrong. They're tapping out a frantic rhythm. My goddaughter is running at full pelt until she comes to a halt at my feet, panting for breath, yet she still looks like a starlet. She's blossomed into a genuine beauty, resembling a taller version of Audrey Hepburn in her white capri pants and black sleeveless top. Her black hair is cropped close to her skull, ocean-blue eyes wide with shock. Lily's expression changes to delight in a heartbeat. When I rise to my feet she hugs me close, then pulls back to inspect me, her hands resting on my shoulders.

'I'm so glad you're here.'

'Are you all right, darling?' I ask. 'Why were you running, just now?'

'I got spooked coming home. Someone followed me again.'

Lily looks so vulnerable I have to remind myself that she's a fully grown adult. She lived in America for three years and thrived there, on her own.

'I wish you'd let me know your arrival time, I'd have waited at the airport. I hope you didn't rush here because of me.'

'Not at all, but I've been longing to see you, and the island.'

'Get a mobile phone, please. It would make life so much easier.'

'I can't stand those shrill ringtones. Were you at Basil's just now?'

'I went to the Cotton House, looking for Amanda, but no one's seen her.' That note of anxiety is back in her voice, impossible to miss.

'Have you seen each other much since she arrived?'

Lily nods vigorously. 'She's her usual self – full of wild energy, the most talkative girl I know.'

'Have you spoken to security?'

'When I went there at lunchtime the building was empty. Did you know there's only one policeman patrolling the whole island?'

'That's because no one ever commits crimes here. Jasper and I know him well, his name's Solomon Nile. He's an Oxford graduate, probably the cleverest man on Mustique.'

'He sounded too laidback for my liking on the phone. Amanda's never let me down before; she'd say if she'd made other plans. We've been together almost every day this summer.' Lily drops her gaze. 'Someone scrawled an ugly message on the side of my boat a few days ago written in Creole. It said *Leave Mustique or die like the coral.*'

'Why on earth didn't you say? I'd have flown here sooner.'

'There was no point in worrying you. The Layton brothers saw the damage before I washed off the paint, but they didn't seem bothered.'

'Solomon's different, he'll find where Amanda's hiding in no time.'

'Let's hope so.' The girl flops into the deckchair next to mine, then kicks off her beach shoes, just like she did as a child.

'Phillip tells me Jose's been acting strangely. Is that true?'

Lily looks surprised. 'He seems fine to me, in fact he's amazing. He spends most of his spare time helping me on the boat.'

'Take care, darling. He's always had a crush on you.'

She looks amused. 'Rubbish, Vee. He's just like you and me, except he can't speak. That's the only difference.'

'I'm concerned for you, that's all.'

'Tell me how you've been,' she says, squeezing my hand. 'Give me all the news about everyone back home. I've been missing the gang like crazy.'

Lily's face fills with delight, when I tell her about the family. She'll be thrilled when they all fly in for her party. Lily is watching me, thoughtful as ever.

'I probably overreacted to those noises in the jungle. I've been a bit strung out.'

'It's a tough time of year for you, isn't it?'

'I haven't been thinking about the anniversary of Mum's death that much, but I'm having trouble with my grant application. If the Oceanographic Society don't renew our funds, the charity will have to rely on private sponsorship.'

'Jasper and I can increase our donation.'

'You're already far too generous.' She stares out at the sea. 'It may sound weird but I feel closer to Mum now I'm spending more time on her boat, completing her project. Do you think she'd have been pleased?'

'Emily was passionate about the island's marine life, like you, but she was a generous spirit. She'd be happy whatever path you choose, if you enjoy it.'

'Why do I miss her sometimes, even though I barely remember her?'

'It's only natural.'

'You've been my real mother, Vee, and Jasper's great too. He may be a crazy genius, but he's always kind.'

'You're easy to love, Lily.'

She leans closer, inspecting my face. 'You were so sad after Princess Margaret died. Are you feeling better?'

'I think about her every day, but that's to be expected. We were together longer than most marriages.'

We fall into silence and let the insects' hum take over. We're gazing in the same direction, at starlight glinting on the ocean's surface. I argued with Jasper for months about where to build our villa. I wanted to live on the island's sheltered side, overlooking the Caribbean, but he insisted we face the wild Atlantic. Jasper wanted to watch every storm gathering on the horizon, before it arrived. I hate to admit that he was right. The ocean's drama still fascinates me. I've spent countless nights on the terrace, watching the sky darken over the shore below our villa, but the unexpected absence of Lily's friend makes me concerned. There may be a new threat here that's unforeseen, capable of arriving from any direction.

I push the thought from my mind and concentrate on Lily instead, teasing her about finding a boyfriend. Her conversational style is just like her mother's, funny and animated. She's completely unaware of her beauty, which adds to her charm. When I check my watch again, two hours have passed in the blink of an eye, and my journey is catching up with me. It's tempting to spend more time chatting, but we'll have the next month to enjoy each other's company. I remind Lily to lock the front door when she comes up, before saying good night. I'm exhausted when I reach my bedroom, but glad that Mustique has retained its old magic.

I'm about to get into bed when I take a final look outside, tempted by the moonlight pouring through a gap in the curtains. The night sky is so clear I can see the impact craters on the moon's face far clearer than in the UK, and the white line it's drawn across the ocean. The scene is perfectly tranquil until I catch sight of movement in my garden. It looks like plants swaying in the breeze, but someone is on my lawn, half-hidden by trees, his pace slow and predatory. I hold my breath until the figure emerges. It's Jose Gomez, my young gardener. He stands on the path for a moment, his face silvered by the moon, then looks up at my window. He's gone in a blink and I can no longer see where he's hiding. Why would a staff member hang around our villa late at night, hours after his duties are finished?

5

Sunday, 15th September 2002

NILE WAKES FROM a nightmare at dawn. He lives through that same Oxford crime scene almost every night, even though his DCI forced him to see a counsellor for a few weeks. He considered resigning from the force, but his new job should help him decide whether to stay in the profession or walk away.

It still feels odd to be back in the cabin where he grew up. It stands in the middle of Lovell Village, a community of small wooden homes scattered across the hillside. The first thing he sees this morning is the coral from Amanda Fortini's room. It's on his windowsill, tainting the air with its odour of seaweed. It's as brittle as dried bone, yet it once pulsed with life, each frond a separate organism. He studies its structure carefully, running a fingertip across the carved arrows, then sets it back on the windowsill. His eyes scan the small room before he grabs a towel from his chair. It was his childhood sanctuary; he spent countless hours here, studying for exams, and dreaming about his future. The desk his father built from old banana crates is still wedged between the door and his narrow bed, suitable for a twelve-year-old, but not a fully grown man. There's nowhere to hang his clothes except a hook behind the door. It's a far cry from the luxurious flat he shared with two other cops in the centre of Oxford, yet part of him is glad to be home. The city's polluted air left a sour taste on his tongue, and night-time brought the sound of juggernauts on the ring road, instead of the sea's slow heartbeat, lulling him to sleep. Nile's reduced circumstances strike him as fitting: no one punished him for his mistake in the UK, but it's a piece of natural justice.

Nile is heading for the bathroom when someone gives a low moan. He steps outside, still in his boxer shorts, to find Lyron stretched out in the porch, mumbling in his sleep. It's not the first time his twenty-three-year-old brother has fallen asleep there after partying all night. Nile marches back indoors for a jug of water, topped up with ice from the fridge. He gets satisfaction from pouring the freezing liquid over Lyron's head, making him sit bolt upright, shouting curses.

'Shut it, Ly. You'll wake the neighbourhood.'

'You bastard.'

'Keep it down, for God's sake.'

Nile lounges against the wall, watching his brother scramble to his feet, still rubbing water from his eyes. There's only a seven-year gap between them, but Lyron still behaves like a child. Nile accepts that his brother got the looks, while he got the brawn. Lyron is a few inches shorter, with a basketball player's lean physique and high cheekbones. But now isn't the best time to offer compliments, while he's spitting out curses.

'I'll punch you senseless one of these days.'

'You never managed it before.' Nile gives an amiable smile.

'I will now, you vicious idiot.'

'Dad's sick, remember? He doesn't need you crawling home drunk every night.'

'Don't give me orders, Sol. You're not in charge.'

'Listen to me, for once in your life. You spend your wages on booze and girls and mine go on Dad's medicine. When are you going to contribute?'

Lyron looks contrite, his anger ebbing away. 'How much does he need?'

'Six hundred a month.'

'Each?'

Nile nods at his brother. 'Food costs money too, and the house needs work.'

'That's most of my wage.'

'Mine too. If there's another way, let me know.'

The heat fades from Lyron's gaze when he grabs Nile's towel and rubs his face and hair dry before tossing it aside. The two men sit next to each other on the front step, without saying a word. When Nile glances at his brother's profile, he looks older than before, his mocking smile absent for once. He remembers his brother's tears at the airport when he flew to the UK, leaving the eleven-year-old kid behind. It hurts that they're no longer close, but the gap seems too wide to fill. He'd like to resume their old friendship, yet they're talking different languages.

'Why are you wasting time, Ly? You're too smart for bar work. I thought you wanted to be a pilot.'

'No one's paying my fees. In case you didn't notice, there

are no good jobs here. Making cocktails is my best bet; at least I get plenty of tips.'

'Move to St Vincent and go to night school. One of us needs to earn decent money.'

'I'm the stupid one, remember? You're the one with all the certificates.'

'What are you talking about? You're just as bright, but that lazy brain never gets used.' Nile gives his brother's shoulder a light punch. 'It's your turn to take Papa to church, but use the shower first, you stink of bourbon and cheap fags.'

Lyron ignores his advice. 'Someone told me a woman's missing. Is that right?'

'Yes. Amanda Fortini is missing; she was supposed to meet a friend on Friday evening and didn't show.'

'What happened to her?'

'I'll find out today, with luck.'

'She can't be hurt, can she? Nothing bad ever happens here.'

Nile is surprised by the tension on his brother's face. He's never shown much interest in the villa owners until now, but the Fortini girl must have visited Basil's often during the summer. Lyron will have mixed cocktails for her most nights, but he rises to his feet suddenly and goes indoors, before Nile can ask questions about the missing woman.

He's about to follow suit when someone beckons from a neighbouring cabin. Mama Toulaine's home is different from the rest of Lovell Village; it's easy to tell she's an artist from the pink geraniums fizzing with colour on her small terrace, the house's exterior painted every shade of the rainbow. Even though she's a friend of his father, he's never learned her first name. Children in Lovell are expected to call anyone from the older generation Mama and Papa, as a mark of respect. Nile can't guess why Toulaine is calling him over, but he raises his hand in reply, before going indoors. He can't exactly pay her a visit dressed in midnight-blue boxer shorts.

Nile washes quickly and puts on his uniform, even though it's only 7a.m. He doesn't have to report for duty until eight, but he can't forget Mrs Fortini's voice on the phone, when he called her yesterday, begging him to find her daughter. Mama Toulaine is watering her plants when he arrives at her cabin. She's a big woman, dressed in a scarlet kaftan, her face framed by a cloud of grey curls, still beautiful despite her years. Mama's from St Lucia originally, and instructs him in French-Creole to take a seat while she fetches coffee. Something about her manner makes it impossible to disobey. The woman moves indoors at a regal pace, leaving him to study the objects on her porch. People in Lovell say that Mama Toulaine practises Obeah, a form of voodoo still prevalent in St Lucia. Nile is almost certain that the walking stick propped in the corner is a coco macaque, a magic tool used to perform spells, decorated with paintings of skulls and feathers. Mama's artistic talents are on display wherever he looks. A painting of Britannia Bay is propped against the wall, the sand glittering with sunlight. He's always wanted one for his father, but Mama's artworks have begun selling for thousands, in big American galleries.

He settles on a turquoise deckchair and waits for Mama to return. When she thrusts a cup of thick black liquid into his hand, it's too late to admit that he takes his coffee white these days, instead of Creole style. It's so bitter with chicory, the first sip makes him wince, but Mama is too busy chatting to notice. She tells him about her kids, working over in St Vincent and Grenada, and her latest exhibition, until he's certain that all she wanted was conversation.

'It's good to catch up, Mama, but I should get to work. Thanks for the coffee.'

'Stay a minute.' She motions for him to remain seated. 'Friday, I took my easel over to Britannia Bay, to paint the sea at dawn. The Fortini girl was there.' She takes the picture propped against the wall and hands it to him. 'She looked pretty, I put her in my painting.'

When Nile studies the scene again, there's a small figure, dressed in a scarlet bikini, her hair golden. He spots the huge yacht that's still balanced on the horizon as pink light floods the sky.

'What did she do?'

The old woman's face gathers in a frown. 'She swam towards that boat and I carried on painting. When I looked up again, she'd gone. I thought she'd climbed on board, or swum round to the next bay.'

'She never came back?'

'I was there two hours and the bay stayed empty, apart from a speedboat going by at a crazy speed. I didn't know they could travel that fast.'

'Was it from the yacht?'

'The sun was too bright to tell. It could have been from Basil's, or one of the villas.'

'Thanks for your help.'

41

'One more thing, before you go.' Her voice drops, her expression suddenly fiercer than before. 'I'm glad you're our new lawmaker, you've got a wise head on your shoulders, but you should take care.'

'I'll be fine, Mama, but I have to help everyone, using the same rules.'

The artist rises to her feet suddenly. Nile doesn't know how to react when she places her hand on his forehead, like she's checking his temperature, but he's too polite to pull away. A rush of Creole words spills from her lips, too quiet for him to understand. When she finally drops her hand there's panic in her eyes.

'I tried to read your spirit just now, but I saw Gede instead. He can't decide whether you'll live or die. It doesn't matter if you believe in Obeah or not; the gods won't protect you. Defend yourself until the threat passes. Do you hear me?'

'Yes, Mama.'

She studies his face at length before her calm returns. 'Don't run away just yet, Solomon. Life's too short to hurry. Finish your coffee first.'

Nile braces himself before knocking back the last dregs. He stopped believing in God years ago, but the fear in Toulaine's eyes looked genuine. Somehow he manages to say goodbye, even though it feels like his mouth is full of sand.

6

I WAKE UP smiling despite the late-night visitor to my garden. My long sleep was only disturbed by a mosquito screaming with frustration, unable to bite me through the netting over my bed. The creatures adore my pale British flesh, no matter how much garlic I eat, or poisons I spray on my skin. I'm determined to speak to Jose today, and put a stop to any odd behaviour, provided there's time for a swim first. Age is just a number, but exercise keeps me fit, and a dip in the sea is one of my greatest pleasures.

I put on my bathing costume and a sarong, before grabbing a towel, but something unexpected greets me when I step out into the corridor. A chunk of coral is lying on the floor outside Lily's room; it's white and calcified, slowly turning to powder. Maybe she put it there to remind me why she's so driven to save the reef, but it seems odd that she's carved an ornate pattern of criss-crossed lines into its surface. The sight of it fills me with sadness. Jasper and I used to spend hours in the sea with snorkels and masks, watching octopuses drift over fields of pink coral, hunting for food. Lily's probably diving there already, her room empty when I peer inside.

I'm still clutching the coral when I go downstairs. Our butler is waiting for me in the hall, straight-backed as a sentinel. Wesley Gilbert has been our right-hand man for twenty years, and he's still an imposing figure. I remember how much he impressed me as a young man when I interviewed him for the position. He had been a soldier in the Grenadian army, recently returned to his native island. I knew immediately that he would make a perfect butler. He answered every question with quiet authority, giving me the sense that he held all the power in our conversation, and offering no clues whatsoever about his personal life. It would be his decision whether he chose to work for us or not, no matter how much I begged. He's in his fifties now, average height, with a keen gaze, and handsome West African features, his bald head gleaming in the overhead light. He rules his small team of one gardener and two part-time maids with a rod of iron. His character is as powerful as my husband's, and he's still intensely private; I can tell he's displeased by his refusal to meet my eye. An uncomfortably long time passes before he says a word.

'You're meant to let me know about your arrival a few days in advance, Lady Vee, not just a few hours before you touch down. That way I can ensure we have everything you need. You know that, but you never remember.'

'Sorry, Wesley, I decided to come early. Thanks for leaving me the buggy. How are you, and your family? I haven't seen you for months.'

'Very well, thank you for asking. What can I get you for breakfast?'

'I'm going for a quick swim. Some juice and a piece of toast will be fine when I come back.'

'Juice? Toast?' He rounds on me, his scowl deepening. 'How will you get through the morning on that? Miss Lily had eggs, bacon and fried tomatoes, before going down to her boat.'

'When have I ever eaten a cooked breakfast?'

Wesley tuts at me. 'Swim for as long as you want, Lady Vee. We'll find you something decent, if you'll only give us time.'

The man shoos me outside, where a new maid is busy laying one of the tables with my best cutlery, then placing passion flowers in my favourite vase. I greet her with a smile, but she keeps her eyes downcast, shyness preventing her from replying. My nerves are perfectly steady when I dump the piece of coral in a plant pot on the terrace. I know from experience that Wesley is glad to see me under all that bluster, but he's got a fierce reputation to maintain. He will take forever to deliver my food, then the process of forgiveness can begin. I let him manage the house and my small team of staff with absolute authority and he's never disappointed me. Most of our conversations are a game of brinkmanship, but I'm almost certain that our relationship will soon be cordial again. I have no regrets about hiring such a formidable man to run the place. He's the only person on Mustique apart from myself with enough guts to stand up to Jasper.

A sense of excitement hits me as I trot down the steps to our nearest beach, a hundred metres below Eden House. It's empty, as usual, the pale stretch of sand hemmed in by

palm trees so thickly laced with vines, the light barely penetrates. The water is still today. Tides don't exist on Mustique;
the ocean only advances and retreats by a few inches each
day, like a shy suitor, afraid to embrace the land. My cares
lift from my shoulders as I walk into the sea. It's only a few
degrees colder than blood heat, just chilly enough to make
my skin tingle. I'm swimming away from the shore when
something nudges my ribcage. A green turtle surfaces a few
feet away. It gives me a surprised stare before vanishing
again beneath the turquoise surface. Time slips away as I
float on my back. I taught my children to swim here in the
days when thousands of turtles lived in the local waters. We
spent hours collecting shells and stringing them together
for necklaces.

My muscles relax as the sun penetrates my skin, reviving
my spirits. When I finally swim back to shore I bask for a
while in the warm air. My love of this place hasn't changed
over the years, fortified by memories. It's got a special place
in the Queen's heart too. I still recall her delight when she
swam in Macaroni Bay, safe in the knowledge that no one
would take photographs. She has never had the opportunity
to relax so deeply again, so the island retains a special magic
in her eyes.

I'm still feeling upbeat when I walk home, but there's no
sign of Jose, and it's the wrong time to ask Wesley to fetch
him, because any request would prompt another rebuke. I
use the interval to go indoors and call my husband, but he
still has the power to surprise me. Yesterday's impatience
with my absence has been replaced by despair. When Jasper
hears that I flew to Mustique early, he bursts into tears,

because he will be unable to join me until the storm warning lifts. I feel a sudden pang of guilt. It must be dreadful to be so ruled by your emotions that the slightest knock can send you spinning off course. I listen until his sobbing quiets, then murmur a few words of encouragement, unwilling to say goodbye until I'm sure he's all right again.

I go upstairs to dress, then take a walk across the garden, where Jose's skills are in evidence. He's growing fruit as well as flowers; lime and lemon trees, passion fruit, and avocados almost ready to eat. I tried to grow roses when we first arrived, but it was no use. Only the toughest plants survive in tropical conditions, the bougainvillea showering the lawn with electric pink flowers. When I stand by the fence the Fortinis' villa is camouflaged by tree ferns, but there's no sign of life. The windows are closed, handfuls of leaves floating across the swimming pool, and the reality of Amanda's absence suddenly hits home. Paulo and Giovanna Fortini are good friends of ours, their large Italian-American family visiting Mustique on a regular basis. They are renowned philanthropists, giving huge amounts of money away since their business expanded, but the wealth gap between Amanda and Lily has never mattered. The girls have been inseparable since childhood, spending each summer playing together, or running down to the beach to meet their friends Sacha and Tommy. Children have always been free to wander as they please here. If one of my brood ever went missing, someone always knew whose house they were visiting, or which beach they'd chosen to build sand-castles. One of Mustique's biggest draws has been the sanctuary it offers to its youngest visitors. I gaze down at the Fortinis' villa again, hoping to see Amanda at one of the windows, but see only reflected sunlight.

Wesley has finally appeared, his expression solemn, when I take my seat. He ushers forward the new maid, who keeps her gaze on the pristine tablecloth. Wesley expects his staff to be seen and not heard, like good Victorian children. Once she has deposited the tray he sends her back to the kitchen with a waft of his hand. Despite his protests, the meal she's prepared looks delicious: sliced mango, Greek yogurt laden with honey, and two large croissants.

'This is perfect, thank you, Wesley.' My butler is about to go back inside when I speak again. 'Could you and I have a meeting about Lily's party soon?'

'I'm at your disposal. The Cotton House is doing the catering and setting up lights and music in Britannia Bay. I've also booked every room at Firefly, as you suggested.'

'Excellent, we can get to work on fine details later. We need everything running like clockwork; I'm keen to get on with it while Lily's out. Could you ask Jose to see me, next time you bump into him?'

'Is something wrong, Lady Vee?'

'Not at all, I just want a gentle word. The garden looks marvellous.'

'I'm glad you approve.'

'Did you hear that Amanda Fortini's missing? I wondered if you knew anything about it.'

He shakes his head. 'The young lady barely speaks to me. She's helping Miss Lily on the reef, that's all I know.'

I can sense Wesley's negativity towards the girl, but our communication is still too fragile for more searching questions, so I inform him that Phillip Everard will be joining me for lunch, then he struts away. It will be hours before he offers me a smile, but he may be willing to share information by this afternoon.

The sea absorbs my attention while I eat. There's no sign yet to announce Storm Cristobal's presence, the Caribbean a shimmering length of pale blue silk. It always strikes me as odd that meteorologists give hurricanes such beautiful names, when they cause such brutal devastation. We normally only catch the tail end of the fierce cyclones that spin across the Atlantic in hurricane season, but this one may be the exception. Cristobal is still whirling down America's eastern seaboard, but Lily tends to ignore weather announcements. She will go on sailing out to the reef, unless there's a force nine gale.

My breakfast is almost finished when Jose appears on the lawn. He's standing over a flowerbed, weeding the soil, when I beckon him over. The young man is still carrying his hoe when he hurries towards me, like he plans to use it for self-defence. Up close he looks boyish even though he's twenty-five, with fine Creole features and an athletic build, his skin golden in the sun, curly brown hair touching his shoulders. I can still remember the day his mother brought him to the villa, answering questions on his behalf. She assured me that he was a good worker, able to understand instructions even though he can't speak, but today his amber stare is unsettling. He doesn't smile when I thank him for taking excellent care of the garden and the pool. Jose's expression remains neutral when I explain that he mustn't follow Phillip around, or visit my gardens late at night, for no valid reason. I feel certain he's understood every word, but the only emotion he shows is relief when I finally dismiss him. My young gardener hurries away, still clutching his garden implement like a musket. The conversation leaves me uncomfortable. I've never been certain how much Jose understands, but I hope his odd behaviour stops or I'll be forced to speak to his mother, who is under enough pressure caring for her large family.

I'm finishing my coffee when another visitor arrives. It takes me a moment to recognise Solomon Nile as the young man Jasper and I sponsored through his university education; it's a pleasure to see him. I can't help smiling at how uncomfortable he looks in his policeman's uniform, his shirt so well pressed the creases in his sleeves are razor-sharp. His thin gold-rimmed glasses look out of place, the rest of his appearance resembling a heavyweight boxer.

'Solomon Nile, you were a gangly teenager last time we met. It's wonderful to see you looking so well.'

He reaches out to shake my hand, but I rise onto my toes to kiss his cheek instead. 'Welcome back, Lady Veronica. You've been away too long.'

'Call me Vee, please. I heard all about your first-class degree, and your decision to join the police. Sit down and tell me everything. Jasper and I assumed you'd stay on at the university.'

He eases into a chair. 'I'd even chosen a topic for my PhD, but I realised I prefer doing something practical, and I wanted to make a difference. I was selected for fast-track officer training with the Oxfordshire police.'

'I never even made it to university, we're both so proud of you.'

'It's all thanks to you and Lord Blake.'

'No gratitude, please, Solomon. You sent us dozens of letters and Christmas cards, which I adored. Your graduation photo is still on our mantelpiece. You looked terrifically handsome in your cap and gown.'

'I didn't expect to get that far.'

'Miss Eveline said you were the brightest child she'd taught. You remember her, don't you?'

His eyes glitter with amusement. 'We're still in contact and she's gentler these days. Miss Eveline cared so much about A grades, she rapped my knuckles with her ruler every time I let mine slip, which focused my mind.'

'I'm thrilled you came back, but a little surprised.'

'The situation changed, Lady Vee. My father's not well.'

'I'm sorry to hear it.'

'He doesn't complain, but Parkinson's disease is slowing him down.'

'That's hard for such a dynamic man. I'm sure he still has a warrior's heart, even if his body's weaker. He had a reputation for fighting to protect the island's fishing rights. I remember the rival fishermen who sailed over from Bequia got rough justice from Hosea and his colleagues. I promise to visit him soon; Hosea's always been a friend of mine. But you're here about Amanda Fortini, aren't you?'

Nile draws a notebook from his pocket. When his gaze falls on me again it's like a laser, precision-sharp. 'What do you know about her, Lady Vee?'

'Amanda's been helping with the Reef Revival project. She's one of my goddaughter's closest friends, as well as our next-door neighbour.'

'Can you describe Ms Fortini for me?'

'People think she's just a socialite, because the gossip magazines love her, but she's becoming an excellent businesswoman, despite being so young. Amanda's art gallery in New York is thriving; that's why she loves coming here each summer to unwind. She's one of those girls that draw attention, like moths to a flame. She looks like a conventional beauty, but she's clever, and good company too.'

'Has she got a boyfriend?'

'You'd have to ask Lily, she's down at Old Plantation harbour. I don't concern myself with the young ones' love affairs, it would deplete my energy.'

'I don't blame you, Lady Vee. I'll speak to your goddaughter now.'

'Stay for a moment, please, I'm enjoying our chat. Don't you miss your history books, Solomon?'

'Every day, Lady Vee, but the past matters less than the present.' Nile's smile ignites for the first time, making his eyes gleam, behind their thin shields of glass.

'Tell me more about your time in Oxford.'

'I'm happy to, if you give me some information. Do you happen to know which islanders own the big speedboats?'

The question forces me to search my memory. 'There's one at Basil's, my friend Phil Everard has one, and so do Dr Bunbury and Keith Belmont. I can't stand the horrid things myself; they consume so much fuel and make a dreadful racket. Why do you ask?'

'It's just part of my enquiry.'

I watch him scribble the names in his notebook, then fire a fresh question at him, until he shares details about his time in the UK. He was placed on the fast-track graduate programme in the Oxfordshire police, which could have led to a lucrative senior position, yet he's chosen to return, rather than send home money for his father's care. I wonder why, but I relax in my chair, thrilled by his achievements, his voice a pleasing baritone. He looks like an athlete not a detective, but Jasper and I were right to buy him an education. Solomon's intelligence shows in the intensity of his gaze and his precise speech. If he can bring Lily's friend home safely, we will be eternally grateful.

7

DS NILE ASKS a few more questions about Amanda Fortini, then says goodbye. Lady Veronica's style hasn't changed since she handed him an achievement certificate on his last day at school. She must be almost seventy but her features are so youthful, she could be in her fifties, her clothes still elegant and unique. She's dressed in white today, a loose-fitting tunic, matching kurta trousers, with a straw hat protecting her face from the sun. Her manner is still playful but firm, her skin so pale she must protect it carefully, her eyes alert and wise. The pressure to find the missing woman feels heavier as he takes his leave. Lady Vee and Lord Blake have sponsored him so generously, he can't let them down.

Nile is travelling on foot today, hoping to see more by taking his time. His walk leads him through the island's northern section. It's the most heavily populated area of Mustique, with villas every few hundred metres. The developers have tried to conceal them behind high walls and fast-growing palms, but the structures swell from the ground like mushrooms. He loved cycling round this area as a kid, fascinated by the ornate buildings. Some look like fairy-tale castles, while others resemble mansions in Tuscany, or English estates. The place is awash with money, yet it's like a ghost town. Most of the rock stars, aristocrats, and million-aires who use their holiday homes just once a year have flown home already. The villas all have delicate names like Hummingbird, Peace, and Lotus Flower, but their windows are battened down with ugly metal shutters.

Lily Calder's boat is moored on the island's sheltered western coast, facing the Caribbean, instead of the rough Atlantic. Old Plantation Bay is the island's smallest harbour, with a dozen fishing boats moored on the jetty. Almost everyone here owns a boat of some kind, from a canoe all the way up to thirty-foot yachts. Bigger craft are forced to anchor at sea, because there are no deep harbours. The mega-yachts must use launches to motor ashore, provided they have an invitation. Calder's boat, *Revival*, is a converted fishing trawler, which has seen better days. There's no sign of her as Nile approaches the quay, but his first duty is to check the two large speedboats moored on either side of the jetty. The huge Bayrider XR7s can accommodate ten guests at least, decked out with leather seats and handrails in shiny chrome. When he checks the licence stickers on their prows, they belong to two of the island's permanent residents, Phillip Everard and Keith Belmont. Both men are from the world of showbusiness, but Nile has never met either of them. Their boats look sleek and blameless, no sign of damage on their fibreglass hulls. With no villas overlooking the bay, he will have a hard time proving that either of them left the harbour the morning Amanda Fortini went missing, but there are still two more boats to check.

There's no reply when Nile calls out for permission to go on board Lily Calder's boat. The woman who emerges from the cabin brings him to a standstill. She's tall and long-limbed, with glossy black hair, her movements as supple as a ballet dancer. The outline of her yellow bikini shows through a T-shirt that skims the tops of her thighs, her sunglasses balanced on top of her head. She assesses him with intense blue eyes before covering them with her shades. He's glad that his are already concealed. Hopefully she won't notice how badly she's blindsided him. He's lost for words, until she steps forward, hand outstretched.

'DS Solomon Nile?'

'That's right, Ms Calder. You called about your friend.'

'Lily, please. I was hoping we'd meet yesterday.'

'I came looking for you here, and at your home. We must have missed each other.' Her expression remains guarded. 'Could you go through the information again for me please?'

She drops onto a bench at the stern of her boat, gesturing for him to do the same. 'Amanda said she'd visit me on Friday night, but never showed up, which isn't her style. She's never let me down in all the years I've known her. I went round to her villa early yesterday morning, but she hadn't slept there. She's not answering her mobile either.'

'Someone from Lovell saw her taking an early swim in Britannia Bay. No one's seen her since.'

When Lily removes her shades again Nile realises that she's scared, not aloof after all. There's a look of horror in

56

her turquoise eyes. 'There's no way she drowned. She's spent the summer reef diving with me; she can swim for miles.'

'It's possible she swam out to the big yacht you can see from here. Do you know the owners?'

'I'm afraid not. She'd have said, if friends had arrived.'

'A big speedboat was seen in the bay when Amanda was swimming, like the ones moored here. Do you know if either ever get taken out early in the morning? It's possible the driver saw her in the water.'

'Neither get much use. I don't know why Phil keeps one; he's got dodgy sea legs these days. Keith takes his out occasionally, but I've been nagging him about how much fuel they burn.'

'Thanks, that's useful. Can you tell me if Amanda has a boyfriend, here on Mustique?'

'She was seeing Tommy Rothmore until a month ago, which hasn't been easy. Four of us have been friends for years: Amanda, Sacha, me and Tommy. We were more like sisters and brothers as kids. He was volunteering on the Revival project too, but he stopped coming out with us after they split up. Amanda hinted that she'd found someone else, but it hadn't worked out. Maybe it was just a fling she didn't want to make public.'

'Why not?'

'Amanda's a celebrity in America, and Tommy's from a well-known family too. I think she wants to keep her love life quiet this time, but she and Tommy were talking about getting engaged earlier this year. She didn't want to hurt his feelings either.'

'Can you think of anything unusual Amanda's done recently? Something out of character?'

The young woman looks pensive. 'A few weeks ago I saw her at the Bamboo Church, which seemed odd. Her parents are religious, but she hardly ever goes to church. Her conversation with Pastor Boakye looked pretty intense. They were sitting together on one of the pews. I asked her about it, but she just changed the subject.'

The Bamboo Church lies close to the airport, a simple outdoor structure, where dozens of ceremonies are held each year. Nile has only met the new pastor Pastor Boakye a handful of times, but he's made a good impression on the local community.

'I'll pay him a call.' Nile scribbles a few words in his notebook. When he looks up, Calder is studying him so intently it feels like he's been placed under a microscope. 'I promise to find out what's happened to your friend.'

Her eyes glisten with tears she quickly blinks away. 'I'm worried, that's why I'm here all the time, keeping busy. Amanda's more like a sister than a friend. What can I do to help?'

'Tell me if she has any enemies on Mustique.'

Calder shakes her head. 'No one, but she and Sacha have argued lately. They were fine until Tommy came between them. I think Sacha was jealous when Amanda started dating him last year. She's been visiting him since the relationship ended.'

'Has Amanda got many close friends here?'

'Everyone loves her. Amanda's this free-spirited golden girl with the world at her feet, but she hasn't changed. She believes in my project so she volunteered to help. We've spent weeks diving together.'

'How's it going?'

'We're grafting live coral onto sections that have been bleached. There are signs of recovery.' The enthusiasm suddenly slips from her face. 'Someone's not keen on my work though. Did you hear about the graffiti on my boat last week?'

'*Leave Mustique or die like the coral.* Who do you think did it?'

She pauses before replying. 'Tommy, probably, to upset Amanda. I care about him as a friend, but he's incredibly sensitive. He doesn't normally drink much at all, but he's hit the bottle hard since their break-up.'

'Is there anything else I should know?'

'Someone followed me home on Thursday, then again last night. I heard footsteps as I came through the trees. The path was empty, every time I turned back.'

'Don't go out alone at night, please, until Amanda's home.'

Her vivid blue gaze travels across Nile's face again. 'You think she's in danger, don't you?'

'I'll find out soon,' he replies, rising to his feet. 'Thanks for your time.'

'Ring me, please, when you have news.'

'You should stay in the harbour today, Ms Calder. If the storm heads this way you could never outrun it.'

'The radio says it won't arrive for days.' A quick smile crosses her face. 'I just need to check if my latest grafts have taken; it won't take long.'

Nile can tell that issuing another instruction would be a

waste of breath. Lily Calder is already stowing oxygen cylinders away, preparing for her next dive. The woman is beautiful enough to leave her imprint on his retinas, but she's from another world. He pushes the attraction aside before it can leave a mark, yet her turquoise stare bothers him as he walks inland.

8

BASIL'S BAR IS one of my favourite places on Mustique, so I walk there for my mid-morning coffee instead of taking the buggy, glad of some exercise. It takes just twenty minutes to follow the winding track to Britannia Bay. I remember when the bar was just a broken-down shack on the beach, with a handful of tables, lukewarm beer and a fire pit for night-time barbecues. The place is much more sophisticated now. The bay looks prettier than ever; the sea is a calm blue ribbon, connecting the ocean to the sky.

When I sit on one of the bar stools, I can picture the place right at the start, with all-night parties, limbo dancing and skinny-dipping at dawn. The island was like a big country estate back then, every face familiar, no cares in the world. The bar only exists because my husband happened to find a young man by the roadside in St Vincent. Basil Charles had been hit by a car, so Jasper took him to hospital and they kept in touch. We both took such a liking to the charismatic young man we brought him to Mustique and helped him set up his bar. I glance around, looking for his distinctive white hair and legendary smile, but there's no sign of him. Basil has so many business ventures now, he's rarely seen in Mustique apart from at the annual Blues Festival that he started years ago.

I recognise a man sitting by the bar as Dexter Adebayo. He's in his fifties now, but I remember him as a handsome young diving instructor, who had just earned his licence to take hotel guests out to explore the reef. He runs his own small business now and he's gained a few stone, a big man with an air of dignity that contrasts with his colourful clothes. He's wearing a vivid Hawaiian shirt, over well-worn jeans, his hair in thick grey dreadlocks. His quiet manner has given him a reputation as a good listener. If Dex sold the secrets of every wealthy holidaymaker who confided in him, while out on his boat, he'd be a millionaire. He looks older than last time we met, but his face splits into a grin when he sees me, and suddenly the years drop away.

'Welcome back, Lady Vee. You're still the most beautiful woman on Mustique.'

'You flatterer, Dex.'

'Let me get you a drink.'

'That's very kind.' I take the bar stool next to his. 'Espresso and some mineral water please. I can't drink like the old days. I have to ration myself.'

'Me too. No liquor until night-time, and most days none at all. But I still love the buzz in here on cocktail nights. I'm only here because a group of tourists are meeting me, before their diving trip.'

'Do you still take them out yourself?'

'Whenever I get the chance.'

'Can I monopolise you, until they arrive? I'd love to hear what's been happening in my absence.'

'Glad to oblige, Lady Vee.'

He asks for two espressos, which the bartender produces at a pace that would never be tolerated in the UK. I notice new tables and chairs have arrived since last summer, the place increasingly polished. Dex and I finally chink our espresso cups, toasting each other's good health. I can feel the man's gaze assessing me as he takes his first sip. Dex is one of those people you can never quite read.

'There's not much to report,' he says. 'The scenery doesn't change. People still come here for a good time. How about you? Why have you neglected us for so long?'

'I went home for the princess's funeral. There were things to sort out.'

Dexter nods at a framed picture of Princess Margaret above the bar. It was taken in her thirties, when she looked more like a movie star than a member of the royal family. 'This place came alive when she was here, dancing with you and Lord Blake.'

'What's happened to her house?'

'Les Jolies Eaux sold a few months ago, to a French businessman. The guy lives like a monk.'

'Pity, that place is built for entertaining.'

'The whole island's excited about Miss Lily's party, in two weeks' time. I hear they've laid on extra staff to get the beach ready and rig the stage for music. She'll have the time of her life. Not every girl gets a serenade from Mick Jagger when she turns twenty-one.'

'He's written a song for her, apparently.'

'Mr Jagger's another one that makes this place buzz.' He studies me again. 'I hear Miss Lily's project's going well. They talk about it on the radio, saying it will help the local economy.'

'Is everyone behind it?'

'Some fishermen in Lovell say they've been tending that reef their whole lives, then the Revival project starts up again, and the girl takes all the credit for doing her mother's work. It sounds like stupid bitterness to me.'

'It could explain why someone painted *die like the coral* on the side of her boat.'

Dexter blinks at me in surprise. 'Anyone with a brain knows she cares about it, just like her mama. She's using her science knowledge to put things right. I see how much good she's doing whenever I dive.'

'They left the graffiti last week, before Amanda Fortini went missing.'

'I heard rumours about that. Hasn't she been found?'

'Not yet. You've been on the island all summer, Dex. Have you ever seen anyone bothering her?'

Dex hesitates, like he's weighing up the pros and cons of telling the truth. 'Tommy Rothmore, one time. The boy came in here shouting abuse and swinging his fists, steaming drunk. He's normally so serious and polite, but he's been out of control since his parents went back to the UK. I felt sorry for him, so I walked him home. He's kept his temper ever since, but he watches her sometimes.'

'How do you mean?'

'Like a child looking at the sun. You want to remember that golden beauty forever, even though it will send you blind. It might be worth the pain, just to look for one more second.' He looks troubled.

'You've got hidden talents,' I tell him. 'That sounds like poetry.'

'He should move on, but he can't tear himself away.'

Our conversation ends abruptly when Dex's party of novice divers arrive, all clutching wetsuits and snorkels, keen to get started. I move outdoors to the shade of a cabana, sipping my ice-cold water. Dex Adebayo's words stay in my mind; I've known the Rothmores for years. They were one of the first couples to buy a villa from us in the early days, so it will take a lot of convincing to persuade me that their only son would hurt his ex-girlfriend, or scrawl a vicious message on Lily's boat. It's just possible the boy has lost his senses. A mixture of curiosity and concern churn in my stomach as I hurry home to ring the Rothmores' villa.

I don't know why tension hits me when I walk through a thick stand of trees. I normally love inhaling the sweet scent of decaying leaves, with overgrown ferns brushing my calves as I follow the path, but I can tell someone's watching me. It's a sense I developed from looking after Princess Margaret, my antennae always raised, in case she received unwelcome attention. When I come to a standstill, there's no one on the path in either direction, no breeze to disturb the undergrowth. I see him only when I stare into the jungle's depths, spotting his face in a sea of green. Jose Gomez is gazing at me intently, but when I call out his name, he vanishes like a puff of smoke.

9

DS NILE IS stuck inside the police station again. His air-conditioning unit is still making a loud coughing sound, but producing no cold air. The noise is so irritating he feels like tearing the machine from its shelf and hurling it outside, but that would end his probation period in dramatic style. He's been knocking his head against a wall of frustrations. The first person he wants to see is Tommy Rothmore; if anyone has hurt Amanda Fortini, her angry ex-boyfriend is the best place to start, but the young man isn't answering his phone.

Nile has spent the last hour waiting for his boss in St Vincent to email a search warrant for the yacht that's still moored in Britannia Bay, but none has arrived. He studies the vessel's details again. The *Aqua Dream* was built in Monte Carlo. It's sixty metres long, an elite-class mega-yacht, fully ocean-worthy, with an immense fuel tank, eliminating the need for frequent shore stops. It sold two years ago for thirty million dollars, registered to a company called Aqua Dream Ltd, with a South American business licence, but no Internet presence. He's checked the boat licences for the Bayrider speedboats owned by Dr Bunbury and Basil's Bar, but the launch Mama Toulaine saw the morning Amanda Fortini was swimming in Britannia Bay may well have come from the yacht. It may even have travelled out to meet her, and she could be on the vessel right now, but he's powerless to act. Nile's shoulders twitch as he stares at the printout again. He needs to question the ship's crew as to whether they saw Amanda Fortini on the morning she disappeared. He can hear the Layton brothers braying with laughter through the closed door, and feels certain he's the butt of their joke. There's no point in twiddling his thumbs until the warrant arrives, so he sets off to speak to the island's only priest.

The church lies on the plain at the centre of Mustique, close to the airport. Nile envies the pastor his workplace when the Bamboo Church comes into sight. It's overshadowed by the elephant tree, which appears in every guidebook. The baobab must be hundreds of years old, its massive trunk listing steeply to one side. Its bark is grey and powdery with age, and a long branch skims the ground, like an elephant drinking from a pool. Nile remembers climbing the tree as a child, pretending to be a mahout riding his elephant through a jungle, until the old pastor chastised him for fooling around on the Sabbath. The church is a simple open-sided structure, roofed with bamboo poles, to keep the congregation dry if a tropical rainstorm hits during services. The only furniture it contains is a simple table used as an altar and thirty or forty wooden pews.

Nile spots the pastor straight away, in a clearing beside the church. He's applying varnish to one of the benches. Pastor Boakye has abandoned his black suit and dog collar, dressed now in shorts and a paint-splashed T-shirt. He looks awkward when the detective approaches, as if he's embarrassed to be caught doing a menial job. Nile doesn't know him well, but they're around the same age, and he's listened to several of his evangelical sermons, because his father can no longer make the journey here alone. Boakye has spoken about arriving from Lagos six months ago, his bishop requiring him to leave Nigeria and travel to far-flung places as part of his mission. The priest's manner is so effusive and eager to please, he seems determined to prove his worth.

Pastor Boakye approaches with hand outstretched like he's planning to draw him into the fold, but Nile is a lost cause. The detective has concealed his atheism until now, but it's only a matter of time before Hosea guesses the truth.

'Good to see you, Solomon. Have you come to help me smarten this place up?'

'Not today I'm afraid. I need your help, Father, if you have a minute.'

'Of course, all the time in the world.' The priest leads him to a shady bench.

'I'm looking for Amanda Fortini. I understand she came here recently, to speak to you.'

The pastor gives a rapid nod. 'She's dropped by several times, even though she's a Catholic and the church is Baptist. Amanda asked for spiritual guidance, but I can't break her confidence, I'm afraid.'

'Please talk openly; her friends are very concerned.'

'I can only say that she's been having difficulties.'

'Amanda's been missing around forty-eight hours, Father. She may be in danger.'

'I want to help, but she'll be upset about me discussing her secrets.' The priest looks uncomfortable. 'Amanda was worried about her relationship with a man. She'd rejected a boyfriend who cared deeply, because she was drawn to someone else. She said he's unpredictable, even dangerous. She was trying to find the courage to stop seeing him.'

'Did she say his name?'

'I'm afraid not.' The priest shades his eyes, his expression regretful.

'This place must seem tiny to you, after Lagos.'

Pastor Boakye smiles. 'Everyone deserves God's love, no matter where they live. Shall we say a prayer for Amanda together, to bring her home safe?'

Nile freezes in his seat. 'I'm not a believer. I bring my father to services, but I stopped attending church years ago.'

'Is there a reason for that?'

'I lost my faith overnight.'

'That sounds painful, Solomon. Remember I'm here if you ever want to talk.' The priest leans forward in his seat. 'Would you like me to request God's help on your behalf?'

'If you wish, Father. I have to get back to work.'

'Come again, any time, if the past burdens you.'

The detective rises to his feet, blurting out a quick thank-you before he leaves. The reason for his loss of belief is too ugly to explain. It's easier to hunt for Amanda Fortini than revisit the past.

10

THE ATMOSPHERE FEELS peaceful when I get back to Eden House, and I've already pushed my gardener's odd behaviour to the back of my mind. Wesley manages a professional smile when I announce my intention to freshen up before lunch, but I call the Rothmores' villa from the landline first. There must be a simple explanation why Tommy doesn't pick up, because people are easy to find on Mustique. The manager at the Cotton House sounds apologetic when she explains that the young man hasn't visited for ages. The last time he ate in their restaurant was with his parents, before they flew home last month.

I intend to enjoy my lunch with Phillip, whatever happens next. There's a danger that Amanda's absence will overtake my life, when I should focus on organising Lily's party, but I hate abandoning a puzzle before it's solved. I put my concern aside when I go upstairs I've always enjoyed applying make-up, like an actor preparing to go on stage; my favourite Chanel lipstick is a great morale boost. I'm satisfied with the results once my makeover is complete, hiding my anxiety from view.

Phillip is waiting when I go back downstairs. He's still my most glamorous friend, even now. No wonder women and men, young and old, still fall at his feet. His black linen shirt, grey trousers and beach shoes may look relaxed, but they probably cost a fortune. The man's wardrobe heaves with Balmain suits and Italian merino jumpers. He is leaning on the balustrade, watching the sea, his face lighting up at the sight of me. The actor's arrival has restored Wesley's spirits too; my butler arrives with both maids following him like a retinue. He places a bottle of champagne in an ice bucket with a flourish, then discreetly backs away. I've realised over the years that Wesley only gets angry because he's a perfectionist, which involves meticulous planning, so spur-of-the-moment changes trigger full-scale panic. Phillip seems wonderfully relaxed by contrast, lounging back in his chair.

'It's great having you here, Vee. Everyone else bores me senseless, or forgets I exist. Never leave, will you?'

'I'm tempted, but my roots lie deep in Norfolk soil.'

'I won't let you board a plane for months. Have you seen Jose yet?'

'He was wandering round the garden last night. I spoke to him this morning, but it hasn't made a jot of difference. He followed me to Basil's just now.'

'What's got into him? He's always been so reliable.'

'Let's hope it ends soon. Tell me what's been happening here, Phil. I've been away so long.'

His eyes glitter, my friend's expression suddenly darkening. 'All manner of strange antics, my dear. Affairs, spats, illicit business deals. Did I mention that I've taken up yoga?'

'Is this a mid-life crisis?'

'Mine ended years ago, thank God.' He looks amused. 'Come and join me. There's a class every Friday morning at Keith Belmont's place.'

'I'm surprised he's got the energy; his last bride was sixteen, wasn't she?'

'The man's got even more skeletons in his closet than me.'

'You never talk about yours, but I'd love to hear.'

'I'd never burden you with the sordid details. I was an ugly, obnoxious child. My poor siblings had a hellish time.'

'Nonsense, I'm sure you were adorable.'

'I was a monster, believe me. Heaven knows why my parents waited until I was sixteen to reject me. I don't blame them for one minute.'

I remember Phillip telling me that he was estranged from his family at a young age, but I know it hurts him to discuss it, so I revert to our earlier topic of conversation.

'It still baffles me why you spend time with Keith Belmont.'

Phillip stifles a laugh. 'He may not be your cup of tea, but I adore the old roué. He's been my partner in crime while you've been away, although the guy's turned over a new leaf. He wants to help Lily's coral project. He's promised a big donation if he can get more involved.'

'I'd take that with a pinch of salt. I don't trust his motives.'

'Keith's the same as me, always looking for entertainment. Old rock stars become obsolete like actors,' he says, his voice suddenly tinged with bitterness.

'Aren't you going to the States soon? I read that you're doing something huge in Hollywood?'

'It fell through, which is a pity, even though star billing is a thing of the past. The director cast me as the star's dad.'

His smile fades suddenly. 'It's the same here; I seem to be going out of fashion at a rate of knots, but it means I can stay till the end of the year.'

'Can't you make the film yourself?'

'I can't rely on the film industry any more, so I'm staying put until an Oscar-winning script lands on my doormat. I'm not having some bastard director casting me as an old fool.' Phillip's eyes gleam with anger, reminding me of his sensitivity; a single unkind remark can cut him to the quick, but he soon regains his composure.

'I've noticed something interesting. You normally have a pack of cigarettes on the table, to fondle, if not actually use. Did you finally give up?'

'Three months ago, but I still keep a packet at home, in case of desperation. I've cut down on the booze too.' He touches my wrist. 'Tell me about you, Vee. You're free at last, no longer a lady-in-waiting. You can step into the limelight.'

'It doesn't feel real. I keep expecting a summons from the palace.'

My old friend's shrewd gaze assesses me again. 'What did the job teach you?'

'Observation skills, mainly. I had to read situations fast, to make sure the princess had the right type of coffee, white cotton gloves, and her favourite whisky. I even introduced her to Roddy Llewellyn.'

'Do you ever regret sacrificing all that time?'

'It was a pleasure most days. We were friends since childhood, and she gave me so many adventures. I visited dozens of obscure countries on royal tours, and she could be tremendous fun.' My friend's gaze remains serious. 'Can we swim this afternoon, Phil? I've been for a dip already, but I'm aching to get back in the water.'

'I'll come to the beach gladly, but only to sunbathe. I've had a wretched ear infection for weeks. The doctor's keeping me on dry land, and banished me from long-haul flights.'

'That sounds miserable, you poor soul.'

'Life's changing too fast, Vee. I'm not ageless like you, more's the pity. Whenever I go to parties I feel ancient. The youngsters see me as a washed-up old dinosaur.'

'Nonsense, darling. Men grow distinguished as they age.'

He suddenly relaxes again, releasing his infectious laugh. 'You'd make a great diplomat.'

Our lunch becomes fun after another glass of champagne, with plenty of flirtation and laughter, but I can tell Phillip's below par, so I keep the conversation light. He's the island's best gossip, telling me about affairs between villa owners, their misjudged financial ventures, and the plans for the island. The island's enchantment lies in its tranquillity; I hope it will keep its charm forever.

The conversation shifts back to Amanda Fortini as we finish pudding. 'Have you seen much of her this summer, Phil?'

'I've been giving her French lessons; she's planning a big trip to Paris, to buy art for her gallery. I'm sorely tempted to tag along. She's getting quite fluent, the girl's a smart cookie.'

When I tell Phillip about trying to get hold of Tommy Rothmore, his eyes widen. He witnessed the ugly scene Dexter described in Basil's a few weeks ago, when the young man staggered in drunk, yelling abuse, and throwing punches. His relationship with Amanda had ended several weeks before, yet he still seemed furious.

'Tommy would never hurt a woman, surely?'

Phillip looks away. 'Anyone can lash out under pressure.'

'How do you mean?'

'His parents expect him to manage the Rothmore Foundation, which is worth billions. It's a heavy burden for such a young guy. Maybe that's why Amanda broke up with him. She enjoys her inheritance, but Tommy's weighed down by responsibilities. Plus, he's just lost the girl he loved. I know from experience that heartbreak can turn us all into monsters.'

'I've been trying not to ask about Carlos. Where is he now?'

'Back in Rio, doing the bossa nova with a guy half my age. I'm determined to fall for a woman next time, older, and preferably someone docile.'

'Poor thing, I know you adored him.' I reach across the table to hold his hand.

'He broke my heart into smithereens. I'm over it now, but victims sometimes attack a partner after a break-up, don't they? Tommy's been at cracking point for weeks.'

'Let's pay him a visit.'

'Is that wise, Vee? It's a police matter.'

'I've got a few innocent questions. He won't pull a gun on us, will he?'

My curiosity about Amanda has grown stronger after two glasses of champagne. Phillip and I don't bother with coffee before setting off for the Rothmores' villa in my buggy, a ten-minute ride away. The alcohol and the company have lifted my spirits. I feel like a tropical version of Miss Marple as we drive up to one of Mustique's loveliest properties. Sunset House has stood at the top of the island's tallest hill since the sixties. It's built in French country style, in pale stone, with cobalt-blue shutters and a lush garden, full of exotic orchids and lilies. The scale of the building is modest, considering the Rothmores' immense banking fortune, but they have the best views. When I stand on the terrace, the entire Caribbean coast of Mustique unrolls before me, from Endeavour Bay down to Old Plantation.

I can sense that something's changed as we approach the villa. The shutters are closed, and no one appears when Phillip rings the doorbell, which is a surprise. Villa owners employ small teams of staff all year round to maintain their properties, yet the place appears deserted. It strikes me again that families like the Rothmores enjoy an extraordinary degree of safety on Mustique. Their UK home must be guarded round the clock, but the island operates on trust. There's an unspoken agreement that everyone is safe, because no one needs to steal, or commit violence. Something isn't right now, though.

'The house feels ghostly,' Phillip says.

My friend is peering through a window into a kitchen that seems to have been lifted straight from an interiors magazine, with a circular table and miles of glittering surfaces, but no sign of recent use. I can tell he's enjoying himself, playing the part of a famous cat burglar, with imaginary cameras rolling. He manages to prise open one of the downstairs windows, without causing damage, but my champagne-fuelled bravado is wearing thin.

'We can't just break in, Phil.'

'Don't be boring; it was your idea in the first place. You're slim enough to wriggle through the gap.'

I'm still grumbling when he boosts me onto the window ledge, but now that my curiosity has been raised, I'm keen to know the truth. The adventure makes me feel young again, my sense of adventure alive and kicking. Once I'm inside the kitchen I unlock the back door for Phillip, who grins like an overexcited schoolboy. We agree to search the ground floor first, for any hint that Tommy could have harmed his ex-girlfriend.

We both know the house well, because we've attended many birthday parties, suppers and celebrations thrown by the Rothmores, but it looks different today. The rooms are replete with shadows, dust sheets covering the antique sofas. The French theme continues in the dining room, which also carries evidence of my friend Nicky Haslam's excellent taste. I feel almost certain the Rothmores employed him to source their bespoke furniture, the lines elegant and simple. It dawns on me that the reason for Tommy's absence could be straightforward: maybe he's staying with a friend while he gets over his heartbreak. Many villa owners have gone home, but some of their grown-up children always stay behind, in no hurry to resume their everyday lives.

'God almighty,' Phillip mutters. 'Is that an original Picasso?'

'I think so, yes.'

We gaze at an abstract portrait of a woman's face, her features dissected then reassembled in vivid blues and reds.

'It's beautiful, whoever painted it, but where are the staff?'

'Maybe they're taking a day off.'

There's no sign of criminal activity on the ground floor. The place seems to have been shut down completely, as if the Rothmores have no intention of returning. I get the same feeling when we explore upstairs. The spacious bedrooms look like a deluxe hotel, bathrooms glistening with cleanliness. I can't understand why the young man has left no trace of himself behind. I'm standing in the corridor when footsteps echo through the stairwell, and Phillip's heard them too. He emerges from one of the bedrooms with a panicked look on his face.

'Hide!' he whispers.

'Don't be silly. It'll be Tommy; let's say we're looking for his mother.'

'That's an outright lie. You'll get us arrested, Vee.'

'Relax and follow my lead, darling,' I tell him.

Princess Margaret taught me never to admit defeat. If circumstances go against you, keep your head up and smile. I make sure to keep my chin raised and look delighted as I march downstairs to face the music.

11

NILE IS SURPRISED that the Rothmores' kitchen door has been left ajar, but it makes sense when footsteps rattle overhead. Tommy must be at home, or the villa's staff are working on the floor above. He's shocked when Lady Veronica hurries down the central stairs, wearing a beaming smile, followed by a handsome grey-haired man of around her own age.

'What are you doing here, Lady Vee?' Nile asks.

'I was hoping to see Tommy Rothmore. His parents are close friends, but he hasn't been answering the phone.'

'So you let yourselves in?'

She blinks the question away. 'Have you met Phillip Everard?'

Nile shakes the man's hand as the penny drops. The guy's an actor from some old films and more recently in TV adverts, but he's never met him in the flesh. The guy looks fit as a fiddle, but less confident in real life. Nile grew up on an island where famous musicians, politicians and royalty are two a penny, but it's still disconcerting to eyeball a big star up close for the first time, particularly when he's in breach of the law.

'Good to meet you, sir. I've enjoyed many of your movies.'
The actor's face brightens. 'That's so kind, thank you.'

'Now could you both step outside for a minute, please?'

Nile is gentle when he warns the pair not to take the law into their own hands. If they have concerns about fellow islanders, they should call him first. Phillip Everard has the grace to look contrite, but Lady Vee observes him through cool eyes that never miss a trick. He's steering a difficult course between upholding the law and respecting a woman whose generosity has improved his life immeasurably. She peers up at him from under the brim of her straw hat.

'Forgive us, Solomon, but this isn't just about Amanda. Someone's been leaving threats on Lily's boat. I won't let that continue.'

The policeman is surprised by the change in his patron's behaviour. Until now she's seemed gentle to the core, a refined British aristocrat, her fierce spirit well hidden. Lady Vee's hands are bunched at her sides, like she intends to fight for Lily Calder's safety, even though he got the distinct impression the young woman could defend herself.

'Why don't we sit down and talk about this calmly?' Nile suggests.

They shelter from the sun under a gazebo by the pool.

'We all want Ms Fortini found,' he says. 'I need your inside knowledge of the villa owners' lives; you have their trust, but I need to stay in charge. If my boss on St Vincent hears about this conversation, I'll be suspended.'

'We'll be discreet, don't worry, both of us are keen to help.' Lady Vee nods at him, her actor friend murmuring his agreement. 'All we know so far is that Amanda's still missing, and we've searched the Rothmores' house. It looks like Tommy hasn't been back for ages.'

'He fired his domestic staff three days ago, according to the villa next door.'

Everard's face brightens. 'What about the summerhouse? I can see it over there, through the bushes. It's the one place we haven't searched.'

They all rise to their feet in unison, and Nile feels a trace of panic. Searching the *Aqua Dream* is his top priority, but the warrant still hasn't arrived and now he's being dragged off course. Lady Vee and Phillip Everard make unlikely recruits, dressed in their immaculate clothes. But they have the one thing he lacks: the trust of every millionaire on Mustique. Nile still believes that the answer to Amanda Fortini's disappearance may lie on the yacht that's still floating on the horizon, or one of the island's biggest speedboats, if he could only unlock the puzzle.

Nile leads the way across the lawn to the summerhouse. The wooden structure is almost concealed by overgrown passion flowers, elephant palms and jasmine. When he glances over his shoulder, Lady Vee is following at a sedate pace, taking care not to dirty her clothes. Her manner has gentled again, now that she's got her way. Nile can't yet decide whether he's made an excellent decision or a bad mistake.

The policeman's concerns about breaking the investigation protocol are forgotten when he reaches the summerhouse. It looks like the place has been burgled. The door has been kicked off its hinges, and someone has been on the rampage, the garden furniture in pieces. There's a mattress against the wall, covered by a crumpled sheet, and whisky bottles littered around. Tommy Rothmore's relationship ending seems to have triggered a meltdown.

'The poor boy,' Lady Vee murmurs.

She's removed her hat, like she's paying respects at a graveside, and the wooden building does have a deathly feel. The knot inside the detective's stomach tightens as his shoes crunch over fragments of bamboo furniture. He comes to a halt when he sees half a dozen large photos of Amanda Fortini displayed on the far wall, each one daubed with red paint, like the graffiti on Lily Calder's boat. The girl's features have been erased, with a few swipes of a paintbrush.

12

I REMEMBER TOMMY Rothmore as a boy, splashing around in the pool with Lily and her pals, or chasing them down to the beach. He was a quiet, courteous child even then, bright enough to understand his role in a world-famous banking dynasty. His manner hasn't changed over the years, always quiet and thoughtful, instead of party-loving like many of his peers. I saw him six months ago, suddenly a good-looking young bachelor, with Amanda Fortini on his arm. The match surprised me, but his seriousness seemed the perfect foil for her fun-loving nature. It's hard to believe he could fall so far, in such a short time. Someone has wasted a great deal of energy in the summerhouse, destroying it from the inside, but not Tommy, surely? Phillip seems upset by the devastation too: his gaze is sober when he studies the ruined photos on the wall, which isn't surprising, so I take pity on him, saying there's no need to stay. Solomon asks him a couple of questions about the last time he used his motorboat, which languishes in the harbour for months, then my friend hurries away, as if chaos were an infectious disease.

Solomon Nile is busy taking photos of the devastation

with his phone, his approach meticulous. I feel some regret over backing him into a corner, but not enough to change my mind. While Lily is in danger I must stay at the heart of his investigation by any means possible. I stand by the door, surveying the mess of ruined furniture and the dusty sheets someone has been using for a bed. It's possible that Tommy has nothing to do with Amanda's absence. He could be staying with a friend, but his options are limited, now so many people have flown home. I'm still wondering where the young man could be when Nile appears at my side.

'I need to see Sacha Milburn. She's visited Tommy recently, but she's not answering her phone.'

I stare up at him. 'I know exactly where she'll be, we can use my buggy.'

'Thanks, but I've got this under control.'

'Have you, Solomon? You need my contacts, remember.'

Nile folds his arms across his chest like he's bracing himself for a hard blow. 'Okay, but just this once, Lady Vee, then please promise to go home.'

I offer a smile, instead of giving my word, then tell him that Sacha Milburn will be at Firefly. The younger crowd go there for early drinks, come rain or shine. Nile still looks disgruntled when we drive south from the villa, cutting through the island's centre.

I can see more evidence that Mustique is changing as we pass the revamped medical centre. It looks like a pair of upmarket bungalows, with the surgery on one side, a small ward, and a couple of private rooms, in case anyone falls ill before the first flight out. The sports ground has a new pavilion, and even the stables have expanded to accommodate more horses. The place looks idyllic today, with three Arab mares grazing in the paddock, waiting for someone to take them for a gallop across Rutland Bay.

Solomon makes a quiet companion, happy to let long silences develop. He's probably thinking of questions for Sacha Milburn. My spirits lift when I catch sight of Firefly, the hotel nestled among coconut palms, with a direct view down to Britannia Bay. I've always loved its relaxed atmosphere. It has just seven guest rooms so Patrick's Bar is never too busy, and the staff serve perfect martinis. I'm crossing my fingers that Tommy Rothmore will be there with his pals, but the veranda appears deserted when we arrive.

'Do you come here much, Solomon?' I ask.

'Never.'

The detective's clever gaze is busy assessing the tropical gardens and manmade waterfalls outside, and suddenly I witness the place with fresh eyes. The empty buckets on the bar are waiting to be filled with champagne that costs three hundred dollars a bottle, an ornate chandelier hanging in the dining area, the tables set with pristine white napkins. I'm about to ask a waiter if Sacha Milburn has visited recently when Nile taps my arm.

'That's her at the back, isn't it?'

I catch sight of the young woman alone at a table, recognising her shock of auburn hair. She comes from a family of famous bohemians, her mother a successful milliner and her father a lifestyle guru, always penning self-help guides on how to gain inner peace. Sacha is scribbling in a journal with such fierce concentration, she doesn't see us arrive. The young woman reacts with shock when I call her name; I notice that her notebook has a vivid red cover that matches her pen. She quickly squirrels them away in her bag and appears edgy as we approach her table. Sacha is no longer the jolly child who played with Lily and Amanda all summer long; I remember her mother saying she had a crisis of confidence at university. It can't be easy having such stylish, successful parents, overshadowing your endeavours. Her hair is badly cut, freckles littered across her skin, her grey sundress so anonymous it almost renders her invisible. It's a shame she takes so little care with her appearance; just a few small changes would turn her into a Pre-Raphaelite beauty.

'Welcome back, Vee,' she mumbles. 'It's great to see you.'

'You too, Sacha. Can we join you? This is my friend DS Solomon Nile. He's just been appointed as the island's new police officer.'

The young woman gives an awkward smile. 'Thank goodness, someone to keep us on the straight and narrow at last.'

'How have you been, darling?' I ask.

'I meant to fly back to the UK sooner, but I'm staying for Lily's party. The villa feels weird without my family filling the place with noise.'

'Come and join us any time, Sacha. You know Lily adores seeing you.'

She gives me a grateful smile, then turns to Solomon. 'Are you enjoying your new job?'

'It's keeping me busy right now, Ms Milburn. I'm trying to find Amanda Fortini.'

Sacha's face blanks. 'We haven't spent much time together lately. I don't have a clue where she is, I'm afraid.'

'How about Tommy Rothmore? He's missing too.'

'That's more of a worry,' she murmurs. 'He's taken things so badly.'

'How do you mean?' Nile asks.

'Tommy's been a mess since Amanda dumped him. He was my first boyfriend, years ago. A lot of water's passed under the bridge since then, but I still want the best for him. I tried to persuade him to see Pastor Boakye. I'm not religious but talking to him has helped me and lots of other people here; I thought Tommy might benefit too, but when I suggested it he flew off the handle.'

'When was this?'

'Saturday afternoon, I haven't seen him since. He yelled at me to leave him alone.'

'Do you know why he and Amanda split up?'

'She's treated him badly from day one. I don't understand why people let her get away with it,' Milburn says, scowling with disapproval. 'Tommy's so conscientious about all the charities he funds, there's little time for his private life. Amanda's too spoiled to support him; she felt neglected and went looking for someone else. She wouldn't say who, even though she and Tommy were together over a year. That's unforgivable, isn't it? He's so upset, anyone near him is in the firing line.'

'Has he threatened you physically?' I ask.

'I was afraid to stay. He was smashing up furniture, and he'd hit one of his staff earlier. The rest resigned on the spot.'

'Did you consider calling the police?'

'It seemed disloyal when Tommy's suffering so badly.'

I reach for the girl's hand. 'None of this is your fault,

darling. We just need to find him. He mustn't hurt himself, or Amanda.'

'I've tried to protect him, but it didn't work.' Sacha's expression fiercens suddenly. 'Amanda never deserved him. If she's come to grief, it's her own fault.'

'Why's that?' Nile asks.

'I see everything that goes on here. Tommy had nothing to do with her disappearing. She's been running off to Lovell at night, by herself.'

'How do you know?'

Sacha's gaze drops to the table. 'It's common knowledge that she sees the wrong people.'

She seems unwilling to reveal her source, despite Solomon's probing. We need to find Amanda Fortini soon; it's always easy to blame a community that isn't your own for anything that goes wrong.

'Sorry to disturb you, Sacha,' I say. 'You looked very absorbed in your writing.'

The young woman forces a smile. 'It's just a few notes, but I'm thinking of doing a children's book.'

'How wonderful,' I say, rising to my feet. 'Come and see us soon, and I'm sure we'll chat again at Lily's party, but please keep it a secret. I'm relying on everyone's discretion. We'll let you get back to work.'

Nile appears preoccupied when we walk down to the next terrace. The swimming pool's tiles reflect the sky, the ocean glassy with calmness, even though the weather reports say the tropical storm is tracking south, but I can tell he's in no mood to admire the view. The detective gives a slight nod before thanking me for my help, then marching away.

13

NILE'S FRUSTRATION IS coming to the boil when he reaches
the harbour in Britannia Bay. It's 7p.m., the sun already
setting, and he's still none the wiser about Amanda Fortini's
disappearance. The police launch is moored by the jetty,
covered in oil cloth. It's gone unused for months. The motorboat is little bigger than a standard dinghy, with the
St Vincent police logo written on its prow in faded paint,
and plenty of scrapes marking its fibreglass shell. Nile still
hasn't received permission to visit the *Aqua Dream*, but his
patience has ended. The yacht still dominates the horizon,
moored just outside the bay. He's surprised when the motor
on the police launch starts immediately, as if the boat's been
waiting for a new adventure.

It takes Nile ten minutes to reach the yacht, its sides
towering above him as he draws close. There's no sign of life
except yellow light beaming from a couple of portholes, the
hull so clean, it sparkles in the moonlight. There's a Bayrider
XR7 just like the ones in Old Plantation harbour, safely docked
on deck, with a hydraulic lift to lower it into the water. Nile
is starting to wonder if anyone is on board when a man in

his thirties appears on deck, dressed in typical boat crew's uniform: navy shorts, a white T-shirt and deck shoes. There's no smile on his face when Nile asks to come on board. The crewman is a few years older than he appeared from a distance when the detective climbs the ladder to board, with a chiselled face and a smattering of grey in his collar-length blond hair, skin roughened by the elements. His face is vaguely familiar and instinct tells Nile that he could be the man Amanda Fortini was drawn to, against her better judgement.

'I captain this boat,' the man says, in a rough English drawl. 'What do you want?'

Nile hears footsteps before he can reply, and another man lurches up from the hold to stare at him. They're both heavyset like nightclub bouncers, wearing the same minimal uniform, observing him like he's an alien species. The two men have noticed the gun belt Nile is forced to wear under local police rules, and for once he's glad of the weapon. The atmosphere feels one hundred per cent hostile.

'I'm DS Solomon Nile. I need to ask a few questions.'

The man gives a slow nod. 'We're listening.'

'I've seen you on Mustique before, haven't I?'

The man shakes his head. 'This is the first time I've visited the Windwards since getting my captain's licence.'

'A young woman's missing from Mustique. She was seen swimming towards your yacht, at dawn on Friday. Her name's Amanda Fortini. Did either of you see her?'

'No one's swum out this far.'

'Yachts normally spend a night or two in local waters then sail on to their next destination. Is there any reason you've stayed longer?'

'We're sheltering here until the storm risk lifts.' He gestures at some wetsuits drying on a rail. 'We've been diving, to keep ourselves amused.'

'Who's the owner?'

'A company called Aqua Dream. I don't have any individual names. We're delivering the boat to St Kitts for them.'

'What's your name, Captain?'

'Dan Kellerman.'

'Did you send a launch over to Mustique early on Friday morning, Mr Kellerman?'

'We haven't used it all week, apart from a few trips to Lovell to buy supplies.'

'Mustique's a private island. You can't go ashore without permission.'

'You wouldn't see us starve, would you?'

Nile glances through a window, into a dining room with simple furniture, and only a few paintings on the walls. The plain décor is out of keeping with such an expensive yacht. 'I need to take a look around.'

'That's not possible, without a search warrant.'

The detective tries a different approach. 'The missing woman's twenty-three, Mr Kellerman. She was last seen swimming towards this boat, two days ago. A big launch was crossing the water, just like yours.' He pulls the picture of Amanda Fortini from his pocket and holds it out, but the captain barely glances at it before passing it to his crew member. The second man returns it fast, like it's coated in a substance that will burn his hands.

'Neither of us have seen her.'

'You could save time by letting me do the search now.'

'Bring me the right paperwork and I'll think about it.'

The guy edges closer, like he intends to push Nile overboard, but physical threats are the one time when his bulk comes in useful, so he stands his ground.

'You'll see me again soon, Mr Kellerman.'

It's ninety degrees in the station when Nile gets back, so he sits on a bench outside, thumbing through his notes. He's searched the police database for Dan Kellerman, the captain of the *Aqua Dream*, but found no trace of him as a registered mariner. Either he's never qualified as a captain, or he gave a false name. The facts are still nagging at him when his senior officer from St Vincent calls. Nile watches the sun dipping behind the horizon as DI Fenton Black speaks. He's a big, avuncular man, with a pleasant smile, but there's nothing gentle about his tone today.

'Amanda Fortini's parents called me earlier, Nile. Don't talk to them again without my permission. I'll share the news from now on, do you hear? They mustn't know about your difficulties tracking the girl down. I need something upbeat to tell them tomorrow.'

Nile provides a quick overview, explaining that he's contacted every household on Mustique, and talked to people in Amanda Fortini's circle. It sounds like her ex could be involved: he's sacked his staff and gone on a rampage, destroying items on his property.

'Arrest him then. Let's close this situation down.'

'No one can find him, and I think this is linked to the *Aqua Dream*. Fortini was last seen swimming across the bay towards it, the morning she disappeared. It's possible the crew are holding her there. I need the search warrant urgently.'

'That may not be possible.' There's a long silence before Black continues. 'It's out of my hands, Nile. My superior's waiting for permission from upstairs.'

'What's the problem?'

'He's dealing with it, all right? What else have you found?'

'Amanda Fortini had a secret relationship, according to the local priest. If I can find the new boyfriend, she might be with him.'

'The island's three miles long, Nile. How hard can it be? Bring him in tomorrow.'

'I'll do my best.'

'You do realise the Fortinis are one of the richest families in the world, don't you?'

'I know that, sir. Can I have some backup, to help me search?'

'Not until the storm warning lifts. Flights are grounded and the marine police have stopped all unnecessary travel.'

'It's hundreds of miles away. They could sail here in two hours.'

'We're meant to uphold the law, remember?' Black gives a loud sigh. 'Don't let me down, Nile. I expect answers tomorrow.'

DI Black rings off without another word, leaving Nile watching a picture postcard sunset, which gives no comfort at all. Nile attacks his work with greater purpose once he goes back inside. He scans the names of every villa owner still present on Mustique, then the electoral roll. Some can be discounted immediately, if they are too old or ill to harm a fit young woman, and he checks travel records too. More than a dozen islanders were on St Vincent or St Lucia the

93

morning Amanda Fortini went missing, including Phillip Everard, but no one else can be ruled out, unless they have an alibi.

There are approximately three hundred inhabitants in Lovell, and less than a hundred on the rest of the island currently. Discomfort twitches in his stomach when he remembers Sacha Milburn's suggestion that Amanda Fortini's secret lover could be from his own community, based on hearsay. The schisms in society drove him to join the police instead of continuing his studies, to try to redress that imbalance. He shakes his head in disbelief, for believing he could change the status quo on his own. Nile's conscience brought him home – a combination of the heartbreaking call from Mama Toulaine about his father's poor health, and his fear of repeating the mistakes that cost a woman her life – but will it be strong enough to keep him here, on the bottom rung of the ladder?

When Nile looks at the clock again, hours have passed while he's been buried in work, his neck aching from staring down at his computer. It's 10p.m. and he should go home and make sure that Lyron has made their father comfortable on the porch. He's locking up the station when he glances north, his keys clattering to the ground. The sun set hours ago, yet he can see a plume of smoke, flames leaping upwards, setting the sky alight. The detective scrabbles in the dirt for his keys, then phones the fire service volunteers. He runs to the dune buggy at his fastest pace, to find out which villa is burning out of control.

14

I'VE ENJOYED MY first full evening alone with Lily for months. We're sitting in the living room, by windows that overlook the sea. I can tell she's concerned, after hearing about our search for Tommy Rothmore. Now she has two friends to worry about, instead of one, but she's doing her best to hide her fears. Lily has spent the past half-hour regaling me with stories about the reef.

'I'm thinking of teaching myself to free dive,' she says.

'What on earth's that?'

'Dex Adebayo used to be an expert; it's diving without oxygen. Some people can go down two hundred metres, holding their breath all the way back to the surface.'

'No, darling, please. It would turn me into a nervous wreck.'

She grins at me, her sense of mischief still intact. 'Let's train together, Vee. You used to dive for oysters in Scotland, when I was small. You've always loved the water.'

'I'm fine in the shallows, but there's a thin line between bravery and madness.'

'That sounds like Jasper. He's the perfect combination of both, isn't he?'

I'm about to reply when Wesley bursts into the room. Our butler normally hides his feelings behind a neutral mask, but tonight his tension is easy to read.

'The Fortinis' place is on fire, Lady Vee.'

When Lily and I dash to the window, flames are dancing behind the neighbouring property's upstairs windows. There's a sudden explosion, like a bomb detonating, and a section of the roof caves in, making fire spew upwards.

'My sister could be in there,' Wesley mutters.

We both follow him when he rushes outside. He runs along the perimeter wall, then chases towards the burning building, with Lily hot on his heels. It takes me longer to scale the wall, snagging my silk dress in the process, but nothing can slow him down. He tries to yank a door open, then hurls a brick through a window and clambers inside. Until now I had Wesley pegged as a control freak, not the type of man who races into an inferno. I'd forgotten about his time in the army.

Lily is already helping the volunteer fire officers; six of them are struggling with the fire hose, while the blaze gains strength. The air resonates with the sound of timbers falling, the fire's crackle deafening me. Acrid smoke fills my airways, making my mouth taste sour, my eyes running. I hate feeling so powerless, but there's little I can do. The fire hose is trained on spikes of flame issuing from the building's roof, but it seems unquenchable. The fire dulls for a moment, then rises again, even angrier than before. Wesley's outline appears behind the downstairs windows. He's running from room to room. It was madness to go inside, but all I can do is watch.

When I retreat by a few metres, a new sound reaches me, grating and incongruous. Someone's laughing at the top of their voice when Lily reappears at my side. The sound is high and out of control, like a child, full of hilarity until exhaustion makes them cry. Smoke gusts from the fire, blurring my view. When the air clears a figure is sitting on the ground. His clothes are tattered, face smeared with the ash that's settled in his hair, but I recognise Tommy Rothmore straight away. He's sitting cross-legged, almost hidden by overgrown plants, enchanted by the conflagration. Lily and I walk closer as his cackling grows more strident. There's a mad look in his eyes. I'm not certain he recognises either of us. Lily crouches down beside her friend, but his gaze latches onto my face.

'Mind the fire,' he yells out. 'Your party dress will burn.'

Lily speaks to him in a soothing voice, but he's unreachable. There are holes in his shirt, exposing burned skin, his eyebrows singed. Something's resting on his lap, and for a moment it looks like he's cradling an infant, his arms wrapped around it protectively. When I kneel down at his side, he reeks of booze, exhaling fumes of neat whisky.

'Come with us, Tommy,' Lily says. 'Those burns need dressing.'

'Nothing hurts any more, thank God.' Another round of laughter spills from his mouth when he points at the flames. 'The bonfire of the vanities.'

'Let's go, please,' she says. 'We'll take care of you, I promise.'

He shakes his head vehemently. 'I know where Amanda is. I can picture the exact spot when I close my eyes.'

I take a step closer. 'What do you mean, darling?'

The ground is littered with cans of petrol and white spirit, half-concealed by the tangled undergrowth, but right now I don't care if he set light to his ex-girlfriend's house, and I can tell Lily feels the same, her arm draped protectively round his shoulders. Tommy's gaze is gentler when he speaks again.

'Don't cry, Lily. She hates people being unhappy.'

'Who does, Tommy?'

'Amanda, of course.' He releases another peal of laughter, as if we're missing something obvious, then suddenly he's on his feet. The amusement on his face has been replaced by fear. 'She's right here. Don't bother looking anywhere else.'

He thrusts something into my hands, but I'm too busy watching him blunder through the trees to care about it. His thin form looks like a scarecrow, burned clothes flapping in his wake. Lily chases after him, but he shoves her away, and soon he's running too fast for anyone to catch him. The entire house is engulfed in flames, and people are rushing across the lawn, using buckets of water from the swimming pool, as if such tiny droplets could stem the blaze. Thank God the villa is surrounded by stone terraces. They're containing the fire, instead of allowing it to reach the trees, or our house would be threatened. Flames still surge from the windows upstairs, tiles slipping from the roof in a long cascade. Bystanders have been drawn to the scene from local villas, to see if they can lend a hand, or to watch the place being razed to the ground. Jose is among them. My young gardener is standing apart from the other onlookers, all observing the huge blaze. I'm too far away to read his expression accurately.

Lily has run back to help the fire officers, but I feel helpless to assist them. I keep remembering the fervour in Tommy's voice when he claimed that Amanda is right here. Could he have buried her body in the gardens, or placed it in her home, before setting the villa alight?

There's no sign of Wesley anywhere when my gaze scans the crowd again, panic making me clutch the object Tommy gave me even tighter. It's a lump of dead coral, like the one outside Lily's door, but the pattern carved into its dry surface is different. Someone has used a knife or a scalpel to mark it with a pair of crossed arrows.

15

THE FORTINIS' VILLA is past saving when Nile arrives. The entire structure is ablaze, volunteer fire officers making little headway. Their truck is dwarfed by the huge building, the jet of water having no impact. Two dozen people are still grouped on the lawn; their faces look demonic, lit up by the flames. He walks through the crowd, telling everyone to leave before the walls collapse. There will be injuries if they stand so close to the fire. But when he glances over his shoulder, he understands the attraction. It's providing drama on an island where every day unrolls at the same pace, under a peaceful sky, the sea barely moving. The fire is mesmerising by contrast, destroying everything in its path.

Nile is sending bystanders home when he sees a man lying on the ground, being cared for by Lady Veronica and Lily. When he gets closer, Nile sees that it's their butler, Wesley Gilbert. The man's eyes are closed while he heaves for breath.

'What happened, Lady Vee?'

'The fool ran into the building, before anyone could stop him.'

'His sister Sheba raised the alarm,' Nile replies. 'She's fine; I saw her just now.'

The man struggles upright, his breathing still hoarse. 'Where is she?'

'Right there.' Nile points at a woman on the far side of the crowd.

'Thank God,' he mutters.

Gilbert is too busy catching his breath to speak again. Nile has known him from boyhood; his stern manner and military background make him seem austere, but tonight his fragility is on display, even though he's already trying to stand up, swaying on his feet. Someone must have called for medical help, because Dr Pakefield is jogging towards them, clutching his medical bag. He forces Gilbert to rest until his breathing gradually steadies.

Lady Veronica lingers at Nile's side while Lily comforts the stricken man. The aristocrat looks out of place, her pale dress making her look ghostly, as the fire throws out vivid flames.

'Tommy Rothmore was talking about Amanda just now,' she says. 'We both tried to help him, but he ran away.'

Nile follows her away from the burning building, deeper into the gardens. His eyes widen when he sees a dozen petrol cans strewn across the ground. He listens carefully while Lady Vee explains that the young man was drunk and rambling, laughing his head off at the fire. Tommy may have hidden the cans of petrol in the garden, then waited until the last staff member left, before starting the blaze. Nile knows from experience that a building can ignite in minutes, after seeing a training video from the London Fire

Service. Furniture and curtains burn in seconds, paint singeing from walls, giving the occupants only the briefest chance to escape. A wooden-framed villa like the Fortinis' could be reduced to a charred shell in less than twenty minutes.

'The boy's in trouble mentally,' says Lady Vee. 'He told us to look for Amanda right here, in the grounds. Tommy gave me this piece of coral then ran off.'

'It's like one I found in her room.'

'There was another at our villa too, the morning after I arrived.'

'I need to see that, Lady Vee.'

The coral is as light as sponge when Nile holds it in his hand. It's different from the cutting on Amanda Fortini's bed. This piece is smaller, hacked from the reef with a sharp blade, its surface so dry he can't imagine it vibrant with colour, swaying in the sea's undercurrents. But why has Tommy Rothmore carved each one with crossed arrows? It looks like a voodoo symbol, reminding him of Mama Toulaine's warning. If Tommy is to blame for his ex's absence, he's using coral as his calling card, for reasons only he can explain. Nile keeps hold of Rothmore's parting gift when he instructs Lady Vee to return to her villa, for safety's sake, promising to keep her and Lily updated. The detective sees regret on her face when she says good night. Tommy Rothmore is in serious trouble; the young man almost confessed as much to Lady Vee. Searching the site will be a mammoth task. Amanda Fortini could lie anywhere below the fallen rubble, or in a shallow grave, among the undergrowth. He'll need more officers and heavy-lifting gear to help him complete the hunt, but that may not arrive for days.

Nile returns to Rothmore's hilltop villa, hoping to find him in his summerhouse, but the place is empty. The island may only be a few miles long, but there are many places to hide, or someone could be offering him shelter. The detective heads for Lovell at a slow pace, stopping to peer into the grounds of empty villas. It's only when he reaches the doctor's house that he sees anything of interest. A row of diesel cans is stacked by the garden wall, the same type as the ones scattered across the Fortinis' garden. He's about to approach the house when Dr Pakefield strides down the path. The man only comes to a halt when he spots Nile, waiting in the shadows, and comes to a sudden halt.

'You gave a me a fright, Detective Nile. Are you here to see me?'

'Sorry to call by so late. I saw your lights on and wanted to ask if anyone else needed treatment after the fire, apart from Wesley Gilbert.'

'The only serious casualty is the house itself.'

'That's good to know. Are you going for a walk?'

'I like a final stroll before bed. It helps my sleep.'

'Do you know why there are so many diesel cans by the entrance?'

The doctor gives him a blank stare. 'They belong to Dr Bunbury; maybe they're for his boat.'

'Have you used it yet?'

'That would be an odd thing to do on my own. My children would love it, but they're not here.'

'Do you know where it's kept?'

'In the boathouse on the beach below the villa. Do you mind if I take my walk now? Tomorrow's an early start.'

Nile allows him to march away. It's well after midnight but the doctor appears glad to escape; his thin form is moving so fast, he looks like he's warming up for a sprint. Instinct makes Nile visit the beach to check on Dr Bunbury's speedboat. There's no light in the wooden boathouse, but something interests him when moonlight floods inside. The boat is older than the others he's seen, but its fibre-glass shell is still pristine, because everyone knows it's Dr Bunbury's pride and joy. It's only when he touches the prow that his fingertips trace a deep scratch in the varnish. He's got no way to prove that Dr Pakefield took the speed-boat to Britannia Bay, on the morning when Amanda Fortini was last seen, but it's definitely been used recently. The owner would have removed any trace of damage, rather than leaving it on display.

16

Monday, 16th September 2002

I CAN SMELL smoke before I open my curtains at 8a.m. The sun is already high overhead, but when I look down at the Fortinis' villa it's a scene of devastation, the external walls blackened with soot. Only the central chimney stack is undamaged; it's still standing tall, like a soldier on a battlefield surrounded by dead comrades. Tommy Rothmore's behaviour continues to bother me, his manic laughter ringing in my ears.

Lily is on the terrace when I go outside, staring at the ruins.

'I can't believe it, Vee. First Amanda disappears, then her house goes up in smoke. Who hates her enough to do that?'

'Tommy was very disturbed last night. I thought he seemed ashamed of something, before he ran away.'

The fear in Lily's eyes proves that she believes Tommy is the likely culprit, but she's too upset to discuss it. Lily is so independent these days, I sometimes forget the trauma she experienced as a child. The Fortinis' villa is one of the few places where she felt safe after her mother's death. Now it's been destroyed, and her closest friend is still missing. It's possible Tommy was trying to confess his deeds last night, but I shift the conversation to a safer topic.

'Wesley paid a high price for his bravery. Inhaling all that smoke did him no good at all.'

'He's invincible, Vee. Nothing can bring him down.'

'Is that how you see him?'

She smiles in reply. 'He was terribly stern when I was small, but always with a twinkle in his eye. I hope he's feeling better.'

'Me too. I'll check on him after breakfast. He turned up for work, even though I told him to rest.'

'See what I mean? The man's immortal.' Her jollity takes a sudden nosedive. 'I wish I could think of a way to help Amanda and Tommy. It's making me feel useless.'

'Solomon's promised to keep us informed. He'll soon tell us what he needs,' I say. 'Stop pacing, darling, please. You'll wear out those espadrilles.'

When the maid delivers our food, Wesley has arranged it with his usual eye to detail, despite last night's drama. There's sliced banana and grated coconut, brioche, home-made jams and a platter of the island's excellent goat's cheese. But Lily only seems interested in the cafetière of coffee. It's only now that I remember the coral I found in the corridor upstairs, so I retrieve it from the plant pot.

'This was outside your room on Sunday morning, Lily. Did you put it there?'

'Why would I bring chunks of coral to the house?'

'I assumed you wanted to show me the reef's in a poor state.'

'You already know, Vee, you and Jasper are my charity's biggest donors. Someone's cut a pattern into it. Do you think it's a spider's web?'

'You could be right,' I say, touching it again. 'But I'm more worried about who left it there. It arrived the night I saw Jose.'

'Let's speak to Detective Nile. Did I tell you Keith Belmont's considering giving me a big donation? His lawyer's sent me a fifteen-page contract to read, all about Keith's potential role.'

'Consider carefully before you accept, darling, he's a slippery customer. But tell me how your grafts are doing.'

'Eighty per cent have taken,' she says. 'But the storm could spoil everything, if it heads our way. Any implants that aren't properly embedded will be torn away.'

'I'd almost forgotten the hurricane. The water looks so peaceful.'

'The forecast says it's coming closer. There's always calm before a storm, isn't there?'

I'm relieved to hear that she will be carrying out maintenance on her boat today, not going out to sea. She'll come home later to work on her grant application for the Oceanographic Society. Lily looks relaxed for the first time when she explains that another year's funding could allow her to recruit more divers, to help bring the reef back to life. Her tension only becomes visible again when her attention shifts back to last night.

'I think Tommy blames me for his relationship breaking down, for some reason. Sacha's been acting weird too. We were all getting along fine at the start of summer, but now the group's fallen apart.'

'Keep your distance if you see him, won't you? Call Solomon Nile immediately.'

'I can't believe Tommy would hurt anyone, but I'll do as you say. It's clear he's not in his right mind.'

'Have you got Solomon's number?'

She pours herself more coffee. 'He gave it to me the first time we met.'

'Handsome, isn't he? I imagine if he took his spectacles off he'd be a dreamboat.'

Lily's gaze hardens. 'I haven't been looking; I just want Amanda found.'

'Why not stay here today, with me? Work on the boat tomorrow.'

'I'll go crazy if I sit still, and the engine needs an overhaul. The *Revival* has to be seaworthy, so I can do the next phase of grafting before the coral spawns.'

Lily drops a kiss on my cheek, then vanishes indoors. She clung to me as a little girl, but she can be implacable. I admire her tenacity, even though I'd prefer to keep her safe at my side.

I gather our breakfast plates, then take them down to the basement, where Wesley is in the kitchen, polishing wine glasses. He looks horrified by the sight of me carrying a tray full of crockery.

'What are you doing, Lady Vee? That's the maid's job,' he says, seizing it from my hands.

I perch on a stool by his table. 'Sorry for barking at you last night. You gave me quite a scare.'

The butler carries on buffing the glass he's holding to a high shine. 'It was nothing to worry about. Everything's in order here.'

'We'd all have been terribly upset if you got hurt.'

'I was never in real danger.' His voice is a fraction softer than before.

'You passed out cold from smoke inhalation.'

'The doctor says I'm fit and well. I saw far worse in the army.'

'Very few people would run into a burning building to save someone. I think you're a hero. Please take a few days off and recover properly.'

'Who would look after you?' He puts down the glass, then turns to face me. 'I had no choice last night. My sister's got three kids, still at school. She's always last to leave the Fortinis' place.'

I blink at him in amazement; that's the longest speech my butler's ever given. I wish that he would lower his guard more often, but the man's sense of privacy protects him like a forcefield. He reveals virtually nothing about his life, even though he understands every detail of mine.

'I'm lucky to have you running Eden House, Wesley. I don't thank you often enough.'

He manages a smile. 'Once a year is plenty.'

'You're irreplaceable.'

'You're welcome, Lady Vee. I'm only doing my job,' he says, his spine stiffening again.

'Can I ask something about Amanda Fortini?'

'Go ahead.'

'I got the sense she upset you. Is there a reason for that?'

He remains silent, gathering his thoughts. 'I don't expect to be treated like an equal by all your visitors; you and Lord Blake are different to the rest, but she never meets my eye.

If I bring her a drink, it's like I'm invisible. After all these years, I bet she doesn't even know my name.'

I can feel his anger heating the air. 'That's an appalling way to behave. I'm sorry, Wesley, I had no idea.'

'Miss Lily and your children are always respectful; you've taught them to be civilised. Now, if you don't mind, these glasses need finishing, and so does the silver.'

The phone is ringing when I reach the hallway. When I hear a woman's panicked voice interspersed with bouts of tears, I know it's Giovanna Fortini. She doesn't seem to care about her holiday villa being razed to the ground. Losing bricks and mortar is nothing compared to her daughter going missing. I can only remind her that police are searching everywhere for Amanda. I don't tell her that the local force consists of one solitary detective. She's more concerned about being unable to reach the island to hunt for Amanda, while airports and ferry services remain closed, but that won't change while Storm Cristobal edges closer, dancing to a tune no one else can hear.

17

DS NILE HAS put out an announcement on the local radio station, which broadcasts across the Windward Islands. It will repeat every hour, advising Mustique's inhabitants of Amanda Fortini's disappearance, and the need to report sightings of her and Tommy Rothmore, but it's 10a.m. and no one has responded. When he looks through the open door of his office, there's no sign of the Layton brothers. Maybe they're doing some work for a change, but as they never explain their movements it will remain a mystery.

He leaves the station to look for Tommy Rothmore again, but his phone rings, just as he's locking the station's door. It's someone calling from Keith Belmont's villa, reporting a break-in last night, when someone was seen escaping from the complex. The news makes Nile grit his teeth. He has to stop himself barking that petty crime isn't his priority: a woman's missing, and a potential murderer is on the loose; but he bites his tongue. If he refuses to look into the crime, Belmont might complain to his seniors on St Vincent.

It takes Nile ten minutes to drive his dune buggy to Belmont's villa, which lies hidden behind a ten-foot-high perimeter fence. Nile studies the name plaque on the wall as he announces his arrival to the intercom; the house is called Blue Heaven, after Belmont's band. Nile isn't a fan of hard rock, but Blue Heaven enjoyed huge success thirty years ago and their fans remained loyal until they disbanded last year. Belmont's private life has earned him almost as much attention as his music; his last marriage to a girl of sixteen made headline news. Nile read somewhere that Blue Heaven's final world tour grossed over five hundred million dollars, even though the band spent all their spare time arguing. On any other day a visit to Belmont's villa would appeal to his curious nature, but the timing's wrong. Nile is bristling with frustration while he waits for the metal door to click open, admitting him to the rock star's empire.

He expected a huge mansion, covered in bling, with an Olympic-sized pool, but Belmont's home is a miracle of clean lines and polished steel. The garden surrounding it is minimal too; the ground is covered in white gravel with a few sculptures and cacti dotted across its blank expanse.

No staff member appears when he walks down the path, but the front door stands ajar. The only sign that Blue Heaven's world-famous frontman lives inside is a Fender Stratocaster guitar hanging from the wall. Nile steps closer to admire it; the instrument looks time-worn, covered in dents and scrapes, plus a few stickers announcing cities the band took by storm.

'You must be a musician, from the way you're checking out my favourite guitar. I bought it from a pawn shop in Nashville, forty years ago.'

When Nile swings round, a thin middle-aged man is observing him. He's dressed in a black T-shirt, faded Levis and Birkenstocks, grey hair worn in a ponytail. There's nothing to announce Keith Belmont's fame, apart from his world-famous features, which look like they've been chipped from the side of a mountain. He seems determined to keep his distance, not bothering to step any closer.

'What instrument do you play?' Belmont asks.

'Drums, but not for a long time.'

'You never lose the knack. Thanks for coming by. I wanted to report the damage, before cleaning up. Can I get you anything? Juice, or iced tea?'

'Water would be great, thanks.'

Nile is surprised to find himself being waited on in Belmont's kitchen. There's a slight tremor in the man's hand when he slides the glass across the surface towards him. Why would someone who has played in front of a hundred thousand fans be nervous, unless he's got something to hide? Up close Nile can see that Belmont has left his face as nature intended, battle-scarred like his guitar, with lines grooved deep into his skin. If the man has been shocked or disturbed by the break-in, there's no visible sign.

'Do you live here year-round, Mr Belmont?'

'No formality, please. Keith is fine.' He drops onto a kitchen stool and gestures for Nile to do the same. 'I've been here six months, with a couple of visits back to the UK. My head was a mess after a brutal divorce, but you're too young to know about that.'

'I'm old enough to know break-ups are hard.'

Belmont rubs the back of his neck like he's massaging

tension away. 'I keep telling myself matrimony's a bad idea, but it's happened three times.'

'Four might be your lucky number.'

'There's no way it's happening again.'

Nile finishes his glass of water and places it on the counter. The exchange feels bizarre: the guy has played Madison Square Garden and the Albert Hall, yet he's sharing personal details. Nile can't yet tell whether Belmont's openness is real, or just another piece of showmanship.

'Could I see the damage, please?'

When the musician leads him to his living room, the air stinks of booze, a drinks cabinet upended, leaving shattered bottles lying on the floor. The bifold doors have been smashed with a sledgehammer that's still lying on the ground, a river of glass fragments pooling on the stone tiles. The paintings on the wall have been slashed to ribbons, a wide-screen TV in pieces on the floor. Furniture has been ruined too, a sofa sliced apart, with padding spilling from the gaps.

'Was much stolen?'

'Bugger all, as far as I can tell. They trashed the place and left; I think it may have been just one guy. I caught a glimpse of him climbing over the back wall.'

'Didn't your staff hear anything?'

'I only employ one assistant. He's here nine to five, Monday to Friday. At the weekends I fend for myself.'

'So it was you that phoned earlier? I thought you'd have a team.'

'An entourage, you mean?' Belmont releases a snarl of laughter, his voice suddenly bitter. 'I can't stand that shit. Being alone is sorting my head out, at last.'

'Do you know what time it happened?'

'Around 3a.m. last night. I sleep well normally, but a noise woke me, so I chucked on some clothes and ran down. The bloke had no time to nick anything. I went back to bed after that and slept till morning.'

Nile stares at him. 'Thieves vandalised your home, but you just went back to sleep?'

'I've lived through worse.'

'Are you sure about only seeing one person?'

'I only caught a glimpse of him, and the damage is nothing compared to hotel rooms I've trashed. I loved breaking stuff when I was young; maybe that's all they wanted.'

'Do you mind if I look outside?'

'Be my guest.'

Nile picks his way over the broken glass, observing how the intruder escaped. The garden is surrounded by white-painted walls, at least ten feet high, so whoever trashed Belmont's sitting room must be agile. The intruder left scuff marks from clambering over it fast, when the musician came downstairs, but he can't understand Belmont's reaction. Even the coolest individual would be too shaken up after a violent burglary to go straight back to sleep when the thieves could return at any time.

Keith Belmont beckons Nile closer and the detective assumes he's got more information about the burglary, but he leads him into a recording studio instead. The musician's only sign of personal vanity is a collection of gold and platinum records that covers the end wall.

'I'm glad they didn't nick this lot. I'd have been gutted, even though I took it all for granted at the time.'

'It's a big achievement.'

'You're only as good as your next album. I'll be recording solo tracks later this year.' Belmont's expression remains impassive. 'Play me a rhythm, can you?'

'I should be going.'

'Don't make me beg. It'll take you a minute, tops.'

Nile senses that refusing will delay him further, but still feels embarrassed. It's so long since he held a pair of sticks that they feel foreign in his hands. The beat is hesitant at first, but memory helps him tap out a few bars of reggae, followed by a long drum roll.

Belmont finally cracks a smile. 'Where've you been hiding? I've scoured the whole bloody island for a decent drummer. Come round Sunday night, some guys will be here for a jam and a few beers.'

'I'm afraid I'll be working, Mr Belmont . . .'

'. . . Keith. I need you, man. Don't make excuses.'

'You must have heard that Amanda Fortini's missing; it's keeping me pretty busy.'

The musician stares back at him. 'That girl's a sweetheart. I saw the smoke from her villa last night.'

'Do you know her well?'

'She does yoga here every week, and we play tennis occasionally. Do you know what's happened?'

'I need to talk to her ex-boyfriend.'

'Tommy Rothmore's pretty strung out. I invited him to yoga too, but he couldn't hack it. The boy can't sit still for five minutes.'

'If you see him, please call me straight away. I'll write an incident report, for your insurers.'

The two men are returning to the living room when Nile spots something on the ground. It's a lump of coral, like the two he's seen before, but the carving is different when he crouches down to examine it. A simple U shape has been cut into its surface.

'Is this yours?'

Belmont drops down beside him. 'It's coral, but not from my collection. The stuff fascinates me. I learned how to dive, so I could see it up close. I've been gathering fragments from all over the world, but mine are harvested sustainably.'

'How come you're so interested?'

'Coral's unique on this planet. It can regenerate from a single cell, it's got thousands of sub-species, and it can break down some of the worst poisons we chuck into the sea.' He shakes his head in disgust. 'Some idiot's hacked that out with a bloody machete.'

'You own a Bayrider XR7 speedboat, don't you? I've seen it in the harbour.'

'What's that got to do with it?'

'Nothing, probably, but do you use it sometimes, to visit the reef?'

'I normally use a kayak these days, if I want to go for a snorkel. It's stopped Lily Calder nagging me about putting a hole in the ozone layer.'

'When's the last time you took the Bayrider out?'

'Weeks ago. Why?'

'A launch just like yours was seen in Britannia Bay, when Amanda Fortini was last seen, taking a swim early on Friday morning.'

'I was here by myself. Getting up late's a bad habit of mine.'

The musician watches Nile pick up the coral, his face unreadable. Belmont repeats his invitation to the jam session on Saturday night, but Nile offers no guarantee that he'll attend. Nile tells him to keep his place secure and consider staying with friends or at Firefly until the culprit's found. It's only after the metal security doors click shut behind him that Nile realises the musician's only flicker of emotion was when he talked about the coral. Their conversation has proved that Belmont has the diving skills needed to harvest the coral that keeps appearing at each crime scene.

18

JASPER IS UNUSUALLY calm when he calls in the morning. My husband is at his best with a task to keep him occupied and he's been busy collecting the costumes for our party guests and getting them stored at the airport. They will be flown over once the storm warning lifts. My biggest fear is that Lily's celebration might be eclipsed by Amanda's absence, but Jasper seems glad of a distraction.

'I'd rather fret about the party than talk to those wretched architects.'

'You'll bring them round, darling.'

'Don't bet on it; they never listen.' His voice quavers when he replies.

'Please don't let it worry you too much.'

Jasper's mental health has been shaky for years. I do my best to shield him from stress, but it's not always possible. My seven decades have taught me many valuable lessons – some unpleasant, others salutary. I have learned that physical exercise stops me worrying about my husband, so I make myself do thirty laps of the pool. After some initial discomfort, it becomes a pleasure. Last night's fire and

Jasper's volatility are distant memories while I'm floating on my back, listening to hummingbirds overhead, and my own quiet breathing.

I'm almost finished when Phillip arrives on the terrace. He's keen to help me plan where to locate our guests, between his home, mine, and the island's two hotels. The man looks like he's stepped out of a play by Noel Coward, dressed in high-waisted trousers and a crisp white shirt.

'Join me,' I call out to him.

'I can't, the doctor would have a fit.'

'Spoilsport.'

'If I swim, my hearing will suffer.' Phillip taps his ear, then motions for me to continue, so I complete another lap. My skin's glowing by the time I stop. Half an hour in the water has cured life's ills, for the time being. I wrap myself in a towel, then wander over to Phillip.

'You look like a water nymph, gliding through the waves,' he tells me.

'More like a crocodile these days.'

'Nonsense, I'm still keen to elope.' My old friend smiles, but I can see he's troubled.

'What's wrong, darling? You haven't been yourself since I got back.'

'I should have told you this sooner.' He hesitates for a moment. 'Tommy called at my villa last week, terribly upset about breaking up with Amanda. I should have listened more carefully. I didn't exactly say there are more fish in the sea, but I was too blasé.'

'Maybe he's been depressed for ages, and Amanda leaving him was the final straw.'

'I should have figured that out.' Phillip's gaze settles on me again. 'Do you think he's hurt her?'

'Whatever happened, it's not your fault.'

'You shouldn't let me off the hook so easily.' He reaches out to touch my hand. 'The boy came to me for advice, but I'm not getting any wiser with the passing years. Rejection hurts me just as much as it did in my teens. I wish I'd given him more solace, but it's enough work keeping myself on the straight and narrow.'

'Don't be so hard on yourself; I can't imagine you being mean to anyone. You've given me and Jasper so much support over the years.'

'What a sweetheart you are, Vee. If you could transport yourself back to any time in your life, when would it be?'

'When my children were small, I think. How about you?'

'Straight after acting school, earning nothing, and playing in off-Broadway shows. I had a dream last night that I was back in a tiny theatre, doing *The Cherry Orchard*. It was glorious.'

'How perfect, I can imagine you as a handsome young thespian.'

I drop a kiss on Phillip's cheek, leaving him drinking mint tea while I go upstairs to dress. I always choose pale colours to combat Mustique's heat, and this morning I pick white linen trousers, a light blue shirt, with a string of agate beads. My friend looks pleased with my appearance, as if a lapse from elegance would be a cardinal sin, but the damage to the Fortinis' property overshadows our chat. The smell of burned timber still lingers on the air, and it's still hard to believe that such a grand building has been reduced to rubble. I make a deliberate effort to focus on Lily's party, instead of fretting about something I can't fix.

'Around a hundred and fifty people are coming. Half of them are flying in on private planes.'

'You're pushing it, aren't you?' he says, narrowing his eyes.

'Josephine and Georgia are flying in next week to give us a hand, bless them. They can take twenty people each at their villas, Firefly are taking fourteen, and another thirty at the Cotton House. I'm sure we can sprinkle the rest liberally across friends' villas, can't we?'

We're talking about a welcoming committee at the airport, and decking the building with night-sky decorations, so the party's theme begins as soon as guests touch down, when I catch sight of someone running across the lawn. There's a fierce look on Jose Gomez's face when he grabs my wrist and pulls me to my feet. He drags me towards the steps, like he's desperate to show me something.

'What are you doing here, Jose? It's your day off.'

A guttural noise issues from his mouth, but he carries on pulling me towards the steps that lead down to the beach, until Phillip comes to my aid.

'Stop that, right now,' he tells the gardener. 'What on earth's wrong?'

The young man backs away, his expression terrified, until Wesley appears.

'Go home, Jose,' my butler snaps at him, until I'm finally released. 'I'll talk to you about this tomorrow.'

'What's happened to him?' Phillip says. 'He did exactly the same thing to me last week, when I was having breakfast.'

Jose is already slipping away between the trees. I still don't know who broke into my villa to leave the dead coral outside Lily's room, but Jose's behaviour is so odd, I can't help suspecting he's involved. He's had many opportunities to watch Amanda in the neighbouring garden, and I know he's been following Phillip and me. My gaze catches on the Fortinis' villa again, while Wesley and Phillip discuss the gardener's behaviour. The property's scorched framework looks darker than ever, my memories of pool parties and dancing in that wild garden reduced to ashes.

'I'd better call Solomon,' I tell Phillip.

'Good plan, we need to get to the bottom of this.'

I hurry inside to call our detective's mobile, but there's no reply.

19

IT'S AFTER 11A.M. when Nile receives a voice message from Lady Vee about her gardener behaving strangely, but working alone makes it impossible to respond. There's a bigger problem to deal with before he can go to Eden House. Someone has seen a fishing boat stranded off Old Plantation Bay, and St Vincent's marine rescue service aren't prepared to launch a rescue with a storm on its way. Nile resents the new distraction but can't ignore it. Currents will carry the boat out to sea if he doesn't act fast. He can't see the fishing boat's outline from the jetty when he reaches the harbour, so the vessel may already have been dragged miles from the island.

He twists the key in the ignition three times before the police launch finally revs into life. He's making slow progress when a large speedboat cuts across the bay, travelling at top speed. Its wash sends artificial waves rippling across the water, the words '*Aqua Dream*' inscribed on its prow. Nile feels discomfort prickling the back of his neck, almost certain the mysterious boat is connected to Amanda Fortini's disappearance, but his boss's refusal to provide a warrant leaves his hands tied. He increases his speed, scanning the ocean ahead, but there's still no sign of the stranded vessel, only the speed-boat racing back across the bay. Kellerman seems to be parading his freedom in front of his face, as a deliberate taunt.

Nile takes half an hour to spot the fishing boat drifting helplessly on the tide. The vessel is like the one his father used to sail, a handmade dinghy, painted vivid yellow, with no shelter from the sun and only a small outboard motor. Hosea still talks about the days when fishermen caught only what they needed to eat, plus a few more for their neigh-bours, then cast the rest back into the ocean alive. These days trawlers operate out of St Vincent, dredging tons of fish from the sea every day, leaving slim pickings for Lovell's tiny fleet. Nile can read the old man's relief in his body language, both hands waving in welcome. It's one of his father's closest friends, Claude Boulez, but he's still annoyed. He'd rather be looking for Amanda Fortini and her disturbed ex-boyfriend than rescuing lost fishermen. The old man is bare-chested, wearing a pair of frayed shorts, with no hat to protect him from the sun.

'What are you doing, Papa? Couldn't another fishing boat tow you home?'

Boulez beckons him closer, and Nile sees that he's had a good morning. The basket at his feet is heaving with flounder, yellow-tailed snapper and squirrelfish. The man should be jubilant, but his expression is blank.

'You need to see why my engine broke.'

'Why? You can fix it after you're back at harbour.'

The old man's eyes blaze at him. 'Come on board right now, Solomon.'

Nile tuts under his breath, but follows Boulez's request. A culture of respect still exists in Lovell, the old free to advise the young. If a village elder makes a request, you're duty-bound to obey, and Nile's police badge makes no difference. He uses his mooring rope to tie the two boats together, then steps aboard. Papa Boulez's age shows when he's up close. The man's chest is covered in knots of white hair, his eyes turning milky, hardly any fat covering his bones.

'What's wrong, Papa?'

Boulez shakes his head. 'I saw petrels all diving together. I thought they'd found a school of grouper, so I sailed out here fast.'

'What did you find?'

'Something so big, I couldn't haul it on board. I'm not strong enough to pull up my net by hand.'

'Is it a reef shark?'

'It's bad luck to talk about it at sea.' The old man shuts his eyes. 'Take a look for yourself.'

Nile steps past the old man, the boat reeling drunkenly on the waves, while sunlight warms the back of his neck. He works up a sweat hauling in the net, hand over hand, with half a dozen red snapper landing at his feet. Something heavy is snagged at the bottom, but the catch still comes as a shock, making his heart rate soar. The sole of someone's foot appears first, tangled in the fishing net. He takes a deep breath and hauls with all his strength until a man's body flops, face down, into the hold. The corpse is dressed in a ripped blue shirt and shorts, a Rolex watch still attached to his wrist. Nile's vision blurs when he rolls the man's body over: Tommy Rothmore's face is almost unrecognisable. One light green eye has been plucked from its socket, his skin littered with cuts, forcing Nile to stare at the horizon, to clear his nausea.

Papa Boulez is on his knees, praying over the body. Nile wishes he still shared his faith, but there are few signs of a divine being's existence today. There's only the pitiless ocean, while Mustique drifts from sight. When he glances east, his gaze catches on the *Aqua Dream*, moored so close by, every porthole is visible. Amanda Fortini disappeared into its shadow and now her ex has been dredged from the same stretch of water. There's a sudden cacophony overhead; birds are gathering again, directly above Rothmore's body, expecting a free meal.

PART TWO

Tropical Weather Outlook

National Hurricane Center, Miami FL

Monday, 16 September 2002

For the North Atlantic and Caribbean Sea

The National Hurricane Center is issuing advisories on Tropical Storm Cristobal, located over central Cuba, causing damage to property. 90 mile per hour wind with predicted storm surges.

Cyclone tracking south, current risk rating: moderate

20

PHILLIP HAS GONE home for a siesta when Jasper calls again. His voice is flat with despair, before I've even said hello.

'The wretched builders are working at a snail's pace. I need you here, Vee. Things are falling apart.'

'It's the same on Mustique. Amanda's still missing, and no one can find Tommy Rothmore either. She hasn't been seen for three days, and it looks like he burned her villa to the ground.'

'Good Lord, are you serious? The boy's a billionaire, isn't he?'

'What difference does that make?'

'He's got the entire world at his feet.'

Jasper's frustration is replaced by curiosity when I distract him with the investigation. One of my husband's strengths is that – although easily upset – he rarely nurses grievances. He demands precise details, like Hercule Poirot, but I'm relieved his voice is steady when we say goodbye.

The phone rings again moments later. Solomon Nile's tone is sober; sea gulls are bawling in the background when he asks me for a favour. He wants the island's only ambulance sent to Old Plantation harbour. I sense immediately that the matter is serious when he issues another instruction.

'Bring Dr Pakefield with you please, Lady Vee.'

My heart sinks at the request; Nile's sombre tone suggests that he's found a corpse, not a living person. It takes me ten minutes to convince the receptionist at the medical centre that the locum's services are needed urgently, even though he's making house calls, but my forceful tone has the desired effect. Simon Pakefield is waiting outside the medical centre when I arrive in my buggy. I haven't seen him since the Fortinis' villa was on fire; he gives me a courteous greeting but the man looks tired, as if some private worry is nagging at him, but it's the wrong time to fret about his state of mind. We work together to empty the ambulance of its contents, piling boxes of medication and bandages in the medical centre's small lobby. It's a typically eccentric feature of island life that the ambulance doubles as a pick-up van and is often driven by the doctor himself. Pakefield looks bemused by my request to go straight to Old Plantation harbour. We set off at a steady speed, because attempting to drive fast on some of the island's worst tracks would result in a broken axle. Neither of us bothers with small talk. We both know that an urgent request for an ambulance rarely signals good news.

Solomon is on an old fishing boat when we reach the jetty, talking to Claude Boulez. I've known the fisherman for years, because he brings his catch to my villa, selling lobster or swordfish steaks to Wesley. Boulez is normally all smiles, but today he barely greets me before hurrying away.

'What's happened, Solomon?' I ask. 'Is it Amanda?'

'Let's talk at the medical centre, Lady Vee.'

Nile says a few hushed words to Dr Pakefield, and my fears are confirmed when they lift a bulky shape from the boat's hold, wrapped in a tarpaulin. Its outline is unmistakably human. When I return to the passenger seat, my hands grip the dashboard like a safety blanket. Neither man speaks as we make the return journey, and I can only stand by and watch the body being carried inside the medical centre.

'Wait outside please,' Solomon tells me. 'You don't want to see this.'

'You need a witness to identify the victim.'

'It should be a relative, or next of kin.'

I stare up at him. 'I see everyone on this island as my extended family. I can't just walk away.'

Nile sighs loudly before allowing me into the room, where the victim's face is already exposed. It's fortunate that I'm standing by the wall, because I need to lean against it hard to remain upright. I've always had a strong stomach, but the young man's injuries will fill my nightmares for weeks. I recognise Tommy Rothmore's ash-blond hair immediately, but his features are ruined. Even our restrained locum appears moved by seeing a young man's life ended so violently.

Solomon is taking photos with his mobile while the doctor removes the tarpaulin. Tommy is dressed in tattered jeans, his torso bare. His form is so slender he looks more like a boy than a man. Now the Rothmores will have to experience the desperate suffering of losing a child, and my heart breaks for them. I've been afraid he might take his own life since witnessing his disturbed behaviour last night.

Dr Pakefield puts on a white coat and surgical gloves to examine the body, while Nile towers over the gurney like a giant trapped inside a lift compartment. The detective is busy scribbling words in his notebook.

'How long ago did you find him?' the doctor asks.

'A fishing boat trawled him from the sea two hours ago.'

'We need a pathologist brought from St Vincent when the storm's passed, but I can tell he drowned. His lungs are full of water. If his corpse had been thrown into the sea, that wouldn't be the case. Dead men can't inhale.'

'He must have been held somewhere,' Nile answers. 'There's a rope around his ankle.'

The locum examines the man's feet, pushing back the torn legs of his jeans, and my breathing quickens. Rope has been bound tightly around Tommy's right ankle, with the end frayed apart, his calves covered in cuts and scratches. I'm coming to terms with the young man's horrible death, but force myself to stare at the poor boy's wounds without flinching. A few chalk-white spikes protrude from an injury on his calf, long and thin, like dismembered fingers.

'It looks like he was tied to the seabed,' I say. 'Those fragments in his cuts are spikes of dead coral, aren't they?'

Nile nods in agreement. 'I'll take one as a sample.'

'There's so much debris in the sea, we can't prove how he got those injuries,' the doctor replies. 'We'll need to keep his body here for the time being. There's a medical refrigerator in the building.'

I watch in silence as Nile places a shard of coral in a plastic tube, then helps the doctor lift Tommy's corpse into a body bag, until his head lolls to one side, like he's desperate to make a final statement. My hands tremble when his one remaining eye meets my face, like he's begging me to find his killer, and I make an internal promise to do my best. When Dr Pakefield zips the bag closed, the boy's brief life is over. His body is wheeled next door, where a drawer is pulled from the wall. The two men handle Tommy's body respectfully but it still feels like an abandonment. Now there's no evidence of his existence, except the number one on the metal drawer, and a blast of cold air.

I bid goodbye to Solomon and the doctor immediately. I know how quickly information spreads across this minute island, and I want Lily to hear the news from me, not another source. Despite Solomon's wish to keep Tommy's death secret until his parents are informed, his chances are slim, so I climb back into my buggy and set off for Eden House at top speed.

21

NILE HAS HATED the smell of hospitals since his father made him say a last goodbye to his mother as a child. He's blocked out the memory, except for that reek of medicine and anti-septic. The corridor has the same odour today and he wishes that Dr Bunbury had returned from his holiday. Pakefield's reticent manner makes it hard to get clear answers; it looks like he's been spending far too long indoors, with no trace of a tan on his pallid skin. The locum always seems ill at ease, but a man can't be arrested just because there's a guilty look about him.

'Can we talk in your consulting room, please, doctor? I just need to confirm a few points.'

Pakefield leads Nile down the corridor, then positions himself behind his desk, his expression solemn, like he's about to share a fatal diagnosis.

'This doesn't sit comfortably with me,' he says quietly. 'Tommy came here last week, suffering with anxiety, insomnia and intrusive thoughts. I prescribed mild anti-depressants and advised him to accept some counselling, but I may have missed something.'

'How do you mean?'

'Psychoactive drugs can trigger delusional behaviour in a tiny number of patients. It might sound bizarre, but he could have committed suicide, couldn't he?'

'What about the rope tied around his leg? It looks like his feet and calves were grazed from scraping across the reef, as if he'd used all his strength to break free.'

'I still think Tommy could have taken his own life. Suicides sometimes fill their pockets with stones; he may have attached a weight to his leg then thrown himself off a boat. A dinghy could drift for miles, carried by a riptide.'

'That's unlikely, doctor. We'd have found it by now.'

'That's a relief. I'd hate to think he'd harmed himself because of his mental state.'

The doctor's manner seems to lift suddenly, his scowl vanishing.

'Do you mind me asking what brought you to the Windward Isles?'

'I trained at London's biggest teaching hospital, staying there for years as an assistant registrar, then fancied a career change.'

'You gave up a senior job, to become a GP here?'

'My wife and I wanted our kids to see the world.' Pakefield blinks rapidly. 'Sorry, but how is my professional background relevant to Tommy Rothmore's death?'

'Forgive me, it isn't. I was just curious.'

'That's fine, but I should phone the coroner then write my report.'

Nile's mind is crammed with information when he leaves the consulting room. The idea of a young man attaching a weight to his body to quicken his death seems unnatural, whatever his mental condition. But when he calls his boss on St Vincent, DI Black latches onto Pakefield's theory. He seems relieved to be handed a credible story for the press and families: the young man took his own life after killing his ex, in revenge for breaking his heart. Amanda Fortini's body hasn't yet been found, but Tommy's fury at her rejection is common knowledge. He may have ended her life then abandoned her corpse at sea, before taking his own.

'The doctor sounds like a wise man, Nile. Get him to put that in his report.'

'It's guesswork, sir, and we both agreed Rothmore was probably abducted while he was drunk, then tied up somewhere to drown. It looks like he was dragged across the reef; we found pieces of coral in his wounds.'

Black scoffs at the idea. 'There's never been a homicide on Mustique, Nile. Phone the parents, then announce the tragic circumstances. Mr Thomas Rothmore has taken his own life and Miss Amanda Fortini is missing, presumed dead. The islanders can draw their own conclusions and the case is closed.'

'His body was found near the *Aqua Dream*. I still need that search warrant urgently, sir.'

'Forget it,' Black replies. 'The CEO of Aqua Dream Ltd has friends in high places, and the crew have diplomatic immunity in our waters. Stay away, do you hear? I expect you to follow my orders; you'll be fired if you go on board. Get that story about the suicide on the radio today, Nile. Make home visits too. The islanders need to know it's over, before they panic.'

The detective shoves his phone back into his pocket, then catches sight of the mega-yacht again on the horizon, its presence taunting him. He follows a path behind the hospital, into a thick group of trees, a remnant of the tropical jungle that used to cover Mustique. Green light surrounds him as he passes between trees, the temperature cooling rapidly. He sits on a fallen stump and watches late-afternoon sunlight sifting between the banana palms. Nile feels calmer as he recalls the names of trees his father taught him to identify as a child: incense, fustic, chenet and cordia. He's glad to inhale the jungle's scents instead of the hospital's raw chemicals. Streamertails and kingbirds fly overhead, a palm crow shrieking in the distance. The island's beauty is unchanged, but he's convinced Rothmore may have been tied up for hours before being killed. He's about to leave when something rustles among the trees. Instinct makes him jump to his feet and follow the sound, remembering that Lily has been followed, but whoever's been tailing him is travelling fast. Birds scream overhead at the sudden commotion, but there's no one in sight.

Nile emerges from the trees unsure how to push his investigation forward on his own. But his gut tells him to follow his instincts; he will always live with the guilt of failing to do so back in the UK. He observes his boss's instruction to make the radio station announce Rothmore's death, and the unexplained disappearance of Amanda Fortini, but there will be no house calls until he knows the truth. He flicks through the notes scribbled in his pocketbook. Sacha Milburn is the one person on Mustique with a history of conflict with both of her former friends. She fell

139

out with Amanda, then Tommy Rothmore was infuriated by her suggestion to take guidance from the island's priest. Milburn would have to be deeply disturbed to kill her ex, but she struck him as a troubled soul.

The detective knows where she lives because her parents' villa lies close to Lovell. He used to admire it on his walk along the beach to school, always arriving with sand in his shoes. The house juts straight out from the hillside, seeming to hover on thin air, by some feat of magic. He takes his time walking there, because it's too late to help Rothmore, and the same attacker may have killed Amanda Fortini. All he can do now is work out why and prove his smug boss wrong.

The path to Stargazer villa winds up the hillside, with only a handrail protecting visitors from a hundred-foot drop. Nile feels relieved to arrive on the terrace, surrounded by waist-high glass fences, allowing drunken partygoers to admire the coastline without fear of tumbling down the rockface. Nile spots four large telescopes placed on each corner of the terrace, and a mosaic depicting zodiac signs by the pool. The house's upstairs windows hang open, with pale curtains flapping from the openings, ice melting in a glass on the outdoor table. Nile recognises the red notebook and pen Sacha Milburn was using last time they met lying on an outdoor table. There's a chance it contains vital information, but he restrains his impulse to flick through the pages.

The young woman looks uncomfortable when she finally emerges. She's wearing another drab outfit that renders her anonymous, her red hair in need of a comb.

'I saw you from upstairs,' she says. 'Has something happened?'

'Have you heard the local radio today, Ms Milburn?'

She shakes her head. 'I've been writing all morning.'

'I'm afraid it's bad news. Tommy Rothmore was found dead a few hours ago.'

Nile watches her reaction, but Sacha Milburn's resilience surprises him. She keeps her head up, blinking tears away, but her voice is cracking.

'I knew something awful would happen, I even wrote about it a few days ago.'

'There's a chance he committed suicide.'

'I don't believe it. Tommy wasn't a coward. The last time we spoke, he told me Amanda's rejection wasn't going to break him.'

'Something you said at Firefly stayed with me, Ms Milburn, about it being common knowledge that Amanda Fortini visited Lovell at night. Is that true?'

She frowns at him. 'I saw her myself. Someone has to keep track of what's happening on the island.'

'That's my job, Ms Milburn.'

'I've kept watch all year. You could call me Mustique's conscience. I saw her walking there, after she met a guy on the beach.'

'You've been spying on people?'

'I'm just monitoring what goes on.' Her gaze is defiant. 'The telescopes aren't just for stargazing, they're good for people-watching too. I keep track of everything and write it down.'

'You said you're writing a children's story.'

'Call it a parable, about good and evil. Some people treat each other with no respect; they break laws and tell lies, Detective. I've been treated badly myself. Don't you care about that?'

'What are you saying, Ms Milburn?'

'A few islanders have been kind to me all summer, like Mama Toulaine and Dex Adebayo, but others don't care how you're feeling.'

'I'm investigating a specific crime, Ms Milburn. That means looking for a murderer, not policing innocent people's behaviour, or spying on them.'

She releases a slow laugh. 'I've been watching that big yacht out in the bay, the *Aqua Dream*.'

'What have you seen?'

'The crew come ashore most nights. They drink at a bar in Lovell, even though no one invited them here.'

'It sounds like you enjoy keeping watch.'

She gives a narrow smile. 'People fascinate me, especially ones like Tommy and Amanda.'

'How do you mean?'

'The beautiful ones. I didn't realise how different they were as a child, but I see it now. They drift through the world so easily.' Her voice is wistful.

'Not this time,' Nile replies. 'Can I use one of your telescopes?'

'Go ahead.'

He chooses one that overlooks the outskirts of Lovell, where dinghies lie beached on the sand like a colourful shoal of fish. The magnification is so high, Nile can read the name of each boat, and see paint peeling from their sides. When a local woman goes by carrying a bag full of vegetables, he can see the beads woven into her hair. The level of detail makes him uneasy. The telescopes have been there since the house was built. Maybe the Milburn family saw him walking to school each day, but more importantly, Sacha has been intruding on people's privacy. He carries on speaking while he looks through the telescope.

'When did Amanda visit Lovell?'

'Tuesday and Thursday, late afternoon last week, I wrote it down in my book. She met a guy on the beach and they walked round the headland together.'

'Do you know him?'

'He works at Basil's Bar. I don't remember his surname, but his first name's Lyron.'

Nile's head jerks back, his vision blurred from staring down the telescope. 'Are you certain?'

'One hundred per cent positive; I've seen him loads of times. He was rough with Tommy the night he got drunk, until Dex walked him back to his villa.'

'Why didn't you say?'

'I didn't think it was relevant.' The young woman's voice tails away.

'It could change everything. Thanks for your time, Ms Milburn.'

Nile stumbles back down to the beach, then instinct takes over. He sets off across the sand at a run, heading for Britannia Bay.

22

LILY STILL LOOKS shell-shocked. I summoned her back to the villa, to share the news of Tommy's death, and she's barely spoken since. She's had to face too much loss already, but there's nothing I can do to shield her this time. It's early evening, the sun sinking onto the horizon, and I'm trying to seem calm, even though the young man's ruined face has stayed in my mind. It terrifies me that Lily's friends are being attacked, one by one, leaving her vulnerable too. I still don't understand how someone entered our villa to leave a piece of coral outside her room, and Lily's fierce independence makes her vulnerable. She's so used to taking care of herself that attempts to protect her can drive her further away, our conversation going round in circles.

'Give me the details again, Vee. It doesn't make sense.'

'I told you, darling. A fisherman found Tommy's body in his trawl net. There was a rope bound tight around his ankle, his feet bare. His lower legs were covered in scrapes, with white pieces of coral in the wounds. They looked like pieces of chalk, sharpened into spikes.'

Lily lifts her head at last. 'Those white quills are called

dead men's fingers; they're sharp as razors after they calcify. I've cut myself on them, when I've been grafting samples onto dead sections of the reef.'

'What are you saying, Lily?'

'It sounds like his body was anchored to the reef by that rope around his ankle.'

'I think it's connected to the coral too, but why would someone go to such lengths?'

'They could have done the same thing to Amanda; I have to look for her.' Lily's face is pale with exhaustion, but she's already rising to her feet.

'Not tonight, please. It's dark, and you've heard the weather reports on the radio; Storm Cristobal may reach Jamaica tonight, if it stays on course.'

'It's still miles away and the biggest section of bleached coral is close to the shore. I'll dive tomorrow, but the boat has to be ready.'

'I'll come with you, and Solomon should be with us too.'

I'm still reasoning with her when footsteps echo on the path, a man's slow tread on the gravel.

'I can't face anyone, Vee. If you want me, I'll be at the harbour.'

Lily dashes away, heading for the pathway down to the beach. I'm hoping to see Solomon Nile, but Keith Belmont appears at the top of the stairs. I like everyone as a rule, unless they're discourteous, but the aging rock star puts me on edge. He's one of the few islanders ill-mannered enough to arrive unannounced, but I adjust my features into a smile. I read an interview he gave years ago, where he claimed to have slept with a thousand groupies, and tried every drug available, during his years on the road. I have to stop myself flinching when he drops a kiss on my cheek. Keith has all the allure of a second-hand car salesman, longing for a deal. His grey hair is scraped into a thin ponytail, lines grooved deep around his mouth, his mud-green eyes assessing my reactions. I'm certain my distaste shows, no matter how much I try to conceal it. If he's heard about Tommy Rothmore's death I have no intention of discussing it.

'Good to see you, Keith. Would you like a drink?'

'Juice would be great, please. I've been off booze for weeks.'

When Wesley appears, I ask for vodka and tonic, and something soft for my visitor, who's studying his surroundings, from the flowering hibiscus to Lily's espadrilles, flung down by the door, as if he's making an inventory.

'Is Lily here, Vee? I was hoping for a word.'

'I'm afraid she's out, but I was touched to hear that you're considering supporting her project.'

'She's doing a great job with the Reef Revival, but someone with a bigger profile should front it, if she wants the charity to grow. She'll need to make changes before I commit myself.'

'I doubt she'll agree. Lily works night and day, she's passionate about the system she's created.'

'That's fine, but I'm talking about publicity. If we call it the Keith Belmont Coral Project, she'll get the media on board. I'd make a substantial investment to get it up and running, including a media campaign.' He pulls out a packet of cigarettes as he speaks. 'Do you mind if I smoke?'

'Go ahead, I'll ask Wesley to bring you an ashtray when he comes back.'

When Keith take a long drag from his cigarette, the glitter

in his eyes makes me grateful that neither of my daughters joined his conveyor belt of wives. I think about all the time Lily sacrifices writing bids for grants, when she would rather be on the reef. The man's cash would liberate her from endless form filling, but is it a price worth paying?

'Why are you so interested in the coral, Keith?'

'I've got a conscience, believe it or not. If I can restore it I'll have done something to benefit the planet, left a legacy. Call it payback for all the private flights I've chartered, and my gas-guzzling cars.'

'You could just support her charity, instead of taking over.'

'I'm a frontman, Vee. It's not my style to stay in the background.' Keith's smile reminds me of a crocodile, anticipating his next meal. 'I'd send that old boat of hers to a wreckers' yard, then buy a new one. That old tub's covered in rust. We need a decent GPS system and more cabin space for divers.'

'The *Revival* belonged to her mother, Emily. It's the final link between them.'

'That's very touching, but the reef needs restoring fast, then we can move on to another island and start again. Lily should sign tomorrow, before I change my mind. My lawyer wants to nail down the details.'

'She's still reading the small print.'

'She'd be mad to refuse a big donation.' The man's sharp gaze scans my face again. 'Did you hear about Tommy Rothmore?'

'Just now. Terribly sad, isn't it?'

'Do you think it's linked to Amanda's disappearance?'

'I've got no idea, but I have every faith in our detective.'

'Solomon Nile? He seems a decent bloke, but pretty inept.'

'What makes you say that?'

'My house was burgled this week. He had no idea what to look for, and he was in one hell of a rush to leave.'

'He's busy, Keith. Amanda Fortini's been missing for days.'

The musician's smile has worn thin when he blows out another mouthful of smoke. I don't know if he came here to bully Lily, or collect gossip, but he's knocking on the wrong door. I won't release a single detail, in case it jeopardises Nile's investigation.

'What have you been up to since you came back to Mustique, Keith?'

He accepts the change of subject with a grimace, then delivers a speech about swimming every day, eating well, and purging his soul. Apparently he spent weeks at a Balinese yoga retreat and came back reformed. He's avoided coffee, alcohol and drugs ever since. The man has even rediscovered the religious faith he abandoned in his wilder years. It sounds admirable, and the large gold cross he wears on a chain around his neck hasn't escaped my notice either, yet his facade doesn't convince me. His gaze is as cold as permafrost when our eyes meet again, the reason for his visit finally exposed.

'Let Lily decide, Vee. I'm only doing her a good turn.'

'I can't influence her; she makes her own choices.'

Keith's reptilian smile slips back into place. 'Get her to call me, please, before I withdraw my offer.'

He drops his cigarette on the marble tiles, then grinds it out with his heel. My heart is beating uncomfortably fast when he finally leaves. Keith Belmont has spotted a way to cleanse his conscience, for whatever sins he's committed, but I hope Lily has the good sense to refuse. Keith Belmont may have enough charisma to rock a stadium full of adoring fans, but a one-to-one meeting with him is like conversing with a rattlesnake.

23

WHEN DS NILE arrives at Basil's Bar the place is empty, apart from a few holidaymakers stranded on the island until the storm passes. They seem happy to extend their holiday, knocking back endless cocktails, thrilled by their unexpected leisure time. When he first spots Dexter Adebayo in the corner, he's surprised by how much he's aged. It's clear that the man still uses Basil's as his office, with his papers and mobile phone spread out on the table, but he's almost unrecognisable from the carefree guy who taught him to dive fifteen years ago. His gaze is vacant, as if his spirit's broken. Nile smiles at him, even though he's preoccupied.

'Good to see you, Dex. How are things?'

'The same as ever, Solomon. I thought you'd stay in the UK, putting that huge brain of yours to use.'

'So did I, to be honest, but circumstances changed,' Nile says, settling on a bar stool. 'I've got a quick question. When's the last time your XR7 went out for a spin?'

Dexter releases a slow laugh. 'If it was mine I'd have cashed it in by now, but the bar owns a half-share. They rent it to tourists on days when I don't need it for diving trips.' He sifts through his papers, then stops to study one. 'The last people to hire it were a French family, from the Cotton House, ten days ago. I make a note for the insurers each time it gets borrowed, in case there's damage.'

'Okay, thanks, Dex. I'll see you around. I need to speak to my brother.'

When the detective turns round, Lyron is polishing a table, his expression bored. The young man's jaw drops when Nile takes his elbow and leads him towards the exit.

'I can't just leave, Sol. I'm stuck here till midnight.'

'You're coming with me,' Nile hisses.

'Why? Is Dad sick?'

Nile carries on glaring at his brother until he finally follows him down to the beach. It strikes Nile that, no matter what, Mustique always looks beautiful. The setting sun is casting lilac and gold streaks across the sky, but his anger is still red hot.

'You're under arrest,' he snaps at his brother.

'Is this some kind of joke?'

'You know exactly why I'm here. I thought you'd help me, but you've blown the whole thing apart.'

'I don't understand.'

'You do not have to say anything, but what you do say could be used against you, in court, if your case goes to trial.'

Lyron's smile vanishes. 'What the hell do you think I've done?'

'You were seen on the beach, twice, with Amanda Fortini, after denying you knew her.'

'If you seriously think I'd harm a woman, you're losing your mind.'

Nile's brother stares at him open-mouthed, but he doesn't care. He grabs Lyron's wrist and drags him along the beach to the police station, where the Layton brothers are playing cards. The two men spring from their seats when Lyron throws a punch, keeping their backs to the wall. The first blow catches Nile's jaw, sending his glasses flying, but his right hook connects squarely with Lyron's shoulder, as the fight continues. It takes several hard punches to win the day. Lyron looks exhausted when Nile finally shoves him into a holding cell and locks the door. The new prisoner punches the wall, rattles the bars, and screams for a lawyer, but Nile returns to the lobby. The Layton brothers eye him with newfound respect.

'Still here, boys? Do you want more of the same?' They shake their heads in unison. 'Leave me to clear this shit up, like always, but give me the keys to your motorbike first, Charlie. It'll get me round the island faster than the buggy. I can't say when you'll get it back.'

Layton hands them over without complaint, then Nile is left by the reception desk, waiting for his brother's yells to subside. Luckily his glasses are scratched, not broken, but it's 8p.m. by the time the station falls silent. When Nile opens the door to the holding cells, his brother is sitting on the mattress in his cell, head in hands.

'Feeling sorry for yourself now, are you?'

Lyron finally looks up. 'Do you know what it's like, being your brother?'

'What are you talking about?'

'The teachers told me how gifted you were on my first day at school. You aced every exam and won medals for running and swimming. There's not one thing in this world I do better than you.'

'Don't give me that bullshit.'

'It's the truth.'

'I thought you'd support me in my job when I came home. You had so much potential as a kid.'

'When did you ever help me? After you left I didn't see you for years.'

The words prick Nile's conscience, but he ignores them. He places his recording device on the floor, then begins to speak.

'I'm taping this interview with my brother, Lyron Edward Nile, because there's no second officer to witness our conversation. I have to remind you again, Lyron, that anything you say could be used against you in court, if your case goes to trial.'

When his brother raises his head again Nile can see he's been crying, but can't afford to care.

'Tell me about your relationship with Amanda Fortini.'

'She drinks at Basil's, that's all. We flirted a few times when I served cocktails to her and her friends.'

'How come you were seen together twice on Old Plantation beach at dusk?'

'We were talking, that's all. I don't have time for girlfriends.' Lyron stares at him, unblinking.

'Where were you, when the Fortinis' villa got torched?'

'Working, like always. Go ahead and check with my boss.'

'I will, don't worry. How come you've got a reputation for drug dealing?'

Lyron hesitates for a beat too long. 'Who told you that rubbish?'

'That's not relevant. I'll search your room tonight.'

'Fine, you know where I live.'

The two men glare at each other, but Nile knows he's got the upper hand. He's not the one behind bars, nursing bruised knuckles from punching the wall.

'Lyron Nile has denied both charges. He'll be held in custody for twenty-four hours, while I look for evidence on both charges.'

Nile gives the recording machine's off button a hard jab with his thumb, then stares at Lyron again. His brother is crying into his cupped hands, a boy again, always too easily led.

'Calm yourself before you make your phone call. You only get one, so use it well. Remember it'll take me ten minutes to walk home and search your room.'

Nile hands his brother the telephone and leaves him to make his call. When he returns five minutes later, Lyron refuses to meet his eye.

The detective feels numb when he walks outside, leaving his brother to contemplate his future. His father will need a long time to drag himself inside, so he slows his pace, following the long route home through a stand of date palms, while darkness smothers the island. Soon he drops onto a boulder and stares at the sand below his feet. He understands his brother's anger; it's hard to make a living on Mustique. Nile always assumed that his brother was savvy enough to stay clean, but maybe he got it wrong.

Half an hour has passed when he finally arrives home. His father is standing by a brazier beside the house, leaning on his stick as he watches flames issue from the metal dustbin, with holes piercing its sides. Nile waits for a while, as ash sifts onto the ground.

'Having a bonfire, Papa?'

The old man's face looks older while he controls the blaze, leaving Nile to complete a professional duty he'd rather avoid. When he goes to his brother's room, his conscience bothers him again. Lyron's pin board is covered with family photos. There's one of him on graduation day, the pair of them running across the beach, then Lyron riding piggyback on his shoulders when he was two years old. Nile searches inside his brother's shoes, under his bed and in his pockets, so he can file a search report tonight with a clean conscience. He picks up the piece of coral that's still lying on his windowsill, then returns to the station immediately, unwilling to face his father's questions.

24

KEITH BELMONT'S VISIT leaves an unpleasant taste in my mouth. Maybe that's because he's so keen to grab Lily's empire. She's always seemed too level-headed to be swayed by money with so many caveats, but I can't be certain. The lure of continuing her work for many years to come may be too strong to resist. When Wesley emerges from the house to check on me, I inform him that I'm taking my buggy down to Old Plantation harbour.

'Maybe I should accompany you, Lady Vee?'

'I'm too old for a chaperone, Wesley.' The look in my butler's eye proves that he's heard about Tommy Rothmore's death, but he's too discreet to mention it.

'I'm sure Lord Blake would want you to stay indoors tonight, where it's safe.'

'I can't let Lily walk home alone.'

Wesley stands between me and the front door, blocking my path, like he wants to corral me indoors and then throw away the key. His protectiveness feels so smothering it's a relief to say good night. Outdoor lights glitter on the swimming pool's surface when I cross the terrace, illuminating the tropical orchids Jose tends so carefully, reminding me that the haven Jasper and I created is under threat. I collect the piece of coral that was left outside Lily's door, in case Solomon is down at the harbour, then hurry to my buggy.

I drive south on the coastal path. Blues music fills the air as I pass Basil's Bar and the wide expanse of Britannia Bay. The lights fade as I drive through a dense thicket. I normally enjoy experiencing the island's wild side, but I'm too edgy to relax: I almost jump out of my skin when a snakebird flies overhead, skimming the buggy's roof. The air feels clammy against my skin, my breathing laboured, but the sensation lightens when I finally drop down to Old Plantation Bay. Lily's mother's old trawler, *Revival*, is lit up against the dark. When I walk closer, tools are littered across the deck, but she's scrubbing the side of her boat. My footsteps make her swing round, her smile only appearing when she recognises me.

'Someone left me another message, Vee. *Leave Mustique or die like the coral,* just like last time.'

'Why didn't you come home straight away?'

'I've got a right to be here. I won't let anyone threaten me, Vee.'

'It's silly for either of us to take unnecessary risks.'

Lily's tiredness shows when she drops onto a bench on the jetty beside me, her head resting onto my shoulder. I feel a stab of fury when I take her hand. The girl has built a strong life from poor beginnings, but someone has her in their sights, and it can't have been Tommy Rothmore, because his body lay in the hospital refrigerator when the vandalism took place. Keith Belmont's time-worn features come into my mind again; he could have left the message on Lily's boat, then strolled up to see me. But why would a man who claims to love her conservation work leave such a toxic threat?

'Have you told Solomon about the message?'

'I was planning to see him first thing tomorrow.'

'I'll come with you. I won't have you risking yourself.'

She lifts her head to look at me, her face calmer than before. 'Me and Tommy were the same age, Vee. I adored him when we were little, but we'd barely spoken in the last few weeks. I feel bad for siding with Amanda after their break-up.'

'It would have blown over, he knew you cared about him. You were bound to stick by your closest friend.'

'Amanda would never scare us like this, if she was safe. I have to look for her tomorrow.' Her gaze shifts to distant lights on the horizon.

'I want to hold a memorial tomorrow evening, at the Bamboo Church, and I'll arrange a wake afterwards. Pastor Boakye can run the ceremony. Tommy won't be buried until his family arrive, but we ought to remember his life on Mustique straight away. He deserves a good send-off.'

'That's a lovely idea, Vee.'

I have a sudden memory of Emily's funeral. The child was as good as gold, sitting between Jasper and me in the Bamboo Church, then watching a memorial stone being laid in Mustique's small graveyard, even though her mother's body was never found. I used to fear such a terrible loss would traumatise her, but she's a survivor like me, which could explain why I adore her. She fights each challenge with boundless energy.

'You don't have to finish your mother's work, Lily. You know that, don't you? Marine conservation projects all over the world could use your help.'

Her lips tremble when she smiles. 'I always finish what I've started, under my own steam.'

'In that case you've got a new recruit. I'll help you clean your boat.'

'Dressed like that?' She stifles a laugh.

Lily's got a point; my clothes are ridiculously impractical: a Liberty sundress and flimsy white sandals.

'I've got my bathing suit on under here. Do you have any overalls?'

'Let me dig something out.'

She returns with a pair of shorts and a T-shirt covered in oil stains. Princess Margaret would laugh if she could see me dressed like a street urchin, scouring paint from a boat, but working together encourages Lily to speak openly. I understand why Keith Belmont is so keen to get involved as she describes her ambitions. If her transplantation system really does regenerate the reef, the method can be used world-wide, and she'll become famous in the science world. Maybe Keith wants to swap his transient fame and a string of failed marriages for a legacy of doing good.

'I'm so proud of you, Lily. You know that, don't you?'

'I wouldn't have got this far without you and Jasper.'

'That's sweet, darling, but you do perfectly well without us clapping from the front row.'

We carry on until the last trace of paint is removed and I can abandon my borrowed clothes and slip back into my dress.

'Shall we have a drink at Basil's on our way home?'

Lily shakes her head. 'I'm almost ready for bed.'

'Me too. Keith Belmont's visit exhausted me.'

'What did he want, exactly?'

'Your signature on his contract. He's prepared to give your charity masses of publicity and cash, provided it runs under his name.'

Lily gives a wry smile. 'I was tempted, I admit, but I can't work for someone that confused. One minute he's talking about purifying his soul, then he's hitting on some teenager in Firefly.'

'Who's he been chasing?'

'Any woman under twenty-five, the younger the better.'

I turn to face her. 'Did he pursue Amanda?'

'She was his first this summer. He invited her over to do yoga, and she had to make it clear she wasn't interested before he stopped sending her flowers. Sacha's the only girl he hasn't bothered asking round for dinner.'

'Was Keith hurt by Amanda's rejection?'

'I don't know. He's not the kind to show his true feelings.'

'Did he flirt with you too?'

'He's dived with me a few times. The guy's genuinely passionate about the coral, but he gives me the creeps.'

My thoughts suddenly slot into place. 'It could be him that's hurting people, couldn't it? He's attracted to you and Amanda. She's missing, and you're getting these awful messages.'

'But why would he attack Tommy?'

'Come on, Lily, you have to admit it seems a bit suspicious?'

'I guess we could mention the new graffiti to Solomon. I'll text him now.'

When I steer the buggy through the trees again I'm glad Lily isn't walking back alone. The thick vegetation and fetid odour rising from the ground remind me that voodoo rituals once took place in the darkest clearings. Lily's behaviour has changed too; she falls silent as the darkness thickens, making me wish the buggy's headlights were more powerful. We've only been in the dark a few minutes when she asks me to pull up.

'I heard it again, Vee,' she whispers. 'This is where I got followed last time.'

When I look back, there are only the black shapes of trees, crowding around us.

'Let's keep going.' When we move on, the sound of footsteps increases until I hear it over the buggy's low buzz. I put the brakes on once more, then call out. 'Show yourself, whoever you are.'

A man's tall form lumbers onto the path and I grab Lily's hand. If he intends to harm us, there's safety in numbers.

'It's just me, Lady Vee, going home from work.' It's Dexter Adebayo. He looks the same as ever, a portly figure with grey dreadlocks touching his shoulders, only his expression more sombre than before. 'I stopped for a smoke in the woods, after a few drinks at the bar. My wife goes crazy if I light up at home.'

'You gave us a fright, Dex,' Lily says.

'Sorry, ladies, but remember the only thing to fear is fear itself. Franklin D. Roosevelt said that, and American presidents never lie, do they?' The bartender's face finally breaks into a smile. 'I'd better go home before my wife files for divorce.'

Lily waits until his footsteps retreat before letting out a peal of laughter. She seems convinced that the sounds she heard before were just Dexter, stumbling through the woods, looking for a place to smoke, but I'm less certain. Lily only falls silent when she pulls her phone from her pocket.

'Solomon's still at the police station, Vee. He's waiting for us.'

The jungle is full of strange echoes as we head south.

25

NILE STARES AT his computer screen while he awaits his visitors. He has compiled a list of every Mustique inhabitant who could have abducted the young heirs to the Fortini and Rothmore fortunes. Logic tells him that the killer is a robust male, fit enough to tackle Tommy Rothmore.

'Let me out, you bastard!' Lyron yells through the door that divides the station from the cells.

Nile doesn't bother to reply. His disappointment with his brother is still so intense, he's not ready for another conversation, even though he's established his innocence. Lyron's manager at Basil's has confirmed that he was working when the Fortinis' villa burned, but he's still got lessons to learn. They did everything together in the old days, but now Lyron is more likely to sail to St Vincent, looking for mischief.

Nile scans his list of salient features from the case. The coral found at each crime scene and in the homes of victims must have a meaning; it's the killer's only direct form of dialogue. DI Black may be correct that the case is a straightforward crime of passion: Tommy Rothmore could have killed his ex-girlfriend, then cast her body into the sea, only committing suicide when his guilt grew unbearable, yet the theory makes him uneasy. Lily Calder's boat has been daubed with the same message as before: '*Leave Mustique or die like the coral.*' There was the break-in at Keith Belmont's house, with coral left there too. If the killer is already dead, who is still harassing members of the island's elite?

When Nile looks out of his window again, Lady Vee is stepping out of her buggy, bearing a lump of coral in her hands, and Lily is heading for the building. He can't afford to be distracted by her looks, but he's only human. Her shorts reveal legs that go on forever, yet she seems to be without vanity; if she's noticed the effect she has on him, there's no outward sign. The two women are just entering the station when Lyron shouts for his freedom again from the holding cells. It's easier to stare down at the pieces of coral he collected from Amanda Fortini's home, and Keith Belmont's villa, lying on his desk.

'Have you arrested someone?' Lady Vee asks.

He hesitates before replying. 'My brother, Lyron. I'm sure now he's not involved, but I won't let him go home tonight. He needs to cool down first.'

'That can't be easy for either of you.' Lily's calm gaze falls on him.

'Don't let it distract you. Show me that coral please, Lady Vee.'

She passes it to him. 'I found this on Sunday morning, outside Lily's room.'

'It's different from the one at Keith Belmont's house.' Nile stares at the three carved patterns: a spider's web, crossed arrows and an upturned cup, or U. 'I know they're Obeah symbols, but I'm not certain what they mean.'

'I still don't understand why the killer's leaving pieces of coral,' Lily murmurs. 'It's at crisis point. Once it's bleached, it's gone forever, unless human intervention kick-starts the growth cycle again.'

Lady Vee keeps her thoughts to herself, head bowed as she studies the killer's calling cards.

'Do you think anyone on the island might resent your work on the reef, Lily?' Nile asks. 'You got a law changed last year, didn't you? Fishermen can no longer use trawl nets inside the bays, and there are some months when they can't fish at all.'

'Most of them supported it. The reef is their livelihood; if they damage it, the fish vanish.'

'That's true, but perhaps it affects illegal activity too. Boats are much more restricted in their movement now.'

Lady Vee peers up at him, 'I still think Keith Belmont's involved. He paid me rather a threatening visit this evening, warning me to keep out of Lily's business. He seems cold-blooded enough to kill someone, and his latest obsession is coral.'

'That doesn't make him a murderer, Lady Vee. If he staged a break-in at his villa to make himself look innocent, he did a good job. He seemed genuinely surprised to see the coral outside his door.'

'He could be writing those threats on Lily's boat to make her fearful enough to hand over her charity, and he pursued both Amanda and Lily this summer.'

'Belmont's on my suspect list, but we've got no hard proof

that he abducted Amanda or Tommy. The answer may lie in the pieces of coral. One was left outside your bedroom door, Lily, two nights ago. Can you tell me who's got keys to your house, Lady Vee?'

'Jasper, Lily and I, my children, and our butler, of course.'

The detective scribbles in his notebook. 'I'll need to speak to Wesley.'

'He's been loyal for decades. I'd rather you didn't bother him.'

'Wesley might be able to guess who's stolen a key to your home.'

'Next you'll be interrogating Phil Everard.'

Nile holds up his hands in denial. 'He was on St Lucia when Amanda disappeared, so he's been ruled out. Our killer needs to be in the right place, at the right time.'

Lady Vee suddenly looks up, her expression startled. 'I think I understand it, at last. This is all about place, isn't it? He's using the coral to give us specific information about where to find his victims. He told Tommy about his method, before he was killed.'

'How do you mean, Lady Vee?' Nile asks.

'Tommy handed me that piece of coral, the night Amanda's villa burned down. He pressed it into my hand and told me to look there for her body. I thought he meant the Fortinis' gardens, but he was talking about the reef.'

Lily's face is suddenly animated. 'It's part of the Staghorn family. There's just one colony that lies north of here; it's in a dangerous spot, in L'Ansecoy Bay. It matches the one from Amanda's bed, with exactly the same carving of crossed arrows.'

Nile can picture the scepticism on DI Black's face on hearing that Tommy Rothmore's killer might be drowning his victims, then leaving their bodies underwater, attached to specific beds of coral, yet he saw the rope around the young man's leg with his own eyes. Someone on the island might be unhinged enough to carry out a unique set of murders.

'If that's true our killer's got access to a boat and diving gear, and he's strong enough to overpower a fit young man,' Nile says. 'If the storm holds off, we can dive in L'Ansecoy Bay early tomorrow morning, before the storm hits, to look for Amanda. It's the only way to prove the theory.'

'Are you qualified?' asks Lily.

'Dex Adebayo trained me years ago, then I got my BSAC qualification in the UK.'

'We can dive together then, using the buddy system.'

Lady Vee raises her head again. 'Shall I bring Phillip? He's not a great sailor since his ear trouble affected his balance, but he can help me on deck.'

'That's a good plan, Lady Vee. Let's meet at the harbour at 8a.m.'

Nile remains hunched over his desk at midnight, long after his two helpers leave, aware that their quest tomorrow may lead to nothing, but it beats doing nothing, like the Layton brothers. He's trying to find criminal records for every Mustique citizen, but the simple act of checking is a major headache. The Internet signal is weak and the Police Records Bureau software is so ancient, it takes hours for basic queries to be resolved. He's about to quit when the window above his desk suddenly blows open, admitting a gust of cooler air. The storm is announcing itself at last, just when he needs conditions to remain calm.

A sudden noise makes Nile yank open his office door, inhaling a lungful of smoke. A firecracker bounces across the floor, igniting a thin stream of petrol. Instinct makes him grab the fire extinguisher and shoot foam at the flames, before the building becomes an inferno, like the Fortinis' place. He runs outside, but there's nothing except the gathering wind. Whoever shoved a Molotov cocktail through the letterbox was fit enough to escape unseen.

Shock only hits him when he gets back inside. If the killer poured petrol through the station door, his brother's innocence has been confirmed, even more forcefully. It proves that the killer is watching him closely, even though it's long after midnight. Sacha Milburn's obsession with keeping watch over everyone on Mustique comes to mind. It strikes him as far-fetched, but he can almost imagine her setting light to Amanda Fortini's villa, after a lifetime of feeling overlooked and believing she mistreated Tommy – but is she crazy enough to try to burn the island's police station down?

Nile abandons his plan to go home. Despite his frustration with Lyron, his brother can't be left in a place that's just been firebombed. He returns to his office and switches off his computer, then tries to get comfortable on his hard chair, but it's a losing battle.

26

Tuesday, 17th September 2002

I WAKE EARLY, wondering if I'm losing my mind. Last night it seemed logical to search for Amanda's body on the reef, but daylight makes me question myself. I could be dragging everyone on a wild-goose chase, but Lily seems determined to press ahead when we meet downstairs. I feel concerned about her and Solomon diving to the coral bed where the dead men's fingers grow, in the most dangerous part of Mustique's coastline, but once her mind is made up, there's no stopping her.

The weather feels different this morning when we get into the buggy. A warm breeze is gusting from the sea, and the clouds are moving again, precursors of the gathering storm. Lily doesn't seem worried by the weather conditions as we pass Dr Bunbury's villa. The two-storey building looks like it's been transplanted from the UK, with whitewashed bricks, and new picket fences. Dr Pakefield is taking exercise on the lawn already, dressed in shorts and a T-shirt, putting himself through a brutal round of star jumps and lunges, while the sun beats down. There's something self-punishing about his regime. He's exercising so hard, he hasn't noticed us, circles of perspiration on his T-shirt when I come to a halt.

'That's a tough workout on a warm day, Simon,' I call to him.

The man swings round to face us. 'Just keeping fit, Lady Vee. It's my only option; I can't swim to save my life.'

'Pity, in a place like this.'

The man gives a tentative smile, using his hand to shade his eyes from the sun.

'I hope we'll see you at Tommy's memorial celebration this evening, Simon?'

'I may be busy at the medical centre, I'm afraid.'

'Please come, it's an island tradition to give people a good send-off.'

'I'll do my best, I promise.'

The man turns away before I can speak again, already dropping to the ground to perform more press-ups. I don't know why enigmatic people always intrigue me. When I glance over my shoulder Pakefield is still following his brutal routine, but Lily appears totally focused on the task ahead.

I drive along the same path as last night, but the island feels benign today; the thick stands of trees never scare me when sunlight flickers through the branches, and parakeets are screeching overhead. Instinct makes me stop for a moment at Britannia Bay, wishing we could go for a paddle instead of a diving expedition. I love the feeling of sand between my toes, unlike Princess Margaret, who hated the scratching sensation with a passion. I always had to provide towels and warm water, so she could bathe her feet after a swim. There are just half a dozen people on the beach this morning, strolling by the shoreline, like the island was the safest place in the world.

Solomon and Phillip are waiting for us on the jetty at Old Plantation harbour. Solomon looks keen to get moving, but my old friend seems apprehensive. These days he prefers to remain on shore, but I'm relieved to share the responsibility of steering the *Revival* while Nile and Lily dive. Lily's manner is changing already. She's more confident now she's the captain, her speech decisive.

'Put on life jackets, please, Vee and Phil. If we capsize, no one's coming to our rescue.'

The bay is calm at first, but the waves pick up as we hit open water. Phillip is holding on for dear life, but I'm still glad of his presence. Someone will need to guard the trail line once we reach L'Ansecoy Bay.

'Do you have a wetsuit in my size?' Nile asks Lily.

'I've been diving all summer, with strapping young guys from the University of the West Indies, so take your pick.' Her face breaks into a grin. 'You're legal to twenty metres depth, but stay clipped to the line. If you drown, my insurance will be screwed forever.'

I stand in the wheelhouse as the *Revival* sails north. The wind is a fraction stronger than last night, giving us an exhilarating ride. Tall waves rock the boat in every direction, making me glad of my strong sea legs. Nile appears comfortable too, after growing up on his father's fishing boat.

The ride to Mustique's northernmost point would be a pleasure on a calm day, but I'm still dogged by the sense that we're making a mistake. I try to concentrate on the scenery instead. When we pass Endeavour Bay I catch sight of a few holidaymakers outside the water sports centre. Two windsurfers are making impressive speed, their red sails skimming across the waves, riding the gusty wind.

When Lily steers past Honor Bay, Point Lookout comes into view. The water grows rougher as we reach the island's northern tip. It's Mustique's worst strait, often dealing out huge breakers in hurricane season, where the Caribbean and Atlantic collide, but today the conditions are manageable. On a good day L'Ansecoy Bay is a great place to picnic, providing excellent views of Bequia and St Vincent. It's part of the island's history too. A French cruise ship called the SS *Antilles* foundered on the reef here three decades ago. The crew and passengers were feted on shore, before being collected by the *Queen Elizabeth*, but the ship fared less well. The burning hulk was abandoned after several attempts at salvage. Its rusting skeleton forms part of the reef now, but there's a prohibition against diving there, and I can see why. Breakers are rocking the *Revival* from side to side, making life uncomfortable, but their assault feels more playful than vicious. My nerves are rising when I stare at the dark water. Soon Lily will be hidden below its surface, prepared to face any danger to find her friend.

27

NILE HASN'T WORN an aqualung for ten years at least. He'll need to rely on memory as well as good instructions to remain safe. Phillip Everard's handsome features still look drawn when Nile zips up his borrowed wetsuit. The actor's gait appears steadier when he helps to drop anchor, standing beside Vee when she takes the wheel.

Lily waits until she and Nile are fully kitted out, sitting on the boat rail, checking their oxygen cylinders' pressure readings for a final time.

'The currents are vicious down there, so stay clipped to the trail line. Don't let the rip current catch you; several divers have died that way.'

'It's okay, I know the conditions.'

'Suit yourself.' She gives a narrow smile. 'We're breaking the law, Detective. The Maritime Agency have outlawed diving here without written permission.'

'Never mind, I may get fired anyway.'

Her smile widens by another centimetre before she flips backwards into the sea. Nile's head spins when he drops into the water. This underworld looks too beautiful to be dangerous, suffused with turquoise light, but invisible forces push him off course. He heads down in a vertical line, keeping track of Lily's flippers, but even the fish are struggling; a school of grouper circle him until an eddy drags them north. He'd like to stop and wonder at this new universe where nothing is safe or predictable. His body feels cumbersome on land, but down here it's like a fragment of driftwood, at the water's mercy.

Lily is powering ahead, her swimming style effortless. Nile is painfully aware that he's putting her in danger too, by agreeing to dive. The reef may offer no clues at all about Amanda Fortini's fate, but the broken hulk of the *Antilles* is already in sight. Nile can see that it's merged with the marine eco-system, outline softened by thick masses of barnacles, seaweed and frothy pink coral. Lily is poring over it already, looking for signs of the killer's presence. When Nile swims beside her she holds up her finger and thumb, checking he's okay. He returns the gesture, but all he can see is the broken hull of the SS *Antilles* that once promised luxury to wealthy French holidaymakers, until it sailed too close to Mustique's shores, hoping to glimpse its famous residents.

Nile spots something glittering on the seabed, but when he follows the trail line deeper, it's just pieces of burned glass, polished by currents after the *Antilles* foundered. He looks through an opening into the hulk, until a red snapper speeds past, almost knocking his mask from his face, startled by an unexpected guest. Nile is still peering through the opening when he sees a black shape tied to some rusting iron. Instinct makes him undo his clip from the safety line so he can look inside, but suddenly his body is spinning out of control. Currents are pulling him away, and Lily hasn't seen he's in trouble. Nile fights hard, but the water is stronger, yanking him away, then hurling him back against the wreck, moving at a tempo he can't match. If he can't grab something solid, the current will haul him into the sea's depths. His heart only steadies again when he manages to catch hold of the ship's anchor chain.

Lily appears at his side moments later. She shakes her head at his elementary mistake, before clipping his harness to the line again. Her face only brightens when he points at the wreck's interior; his near miss is forgotten when they stare through the opening together. Lily taps her watch, but he's not prepared to leave that mysterious black shape behind. He grabs hold of it through the opening, but it takes several hard yanks to pull it free. When the black object emerges at last, it's a body bag, like the one Tommy Rothmore is zipped inside at the medical centre. Lily's face tenses behind her mask.

They rise to the surface, with the bag drifting behind. The first thing Nile sees when he breaks the surface is Phillip Everard, reaching out to help him aboard. The actor looks stronger than before, but upset by their new piece of cargo.

'Is it Amanda?' he murmurs.

'I need to look inside to find out.'

Nile waits until Lily is safe on board, sensing her tension as he tells his three helpers to step back. If there is a body inside, he can't forecast its condition. His breath is coming too fast when he unzips the bag by a few inches, releasing a stream of water. He freezes in place when a lock of blond

175

hair flows through the opening. That pale gold shade is instantly recognisable, but he peers inside the bag to make sure. Amanda Fortini no longer looks like a society girl; her skin is mottled, blue eyes milky. He's about to zip the bag shut again when a piece of coral tumbles onto the deck, bearing crossed arrows. The killer must have thrown it in just to prove that he's in control. Nile doesn't care what the symbols mean; they're no more than a taunt, the killer mocking him in a foreign language. His teeth are gritted when he zips the bag shut.

'Let's get back to shore,' he calls out.

Phillip Everard has slumped onto a seat in the prow, with Lady Vee clutching his hand. When Nile joins Lily in the boathouse she's too busy steering between the rolling waves to make conversation, but her distress is obvious. She has just found her closest friend's body anchored to the coral she's so keen to preserve. Tears roll down her face but she blinks them away. Nile wants to offer comfort, but the waves are so choppy, she needs to concentrate. The detective walks to the prow to phone DI Black. He's forced to yell the news of Amanda Fortini's death into his phone, the wind stealing his words before they connect.

28

PHILLIP LOOKS EXHAUSTED when the *Revival* moors again in Old Plantation harbour, so Lily offers to drive him home to recover. I hear Solomon thank them both for their help, but it's Lily's bravery that lingers in my mind when I survey the body bag, still lying on the deck of her converted trawler. Many people would crumble on realising that a friend had died in such horrible circumstances, but she steered us home through rough water without complaint, her previous suffering making her mature beyond her years. I shiver for the first time since we returned to Mustique; even though the wind is still warm, my clothes are soaked with sea spray.

'Can you come to the hospital, Lady Vee?' Solomon asks. 'I'd like to compare notes with you afterwards.'

I'm glad to be included in his investigation, even though I dread seeing Amanda's body. Mustique's only ambulance is arriving already, with Simon Pakefield at the wheel. The medic seems as remotes as ever, but his mental state isn't my biggest concern. Amanda Fortini may have been lying on the ocean floor ever since she went missing four days ago, and we need specific details to explain who put her there.

No one speaks as the ambulance heads back to the medical centre. The medic's habitual silence bothers me as he steers the vehicle; I've realised that he rarely speaks unless he has facts to report. It's clear he takes his job seriously, but a more confident doctor would offer emotional support.

Once the body is carried inside the medical centre, Nile explains what's happened. The doctor appears shocked by the announcement, but maintains his professionalism, nodding at Solomon once he's opened the bag.

'Put on gloves and an overall, please. I need help lifting her onto the table.'

Solomon selects the largest white coat from a hook on the wall, then I catch sight of Amanda's hand protruding from the bag, like she's trying to claw her way out. Our new detective falters for a moment but soon gets his feelings under control.

'Sit down if you feel faint, Detective.'

Nile shakes his head. 'Let's get it done, I'm fine.'

It only takes a moment for the two men to lift Amanda's body onto the table, then I understand Solomon's reaction. I can't tell how much of the damage is due to violence. Time may have left the green bruises that cover much of her skin; her flesh looks swollen too, a scarlet bikini cutting into her thighs. The young woman's face is no longer slender and fine-boned, there's an ugly wound by her right temple, her features broken. Only her hair has retained its glamour, still tinted an expensive gold.

'You bastard,' I hiss under my breath.

'My thoughts exactly,' the doctor agrees. 'Her body looks

like a car crash victim's; something piled into her right side at speed. I can tell she's got a broken skull, fractured ribs and a broken pelvis just by looking at her. I imagine she died instantly.'

'Could she have been hit by a speeding motorboat?' Nile asks.

'That would do it, yes.'

Anger floods through my system as we all gaze down at Amanda's body. No matter what mistakes she made, she didn't deserve such a violent death. The most obvious explanation is still that she was mown down by the speedboat Mama Toulaine saw in the harbour. I can't imagine anyone on the island, including Keith Belmont, being unhinged enough to kill someone so violently, then drag her body down to the ocean floor.

'Tell me about the body bag,' Nile says.

The doctor looks up at him. 'The medical centre's crest is stamped on the back, but I can't say when it was taken, I'm afraid.'

'Why not?'

'I'm a locum, remember? I've had no reason to check the hospital's supply. No one's died here recently, except the Rothmore boy.'

'Who could have stolen one from the storeroom?'

The medic shakes his head. 'I wish I could say, but we don't have CCTV. This place is open all day, so patients can receive treatment.'

'I'm sure we can get that information from another source,' I say. 'We need to keep our discovery secret, until her family are informed, don't we? I think we should announce

Amanda's death to the islanders at the memorial service I've arranged for Tommy Rothmore this afternoon.'

'That's your decision, Lady Vee.' The medic strips off his gloves and drops them in the sink. 'This is very unfortunate. People are already shaken by Tommy's death, without another young person being killed.'

Simon Pakefield gazes first at Solomon then at me, as if we are both potential murderers. The silence thickens as Nile helps him place the young woman's broken corpse back in the bag, then wheel it next door. When Amanda is deposited in the refrigerator unit, only a thin layer of metal separates her from Tommy Rothmore, the two victims reunited in death, even though their relationship ended weeks ago.

I feel too numb to cry, and Solomon's face is blank when we stare at the drawer that holds the girl's body. The severed rope around Rothmore's ankle makes more sense now; the killer may have tethered him to a different section of the reef, the ties worn thin by waves rubbing against spikes of dead coral. I glance at the room's only window; it's made of frosted glass, designed to protect the privacy of the dead, the midday sun muted to a dull blur.

29

NILE IS FASCINATED by Lady Vee's reaction to seeing Amanda Fortini's body. Her manner is brisk and resolute when they sit down together on a bench, a hundred metres from the medical centre, where they can't be heard. He's impressed that she can put personal feelings aside, to concentrate on justice for the victim.

'It's someone who can dive, with an appetite for danger,' she says. 'They could have left Amanda's body in a far safer place, but chose the hardest bay to access.'

'He picked somewhere with plenty of history; the wreck of the *Antilles* is still talked about now. My father remembers sailing out to check the passengers were safe.' Nile shuts his eyes against the sun's glare, trying to picture the killer diving down to the reef, dragging the body bag behind him. 'I still think the *Aqua Dream*'s involved.'

'Are you sure? We keep referring to a male killer, but it could be a woman, couldn't it?'

'She'd need to be very physically strong. Whoever's doing this attacked two fit young people, then dragged them into a boat, to ferry the bodies out to the reef.'

'I see what you mean, but it must be someone who knows the terrain intimately. Mustique is built from coral. They've chosen part of the island's DNA to use as clues. I'll try to find out exactly what the symbols mean today. I'm going to call on your father, Solomon, before Tommy's memorial, but I'll get to the church early to see Pastor Boakye.'

Nile watches her walk away, dressed in her pale clothes, the quintessential Englishwoman abroad. He could never have guessed that she would become his closest professional ally on Mustique, but her wisdom and insight make her an ideal partner. She receives a warm welcome in any house on Mustique.

The detective's frustration returns when he walks back inside the medical centre to see the part-time nurse. The young woman says that the storeroom is locked at all times, but Nile has his doubts. There will have been occasions when the desk is unattended, leaving any casual visitor free to steal a body bag and escape by one of the fire exits, without being seen.

He keeps his anger in check when he leaves the building at 2p.m. He knows he faltered in the examination room because the sight of Amanda Fortini's body chimed too loudly with the woman he failed in Oxford. He stares out at the *Aqua Dream*, balanced on the horizon, rooted to the spot. DI Black has cautioned him to stay away, but sticking to protocol didn't protect that victim, or Amanda Fortini. This time he must follow his instinct, before another life is lost. He walks back to the harbour at his fastest pace. It takes several attempts to start the police launch's engine, and the waves are higher than before, long and undulating.

They're not yet tall enough to surf, but the storm is making its presence felt. This stretch of the Caribbean is reacting to the weather system that's heading for the Windward Isles, which provides Nile with a perfect excuse.

There's no sign of Dan Kellerman when he motors out to the *Aqua Dream* in the police launch, so he circles the yacht, taking photographs on his phone. He approaches close enough to hold the camera up to each porthole, photographing the interior. He takes images of the speedboat that's stationed on deck too. There's no sign that it's caused human damage, but a swimmer could never escape its huge engine. He's tempted to scale the ladder and go on board again, when the captain suddenly emerges, infuriated by the sight of Nile's camera.

'What the hell are you doing here?'

'Good afternoon, Captain. Mind if I join you?' Nile calls out, offering a beaming smile.

'I told you, no one comes on this boat without a warrant.'

'I'm only here to offer you shelter. You've got my permission to approach the shore. Choose any bay, and keep safe if the storm hits us. Feel free to dock, until it passes over.'

The captain glares at him. 'Were you taking pictures just now?'

'Yes, indeed. I'm a marine life enthusiast. Did you know that a whale shark was spotted near here, last year?'

'Shut up, you idiot. I'll get you fired for this.'

'Stay safe, Captain, like I said. Come ashore if the storm comes this way.'

Nile feels satisfied when he returns to harbour; at least he's got a visual record of the yacht's layout. He collects

Charlie Layton's motorbike from the station and heads back to Lovell. Wesley Gilbert's cabin is the highest property in the village, giving him a view of dozens of brightly painted cottages cascading down to the beach. Gilbert's home looks austere by comparison, suitable for an ex-soldier with its sombre dark blue walls, and white picket fences.

Lady Vee's butler has the radio on when Nile approaches his property. Spanish flamenco drifts through the door, low and tuneful, every note perfectly in time. It's only when Nile walks closer that he realises his mistake. Gilbert is cradling a guitar on his lap, eyes closed as he plays. Nile waits until he's finished before announcing himself.

'That's quite a talent, Papa.'

'I should practise more.' Gilbert doesn't seem fazed by the arrival of a visitor. He props his instrument against the wall then beckons him inside. 'Don't call me Papa just yet. Wesley's fine until I retire.'

Nile smiles in reply, but Gilbert's manner doesn't allow for relaxation. The man is studying him like a headmaster considering a variety of punishments.

'You're not here for idle conversation, are you, Solomon?'

'I need to find out what's been going on at Lady Vee's villa. The violence is linked to Lily Calder's coral preservation project in some way.'

'Do you want a beer, while we talk?'

'That would be great, thanks. Is this your day off?'

'Lady Vee sent us all home; some of us are helping with Tommy Rothmore's wake later. Most of the island's domestic staff are involved.'

Nile looks around while Gilbert fetches their drinks. The

man's furniture is made from simple dark wood, the walls adorned with paintings of the island's vivid foliage, tangled with the white flowers of vespertine. He recognises Mama Toulaine's style but never expected to see her work in Wesley Gilbert's home. Nile follows him outside when he fetches two bottles of lager and a bowl of nachos. Gilbert settles in a deck-chair, putting his feet up on the rail, his expression relaxed.

'How can I help, Solomon?'

'You must have seen plenty of Tommy Rothmore and Amanda Fortini this summer. Has there been any odd behaviour at Eden House?'

'I try not to look too closely. My main duty to Lady Vee and Lord Blake is as their butler, discretion guaranteed.'

'The rules have changed, Wesley. We just found Amanda's body.'

Gilbert's eyes widen. 'I'm sorry to hear that. So young, wasn't she?'

'Twenty-three a few months ago.'

'Tommy and Amanda were young heirs to huge fortunes. Money was handed to them on a plate, and I guess that can be a blessing and a curse.' His voice is neutral; he's stating a fact, not griping about the wealth gap. 'Tommy quit visiting Eden House straight after their relationship ended.'

'Can you think why they were targeted?'

Gilbert takes a gulp of his beer. 'People like that can be oblivious sometimes.'

'Meaning what?'

'They're too high class to snap their fingers, but if you're a waiter, a cook or a maid, you're invisible. Some people hate being overlooked.'

185

'Including you?'

'I couldn't do my job if it hurt me that badly. Working as a butler wasn't my first choice after the army, but the job suits me.' Gilbert returns Nile's gaze. 'That's because Lady Vee and Lord Blake treat me fairly. They may not be the richest couple on Mustique, but they've got the most class. They've passed those values down to Lily.'

Nile finds the conversation frustrating. He was hoping for answers, not a statement of professional loyalty. His next line of questioning will damage the relaxed atmosphere, but there's no avoiding it.

'Whoever's hurting these people is leaving pieces of coral in their homes, and it must be an insider, unless they can walk through walls. Someone entered Eden House on Saturday night without breaking a window or forcing a door. They went up to the second floor and left coral outside Lily's door. It has to be someone with a key, who knows the layout.'

'The only people in that category are Lady Vee's relatives and me. If you're asking whether I got copies made and handed them out, surely I'd have done that sooner, if I wanted to hurt the family.'

'How about Jose Gomez? She saw him in her garden at midnight.'

'Jose's dumb, not stupid. He'd never hurt anyone.'

'How did you spend Saturday night and Sunday morning, Wesley?'

'I knew you'd get there eventually.' Gilbert gives a narrow smile. 'I went to Patti Toulaine's straight after work and didn't leave till 8a.m. the next morning.'

'I knew you were friends with Mama Toulaine, but not that you're a couple.'

'You were away a long time, Solomon. Patti likes her independence too much to co-habit, but we've been together years.'

'That explains your fine artwork. Who else could break into Eden House at night?'

Gilbert looks thoughtful. 'I can't account for Lady Vee's family. One of them may have been careless, so someone's taken a copy.'

'How about friends? She's relaxed about letting people inside, isn't she?'

'The Blakes have plenty of dinner parties.'

'What about Phillip Everard? He's been close to the Blakes for years.'

Gilbert releases a laugh. 'That guy's half in love with Lady Vee, and he wouldn't hurt a fly. He's so mindful of people's feelings he even remembers my birthday. Last year he gave me a Cartier watch. The guy was over on St Lucia helping Lord Blake when Amanda went missing, wasn't he?'

'I'm just wondering who may have borrowed a key, then been careless enough to leave it lying around.'

Nile thanks Gilbert before he leaves. He's glad that the man's alibi rules him out, but he needs hard information. It interests him that Mama Toulaine has chosen such a restrained character for her partner, but the man's true personality showed this afternoon. Gilbert spoke about being ignored by the young people he's served all summer long, apart from Lily Calder, and it's possible that someone with a less calm disposition might have taken offence. Until now

Nile has believed that Jose Gomez had no role in the violence, too childlike to harbour such murderous anger, but the young man has been behaving oddly for weeks.

It doesn't take Nile long to walk down to the waterfront, to look for Jose. The Gomezes' cabin is a ramshackle structure, raised on wooden stilts to protect it from storm swells, but it still looks vulnerable. Several of the wooden steps leading up to the porch are broken, the whole structure in need of maintenance. Nile waits several minutes after knocking on the door, but the place is empty.

30

MY SPIRITS ARE still low when I head for Lovell on my buggy, but I promised to visit Hosea Nile, and I can't back out, even though Amanda Fortini's death fills my mind. Time shifts backwards to a happier period once I see Lovell's cabins ranged across the hillside, picked out in pastel colours that glow in the Caribbean sun. When Jasper first brought me here forty years ago, the community lived in different circumstances, with no running water, electricity or health care. Now the place has a school, church and a library. I can tell the community is prospering on its own terms, from the gardens full of lime trees, banana palms and geraniums flourishing on people's doorsteps.

Hosea Nile's house lies at the centre of Lovell overlooking the sea. He's sitting on his porch with Mama Toulaine, rising slowly to his feet at the sight of me. I have to hide my shock at how thin he's become, and the tremor in his hands when he holds mine. Mama Toulaine stays in the background, but it's a pleasure to see her too. The artist looks resplendent in a peacock-blue dress, decorated with scarlet embroidery, her bearing regal. She kisses my cheek before accepting the cake tin I've brought, leaving Hosea and me on the porch. He's changed a great deal from the confident young fisherman who spent days showing us the different coves from his boat, back when the jungle was so thick that much of the shore was inaccessible. He seems delighted to have a visitor, but his speech is slow, and he's easily distracted, his gaze drawn constantly to the sea.

Mama Toulaine carries the conversation when she returns with slices of cake arranged on plates. It could be my imagination but the painter seems burdened by something, even though the news of Amanda's death hasn't yet been announced. I can't tell whether she's worried about Hosea, or has troubles of her own.

'How's Solomon finding his new job?' I ask.

Hosea's reply takes a long time to arrive. 'He should have stayed in Oxford. His sense of duty brought him home.'

'That's an admirable quality in a young man. I've always believed in loyalty.'

'Me too, Lady Vee, but one of my sons has too much, the other too little.'

The sadness on the old man's face makes me change the subject. Hosea has always had an uncanny knack of reading the sea; he says that Storm Cristobal could take twenty-four hours to choose which island to attack next. There's time to lock our storm shutters in place and batten down the hatches. It's been decades since a tropical storm caused serious damage on Mustique. Typhoons normally pass us by, uprooting trees and smashing down buildings in the Bahamas instead.

Hosea is soon tired, even though I've only been in his home for half an hour, his speech becoming slurred.

'Why not take a rest inside, before your strength goes?' Mama Toulaine asks him.

When Hosea finally complies she helps him up from his chair; his brisk walk has been reduced to a stagger by Parkinson's disease and I sit in silence, unable to help. After a few minutes Mama Toulaine emerges again, her expression solemn.

'Are you going to the memorial service, Mama?' I ask.

'Of course, I always pay my respects when a soul passes over. It's an Obeah custom.'

'I wanted to ask you about it. Obeah's a kind of sorcery, isn't it?'

She gives a firm headshake. 'It's a religion like your Christianity. It's followed by thousands on St Lucia, and here on Mustique too. There's enough room in the sky for plenty of gods.'

'No offence intended; I only want to understand it better.'

'Obeah magic can be used for good or evil, but few people have the gift like me.' When she turns to face me again, her gaze is unsettling. 'Hosea's worried about his son, Lyron, that's why he's tired. He didn't mean to be rude, going back inside.'

'I loved seeing him, there's no need to apologise.' My glance falls on two faint symbols etched on the backs of her hands, just like the carvings on the pieces of coral. 'Do you mind me asking what your tattoos mean, Mama?'

'Life and death.' Toulaine holds out her hands, showing me the symbols. 'The open cup is the god of life; he's the water and wine that never runs out. The crossed arrows symbolise Gede, the god of death. He stands on the crossroads between

191

this world and the next, dressed as an undertaker, with his gang of coffin bearers. Our fates are in his hands.'

'That's fascinating. Are there more Obeah symbols?'

'Most come from the natural world. We believe that birds are spiritual messengers. If you see a white owl, death or illness will come to your community in three days' time.'

'What does a spider's web mean?'

'They're bad luck too, they symbolise confusion. If you find a spider's web it means someone is getting in your way.'

'Are the crossed arrows very powerful?'

Mama gives a slow nod. 'It's the worst sign of all. The arrows show that Gede will come for you, straight away, if you've done something wrong.'

'The young never understand how closely life and death are linked, do they?'

'They expect to live forever, but you've got your own troubles, Lady Vee. I can hear it in your voice.'

'Haven't we all?'

She gives a low chuckle. 'Second sight can be a burden.'

'I don't envy you. It's complicated enough dealing with the present. Do many people here practise Obeah?'

'Dex Adebayo was raised that way, like me, but there are plenty of others. Some of the villa owners put faith in our rituals too.'

There's so much wisdom in Mama's face I'd like to confide in her, but can only offer generalities. 'Someone's hurting young, privileged members of the community, and leaving Obeah symbols behind.'

'Look at the ones closest to you. Take that Dr Pakefield,

for example. He's been sailing out at night to that big yacht that stains the horizon, like a shadow.'

'Why would he do that?'

'You can find that out yourself.' Mama Toulaine gazes into my eyes again, so deeply it's like she's reading my soul, until she recoils suddenly, her smile vanishing.

'What did you see?'

'Nothing I can say out loud. You love that girl of yours, so keep her safe. Do you hear me?'

'Loud and clear, Mama.'

The conversation becomes awkward after that. Whatever fate the artist saw written in my eyes has made her retreat into silence.

31

Nile is not looking forward to his next task at the station this afternoon, but it can't be avoided. He can only hope that his brother's short incarceration has improved his attitude. Lyron is standing under the overhead window, his expression calm while he gazes through the bars. The young man keeps his distance when the door is unlocked, showing no inclination to fight. When he sits on the bench outside Nile joins him. The two brothers watch the sea slowly turning grey.

'I was looking forward to you coming back, believe it or not,' Lyron mutters.

'Me too. I thought we'd hang out on St Vincent, looking for girls.'

'Why bother? They never pick you.'

Nile can't help grinning. 'The same old taunts.'

'I got the sex appeal, you got the brains.'

'It's time to move on, Lyron. You're smart enough to be a pilot. If you want money for training, I'll help you raise it.'

'I'd have to pass the entrance exam first.' There's silence

before the younger man speaks again. 'Something's bugging you, Sol, isn't it? Did you get fired over there, in the UK?'

'I made a mistake. Just like you did. I'm trying to find a way to live with it.'

Lyron studies him with a calm gaze. 'You've been remembering other things from the past, haven't you?'

'How do you mean, Ly?'

'I changed your life, didn't I? Our mother died because of me.'

'Are you serious?'

Lyron kicks at a stone on the ground. 'It's what happened; I can't change it.'

'Have you carried that round all this time?' Nile wants to reject the claim out of hand, but the truth slowly registers. 'I hated you when I was seven years old, but it ended long before I turned eight. How could I stay angry with a baby, just learning to walk?'

Lyron sits up a little straighter. 'You're sure about that?'

'Positive.'

'And you'd help me go to aviation school?'

'I'll equal any amount you save, as long as you stay away from trouble. If you need money, ask me. Okay?'

Lyron gives a slow nod, then rises to his feet, but the detective can't accompany him home. He gives his brother's shoulder a light slap, then turns away, grateful for the chance to clear the air.

Nile's mind is back on the case when he rides Charlie Layton's motorbike to Lady Vee's villa. He doesn't care that the rising wind is shaking the trees' branches and nudging the bike off course. All he wants is to find out how the two victims died, to remove their weight from his conscience.

Nile parks outside Eden House, his skin clammy from the moist air. He catches sight of the Fortinis' ruined villa, only a hundred metres away, remembering that the family have suffered a far bigger loss today; Amanda's mother wept hard on the phone when she heard about her daughter's death. The collateral damage is severe too, their mansion reduced to piles of rubble, melted glass and trees damaged by the fire.

Lily Calder has regained her calm when he spots her on Lady Vee's terrace. She rises from her sun-lounger in one fluid movement, like a gymnast, her turquoise gaze studying him intently.

'Are you on your own?' he asks.

'Vee's going to the memorial after visiting your dad.'

'You should have gone with her. It's not safe to spend time alone.'

'I'll be surrounded by people for the rest of the day.'

They sit down together at the outdoor table. 'Are you okay, Lily?'

'More or less,' she says, but her smile is unsteady. 'Except I've just lost two of my closest childhood friends.'

'I hate saying this, but you might be the killer's next target.'

'How do you mean?'

'You're the island's coral expert, he's left death threats on your boat, and he's killing people you love. He even broke into your villa at night to leave his calling card outside your door.'

'It doesn't make sense. I don't have any enemies here.'

'Amanda and Tommy probably thought that too.'

She shivers in the breeze. 'Are you saying this to scare me?'

'The opposite, actually. I want you to keep safe.'

'Me too.' Her smile widens at last. 'There are plenty more reefs that need my help. You must have suspicions, Solomon. Who do you think's doing it?'

'The last time Amanda was seen, she was swimming towards the *Aqua Dream*. I'm not authorised to go aboard, but I went out there a few hours ago to take photos. The two crew members have diplomatic immunity, so they can't be prosecuted.'

She shakes her head in disbelief. 'Can I see the pictures?'

Lily sits beside him to peer at the images on his phone. One shows the Bayrider speedboat stationed on deck, waiting to be lowered onto the water by a hydraulic pump, but others show the yacht's interior. The cabins Nile photographed through the portholes are surprisingly modest for such an expensive vessel, with basic wooden furniture, grey linoleum floors, and no luxuries. One of them has diving gear and oxygen cannisters stacked against the wall.

'There's no sign they've hurt anyone,' she mutters.

'Maybe they bury them on the reef straight away.'

Lily's eyes suddenly blink shut. 'Those bastards might have kept her there. God knows what she suffered, before she died.'

'Dr Pakefield thinks she died instantly, in the water.'

'That's a small mercy.'

'Tell me about her. I know I'm missing something; I need to understand the link between her and Tommy.'

'She was funny, kind and generous, but not always great at empathy.'

'Arrogant, you mean?'

'Amanda adored her life, but Tommy was more cautious. They could both be self-absorbed. That can make you ignore warning signs, can't it?'

Nile shakes his head. 'My boss wants everyone to believe that Tommy killed her then drowned himself.'

'He was too gentle to do that, even though he was suffering.' Lily's eyes cloud over and Nile bites his tongue; he'd forgotten the story about her mother walking into the sea.

'Sorry, that was clumsy of me.'

'I'm normally fine about it, but today's the anniversary of her death. I always try to keep busy, instead of sitting at home feeling sad.'

'I know how that feels. My mother died young too.'

He's surprised by the sympathy in her eyes. Her hand settles on his wrist for an instant, like a butterfly brushing his skin, then she jumps to her feet.

'It's almost five, I mustn't be late for Tommy's memorial.'

'Do you want a lift?'

'Thanks, I'll just get ready.'

Lily rushes away, taking the steps two at a time. When she reappears on the terrace five minutes later, she's wearing a short black dress, high heels, and huge shades covering her eyes. She should be climbing into a limousine, instead of hitching a ride on an old motorbike, but she doesn't appear to care. When Nile kick-starts the motor Lily's hands settle on his waist like it's the most natural thing in the world.

32

TIME OPERATES DIFFERENTLY on Mustique. Events always start later than advertised, even memorial services. I'm one of the first to reach the Bamboo Church at 5p.m. but I was keen to escape my tense conversation with Mama Toulaine. I admire her painting, but her otherworldly aura puts me on edge, as if she really can see life's hazards clearer than the rest of us.

The church lies inland from Lovell, on a flat stretch of ground. There are no stained-glass windows, vaulted ceilings or steeple, yet the wooden-framed building appears in many visitors' holiday photos. I have a perfect view of the elephant tree from my seat. The tree's massive form leans towards my pew, as if the elephant is reaching out his trunk. Everything on Mustique grows on a giant scale because of the climate, including the centipede that crawls across the bench in front of me as mourners arrive. Whoever killed Tommy and Amanda may put in an appearance. They must still be on the island, because no one is free to leave. This is the ideal opportunity to watch for tell-tale behaviour.

I hurry over to speak to Pastor Boakye once he arrives.

He may be a new arrival on Mustique, but he's already well-liked; the man always looks well-groomed with hair styled in cornrows, his expression earnest. He's struck me as a force for good, taking youngsters under his wing. His kind smile always reassures me that most problems can be fixed, but his expression is solemn when I inform him of Amanda Fortini's death. I want him to announce it at the start of the service, so we can commemorate both their lives.

'How can this be happening, in such a quiet place, Lady Vee?' he murmurs.

'I don't know, Father, but I wish it would stop.'

'It's tragic for their families. I'll pray for them both, I promise.'

I've always found solace from attending church, but praying for Amanda and Tommy seems too little too late as I slip back into my seat.

Sacha Milburn doesn't notice me when she hurries down the aisle. The girl is wearing a dark blue dress with a high neck that makes her look like a Victorian governess, its hem trailing the ground. I can tell she's been crying, but her behaviour at Firefly has stayed in my mind. She was such a sweet young girl, playing with Lily all summer long, but now seems encumbered by worries, as if she's finding the adult world hard to navigate. The young woman is dabbing her eyes when she sits in the pew opposite, and suddenly my own losses crowd my mind. The last funeral I attended was Princess Margaret's. She planned every aspect of the ceremony herself, requesting an intimate service for family and close friends in St George's Chapel at Windsor Castle, with no outsiders to witness our grief. I shut my eyes to recall happier events at the Bamboo Church; weddings held here on a perfect summer day, throwing cups of rice over the bride and groom, instead of confetti.

It's a relief when Phillip arrives, clearly recovered from his seasickness. He looks immaculate in a dark linen suit, and always knows how to help me, taking my hand immediately.

'I bring good news from St Lucia. Jasper's making progress, at last. He was very upbeat on the phone just now,' he whispers.

'Thank goodness, I'll catch up with him this afternoon.'

I'm too interested in watching people arrive to pay full attention to Phillip's voice. Over half the attendees are from Lovell, and I catch sight of Dex Adebayo, wearing one of his loud Hawaiian shirts, with pink flamingos flying across his chest, but his expression looks less jubilant, and his body language is jittery. Could I have misread him for all these years? Maybe he's grown to hate the wealthy young visitors he teaches to dive, who can jet off on fresh adventures, while he remains stuck in one place? Dr Pakefield has come to the service after all; he's sitting in an empty pew, his severe expression scaring people away. I need to tell Nile about his late-night trip to the *Aqua Dream*, which he's chosen not to disclose. The medic could have directed all his simmering anger at the island's youth. He wouldn't be the first doctor to take lives, instead of saving them.

My attention focuses on Phillip again; I try to imagine him as the killer, like every other member of the congregation. He's one of my longest-standing friends, great fun to be around, but incredibly thin-skinned. The poor man suffers agonies if his acting performances are ever criticised. His sensitivity seems to be a blessing and a curse. He's too quick to empathise, picking up every vibration in the room, like an over-tuned violin string. I know his bisexuality has troubled him over the years too, and his childhood sounds terrible, but he's given me unconditional support in the thirty years we've known each other. He was over on St Lucia helping Jasper the morning Amanda Fortini went missing, so it's a relief to cross him off the list I'm carrying in my head of potential killers.

I glance over my shoulder when the pianist begins a quiet tune. All the staff from my villa have turned out for the ceremony. Wesley looks handsome in his black suit, shepherding Jose Gomez into a front pew, in case the gardener should misbehave, my two maids following behind. My butler's demeanour hasn't changed over the years. He's always been immensely dignified, serving my family with professionalism, while maintaining his privacy. Our recent talk in the kitchen is the most candid conversation we've held for years.

Jose Gomez is another matter entirely. My young gardener seemed like a gentle soul, but he's been behaving strangely and I can't identify a reason. I feel an odd prickling in my hands when Mama Toulaine sits down at the end of their pew, as if the temperature has just plummeted. She's still dressed in her vivid outfit, beads and crimson feathers woven into her hair. The artist is an expert on the Obeah symbols left on the pieces of coral. It's possible that she's seen more than she's saying.

The pastor is standing by the altar, under a large wooden

cross. He's dressed in a starched white chasuble, his manner gentle when he announces Amanda's death. The whole congregation takes an in-drawn breath, then images of Tommy Rothmore appear on a battery-powered projection screen, reminding me of his golden-haired boyhood. Photos show him leaping into the sea, picnicking with friends, then in evening dress, with his arm draped around Amanda Fortini's shoulders. The pair look so alike they could almost be brother and sister, two beautiful aristocrats with the world at their feet, who appeared to have no enemies.

My attention shifts when Phillip nudges me. Lily is arriving late with Solomon; the detective is wearing a smart jacket over his uniform and I've never seen her look so comfortable in a man's company. They choose a pew at the back, sitting side by side. Lily needs someone clever enough to keep her interested, and it's possible that Nile could tolerate her independent spirit, but I mustn't speculate. If Lily feels she's being pushed, she's sure to run in the opposite direction.

When Pastor Boakye addresses us, my mind returns to the two victims. The priest exhorts us to celebrate their lives, while mourning their untimely deaths. I catch sight of Dr Pakefield again, the medic keeping his mouth shut while the rest of us sing 'Amazing Grace', gazing down at the words in his hymnbook. His manner is still so awkward, I can't imagine him having the confidence to go on the attack. None of the music stirs me until a young girl from Lovell sings an African prayer unaccompanied, except for birdsong outside. The purity of her voice undoes me at last and I find myself crying for Princess Margaret and the lost ones from my family, as well as Amanda and Tommy, with Phillip still gripping my hand. My friend is stifling his tears like everyone else, except Keith Belmont, who I've only just spotted. He's at the end of our pew, eyes hidden behind dark glasses. I remember him claiming to have revived his faith, and the ugly gold cross hanging round his neck, but his body language frightens me. He's completely motionless, like a snake waiting to strike.

33

NILE WATCHES THE congregation rise when the hour-long service ends. Keith Belmont is first to leave, the musician giving him a short-lived smile before slipping away. Lily is comforting her friend Sacha Milburn, who is the most openly emotional person at the service. The redhead's odd habit of watching the island's population keeps her on Nile's suspect list but right now it would take a leap of imagination to see her as a credible murderer, while she cries uncontrollably.

The congregation is in no hurry to leave, apart from Jose Gomez. When Nile spots him on the far side of the crowd, Lady Vee's gardener backs away. Before he can reach him, he's disappeared into the surrounding trees, leaving Nile with a list of unanswered questions. Staff from the Cotton House have laid out refreshments under the shade of the elephant tree, the refreshments paid for by Lady Vee. The scene looks like an upmarket garden party, and tonight there will be music, drinks and dancing on Britannia beach. It's a time-honoured tradition on Mustique to celebrate the lives of the dead with parties, instead of bleak funerals.

Nile is heading outside when Pastor Boakye stops him.

'Can I talk to you please, Solomon?' The man's tuneful West African lilt sounds the same, but he looks tenser than before.

'Of course, Father. Let's find somewhere private.'

The priest leads him to a deserted spot, overshadowed by tree ferns. Nile notices changes in Boakye's manner. His hand gestures are twitchy, and a line of sweat is forming on his upper lip. The pastor takes out a handkerchief to blot his forehead before speaking again.

'I should have said this before. Tommy called at my cabin on Sunday night, around 2a.m.'

'The night Amanda's villa burned down.'

'His speech was slurred, burns all over his clothes. He said someone had attacked him. They'd left curses on his property, carved on pieces of coral. He'd thrown them away, but I could see he was suffering. He thought someone had put an Obeah curse on him, so he could never rest. He kept babbling about the coral. Tommy said it was dying, like him.'

'What did you do?'

'Not enough,' he says, his eyes blinking shut. 'He said he was afraid of dying, but after a while he seemed to calm down.'

'Did he say any more about his troubles?'

'He told me his attacker hates the coral. He wants it all to die. I asked who was bullying him, but he was too afraid to name him.'

'That doesn't make sense.'

'I got Tommy to stay with me, so he wouldn't be alone while his mind was disturbed. I made up a bed for him on the couch, but by morning he'd vanished, leaving the front door open. That concerned me too.'

'Why's that?'

'Obeah law is like the old beliefs in Nigeria. They think you should always leave a door or window open, so bad spirits can leave your home freely, without getting trapped. I should have sat up with him till morning. It might have saved his life.'

'It's not your fault. If someone wanted him dead, they'd have killed him anyway.'

The priest looks startled. 'You don't think it was suicide?'

'I'm a detective, Father. Nothing's certain until it's proved.'

Boakye's expression is mournful when he vanishes into the crowd, which grows more voluble as the Pimms flows. The priest's manner is a marked contrast with his congregation. He seems burdened by private troubles he's unwilling to share, but there's no time to consider that now. Tonight there will be singing and dancing on the beach, everyone keen to remember two young people's lives with fun instead of sadness, yet Nile can't relax until he's discovered the missing link. When his gaze catches on Lady Vee and Lily he sets off in their direction. The crowd parts like the Red Sea when a man of his stature heads towards them.

34

I NO LONGER enjoy wakes, since losing so many loved ones. Death may be life's one inevitability, but I'd rather not welcome it with open arms. I'm glad of the distraction when Solomon invites Lily and me to the police station. We'll reach the truth quicker if we all pull in the same direction. Solomon looks like an earnest young teacher instead of a cop when he makes his request, his gold-framed glasses glinting in the sun. It interests me that Lily chooses to ride on his ancient motorbike to the police station, rather than my buggy, so I'm alone when I follow the track towards Lovell.

When Solomon leads us inside we're met by a wall of heat, and the odours of cigarette smoke and stale coffee. His gaze is still bright with curiosity when we sit together in the reception area.

'I want us to plan tonight's party, but this is a good time to share information. Have you found anything new, Lady Vee?'

'Dr Pakefield's been seen going out to the *Aqua Dream* in a speedboat, late on Monday night, which breaks his contract.

Mustique's doctor is meant to stay on the island round the clock, in case someone falls ill. Keith Belmont still bothers me too. He seems so sincere one moment, and then creepy the next.'

'We don't have any evidence against Belmont, but I'll check on Pakefield soon. How about you, Lily, anything to report?'

'Maybe we're getting too hung up on the coral. The symbols he carves could matter even more.'

'Mama Toulaine explained their meaning today,' I say. 'The crossed arrows symbolise the death god, Gede, and the open cup is the god of life. The spider's web mean someone's getting in your way.'

'That's interesting,' Nile replies. 'The death sign was left at Tommy and Amanda's homes, but the life sign was at Keith Belmont's. The one left outside your bedroom door was a spider's web, wasn't it, Lily?'

'So I'm blocking his way, but there's a chance I'll stay alive,' she says, with a shaky laugh. 'That's good to know.'

'It could be someone from Lovell, steeped in the old folklore,' says Nile. 'Or a villa owner, trying to camouflage themselves.'

'Mama told me Dex Adebayo believes in Obeah.'

'His only alibi is his wife's claim that he was with her when the villa burned, so I'll be keeping an eye on him. We still haven't worked out who broke into Eden House on Saturday night. It's likely to be someone who knows your property intimately. Jose Gomez has been behaving oddly, hasn't he?'

I shake my head. 'He's vulnerable, but he loves working

in the gardens, and until recently he's been a model employee.'

'But now he's changed, Lady Vee. He's been following you and Phillip, and maybe Lily too. Whenever I get close he runs away.'

Lily looks unconvinced. 'Jose's been volunteering on my boat, so I let him work on shallow sections of the reef, with a snorkel and mask. He showed a real skill for grafting, but he hasn't shown up at the harbour all week.'

I catch sight of what's written in Nile's notebook while he speaks. It's a list of names, with Jose's at the top, followed by Keith Belmont, Simon Pakefield and Dex Adebayo. The words 'Aqua Dream' are scrawled at the bottom. It almost matches the set of suspects I'm carrying in my head. Solomon passes me his phone, showing me photos of the *Aqua Dream*'s interior, which is far plainer than I expected. Mega-yachts are normally decked out in ultra-modern style, with sleek bespoke furniture and exquisite light fitments, but this one has lino floors and wooden store cupboards lining the walls. It looks too simple to please a billionaire's tastes.

'I expected gold leaf and crystal lamps.'

'Me too, Lady Vee, but the most important thing is to keep you both safe. I want you to invite Phillip to stay, and ask Wesley to sleep at Eden House, until the violence ends.'

'That should be easy; they're both worried about us.'

'There's safety in numbers. Tell me what you've arranged for the beach party tonight please.'

'People need the chance to speak about Tommy and Amanda; we've all been deeply affected by losing them. I've got Basil's Bar to arrange everything tonight on Britannia Bay, with music, drinks and a barbecue. Everyone on the island's welcome.'

'The killer's likely to be there. I imagine he was at the memorial service too, witnessing the pain he's caused. We all need to keep our wits about us and look for any odd behaviour.' Nile scribbles a note in his book. 'It's still important we find out who could have got a key to your house, Lady Vee. Think hard if anyone's been inside alone, please, with time to go through your things.'

'I will, Solomon.' I stumble to my feet, suddenly energised. 'I need to check our house is secure. Don't worry about me getting home, I'll be fine on my buggy.'

I say a hasty goodbye to Lily and Solomon, before hurrying outside. The building's heat felt so oppressive, I'm eager for fresh air. We're stuck on an island where someone is playing vile tricks on us. It bothers me more than anything that the killer left a piece of coral outside Lily's room. She could be next on his list, but it's a threat I don't fully understand, despite knowing more about the Obeah signs. I've taken care to lock every door since Amanda went missing, even though Jasper and I spent years there in perfect safety. It would require nerve to break into a locked house at night to leave your message of doom. Whoever did it has courage, or they've lost their mind so completely they don't care about getting caught.

35

NILE EXPECTS LILY to chase after her godmother, but she's still sitting on one of the station's ugly plastic chairs, inspecting fragments of coral. His phone rings before either of them can speak again. He hears a woman's sharp cry for help, before the line dies.

'Sacha Milburn's in trouble.'

When Nile rushes from the police station, Lily follows, the island a blur of green as the motorbike revs faster. Stargazer villa looks peaceful when they pull up, the terrace still guarded by telescopes on raised plinths. It's only when they reach the terrace that Nile sees a pink tinge to the swimming pool, and a dark shape at the bottom.

Lily kicks off her shoes and dives in first, dragging Sacha Milburn to the surface. The detective hauls her inert body onto the marble terrace, keeping his panic locked down. Sacha's skin feels cold as he lays her in the recovery position then pummels her stomach until water gushes from her mouth. When he presses two fingers to her throat her pulse is barely perceptible.

'Not you as well,' he mutters under his breath.

He can tell she's slipping away. The girl is unnaturally pale, blood dripping from the back of her head, her long dress plastered against her skin. Lily keeps Sacha's airways clear as he pumps his hands up and down on her breastbone. He remembers the first aid training from his police induction, but it may be too late. Blood is still dripping from Sacha's head wound, her jaw slack, until her body shudders back into life. Lily cradles her friend's head as she coughs up water and Nile feels his shoulders relax. He's found two corpses already this week; he couldn't forgive himself if another victim died.

Dr Pakefield remains silent when Nile calls his mobile, finally giving a few terse instructions before hanging up, but Lily is already using a towel to stem the blood from Sacha's wound. Nile glances around the terrace, trying to gauge what happened. There's a glass of juice beside her red pen on a table nearby, but her notebook is missing. He's willing to guess that she came back from the memorial service and buried her sadness in writing, but the killer stole her journal, in case it held incriminating information. The story grows clearer when he sees blood spattered on the ground. When he traces it back he can tell she was struck near the stairs up from the beach, then ran towards her house. The young woman must have been holding her phone; she called him before being shoved into the water, her mobile phone still lying at the bottom of the pool. The killer must have believed his work was done, safe in the knowledge that her staff were at the Bamboo Church, enjoying the hospitality after Tommy Rothmore's memorial.

Sacha is reviving when Nile crouches beside her again. 'Did you see who hurt you?'

'He caught me from behind.' Her voice is groggy, eyes closing like she's desperate for sleep.

'Stay awake, sweetheart,' Lily whispers. 'Dr Pakefield's on his way.'

'Not him, please. I don't want to see him again.' Tears spill from her half-closed eyes.

'Why are you scared?' Nile asks. 'It's okay, you're safe now.'

Dr Pakefield's face is solemn when he arrives. He's still wearing the dark suit he wore to Rothmore's memorial, his appearance anonymous, yet his arrival upsets the victim. She tries to squirm away when he approaches.

'Leave me alone!' she cries out, then her eyes suddenly fall shut.

'Don't worry about her behaviour. Head injuries can make patients hallucinate,' the medic says. 'Help me lift her into the ambulance please.'

The young woman is drifting in and out of consciousness. Lily clambers into the vehicle, leaving Nile alone on the terrace. There's blood on his white shirt, trousers soaked by chlorinated water, and Lily has forgotten her sandals. She was so keen to help her old friend she stepped into the ambulance barefoot and soaking wet. A smile of admiration appears on his face when he remembers her plunging into the pool fully dressed, but Sacha had a narrow escape. Only a combination of luck and good teamwork kept her alive.

Nile is about to drive back to the police station when someone appears on the steps to Sacha's villa. The man's figure is distinctive, with grey dreadlocks and a garish shirt, his jeans bleached pale by time. Dexter Adebayo's sartorial style hasn't changed in decades, but he looks strained when their eyes meet. He keeps his sunglasses on when Nile approaches, scanning the terrace before giving his greeting.

'Where's Sacha? Is something wrong?'

'She was attacked. The ambulance just took her to the medical centre.'

Nile is interested by his reactions. Adebayo seems shocked, but he's also struggling to keep still. The sheen of sweat on his face and rapid hand movements suggest intoxication.

'Why are you here, Dex?'

'Sacha invited me, but didn't say why. She's a pal of mine, and I know she's having a hard time. I guess she had a thing for Tommy Rothmore, and now he's gone.' Adebayo shuffles backwards, trying to escape Nile's stare.

'You seem tense today, Dex.'

'The memorial put me on edge. I moved here from St Lucia for peace and quiet, not violence.'

'Tell me what you know about coral, please. You're a diver, after all. You see it every day.'

Adebayo nods his head. 'I've known its importance since my childhood. My dad was a fisherman, like yours. He taught me that it protects marine life. If it dies, we all go hungry.'

'You were raised the Obeah way, weren't you?'

'It doesn't mean anything to me now, just old voodoo that stopped working a long time ago.'

'Tell me more about that Bayrider you share with Basil's. Don't you ever take it out, early in the morning, for a solo dive? You were passionate about it, back in the day.'

'Every ride has to pay for itself; I never take it out alone,' the man replies, his gaze slipping to the ground. 'Give Sacha my regards, please. That young lady's a favourite of mine.'

Adebayo backs away, leaving Nile alone on the terrace, the swimming pool's filtration system already removing the pink tinge from the water, like nothing had happened. He searches for the killer's calling card, but finds nothing, until he walks down the steps to the beach. A piece of coral has been dumped near the top, just like the pieces Nile found in the victims' homes. The detective takes a photo of the carved spider's web cut into its pale surface, but something snaps in his mind when he looks at it again. He's so sick of the killer's games he hurls it onto the beach below. Dexter Adebayo could have attacked Sacha earlier, aware that she'd be alone, then returned to gloat over his success and leave his calling card. The case is forcing him into unfamiliar territory, where people he's liked and trusted all his life are starting to look like murderers.

36

WESLEY'S ATTENTION TO detail shows when I enter the kitchen. Platters of salad, pâté and cheese have been left in the fridge, as if Lily and I would starve without his expertly prepared food. The idea that someone may have taken my spare set of keys to Eden House has left me jittery. I wander from room to room, checking every window and door, but the locks are intact. The keys lie in my desk drawer inside an old cigar tin, exactly where I left them, until I slip them into my pocket. The island still looks idyllic, but the storm is making its presence felt. A hot breeze is blowing through my garden, tearing petals from the orchids, young banana plants swaying in the breeze. The forecast says that Storm Cristobal will arrive tomorrow. The chances are even that it will skim past us, or leave Mustique ravaged, and the island's fragility has never seemed more obvious. Mustique is just a speck of coral, caught between the Caribbean and the Atlantic, at the mercy of competing forces.

I'm still thinking about the storm when I call Jasper's hotel, on the off-chance he's there. It's a relief when he picks up immediately.

'This is extraordinary, Vee. It's the first time you've phoned me in forty years.' The delight in his voice echoes down the line.

'That's a huge exaggeration. I'm just checking how you are.'

'Ecstatic, actually. The contractors are listening for once, and the second shipment of marble is perfect quality.'

'Well done, darling.'

There's silence before he speaks again. 'What's up, Vee? You sound low.'

'It's awful news, I'm afraid. We found Amanda's body this morning. I've organised a wake tonight, for her and Tommy, but I feel like going to bed and crying.'

'You phoned for moral support?'

'Something like that, yes.'

'Listen, darling girl, I'm worried about you, and promise me you'll take care of Lily. You matter far more than these stupid villas.'

'You really are the oddest man. You drive me mad with worry about your building project for days, then you say something incredibly sweet.'

'I mean it, Vee. I'd go to hell in a handcart without you.'

Jasper rarely expresses his emotions, as if it would involve a loss of face, so his words linger as I replace the receiver. My husband may be heedless sometimes, but he struck exactly the right tone, reviving my spirits in moments. I set off to Phillip's villa on my buggy without calling in advance. I feel bad about abandoning him after the church service without saying goodbye. It's only a short ride on the buggy, but the humidity levels are rising with the oncoming storm, my clothes sticking to my skin.

Phillip's villa looks appealing as I pull up outside, even though the wind is shaking blossoms from his trees, purple flowers scattered on the ground. Jacaranda may be one of the smallest homes on Mustique, but I love its quirky style. The swimming pool looks like a tropical spring, surrounded by slabs of petrified coral, with wildflowers growing in between. My friend is sitting outside, gazing at the water's surface like it holds the answers to life's deepest mysteries. He's abandoned the Armani suit he wore to Tommy Rothmore's memorial, dressed now in shorts and a white linen shirt that accentuates his tan. I can tell that something's wrong. He doesn't notice me crossing the lawn, his expression shell-shocked when he finally looks up.

'Jesus, Vee, you frightened the life out of me.'

'Sorry, darling. Are visitors here really so rare?'

He manages a shaky smile. 'My nerves are shot, that's all.'

'Let me get us both a drink, I know where you keep everything.'

'Don't go inside, please. The place is so infested with bloody mosquitoes I've sprayed everywhere with Deet. I won't let you inhale those nasty chemicals.' He gazes back at me. 'Did Lily get hold of you? She just called me from the medical centre.'

'What's happened?'

'Sacha Milburn was attacked just now. She's okay apparently, but I can hardly believe it.' His face looks haunted.

'All of this hurts you a great deal, doesn't it?'

'My childhood was a warzone, Vee. It's ringing all the wrong bells.'

'I wish you'd tell me about it.'

'It's not a pretty story. My parents were too poor to feed their big pack of kids, so we ended up fighting for scraps of food and affection. There was never enough to go round, so the attacks were brutal.' He gives a shaky smile. 'Isn't it weird how the past seems to get bigger, instead of fading, as we age? I thought it would get easier with time.'

'Have you seen a therapist?'

He shakes his head. 'Too many Hollywood shrinks sell your secrets to the press. I've always hated being talked about, unless it's for a stellar performance.'

'There must be someone discreet, darling, if the past still troubles you. I promise this place will soon be calm again.' I lay my hand on his arm. 'If we let it scare us, the killer's won. Would you mind staying with Lily and me at Eden House until the danger's over? I'm going to ask Wesley too. We'd both feel safer with you around.'

His face brightens immediately. 'I'd love it.'

'I've brought you keys, so you can come and go as you like. Lily will be overjoyed, and there's safety in numbers.'

Phillip plants a kiss on my cheek, leaving me wondering why I didn't invite him sooner. The man's been alone all summer, with a broken heart. I remember hearing about the misery of his childhood in Canada, on a rundown farm. His mother and father blamed each other for their poverty, leaving Phil and his siblings caught in the cross-fire. I feel a fresh wave of admiration for the man he's become and notice the spring in his stride when he dashes off to fetch us both a drink. He returns with two Manhattans on a silver tray, the blend of rye and vermouth just right, with a maraschino cherry to sweeten the mix.

His impeccable style will be an added bonus to having him as a house guest.

'Let's forget our troubles, Phil. I want to enjoy tonight's soirée; all we have to do is stick together, and keep watch. I've got the oddest feeling that the killer's right under our noses, if we could only see the wood for the trees.'

'I love your fighting spirit, Vee.' Phillip's face breaks into a grin at last.

'I'll find the bastard that's doing this, believe me. When I discover who it is, I'll have him locked up for good.'

'Don't take any risks, and promise me one thing. Carry a phone from now on; I've got a spare you can keep. It's madness to be out of reach at a time like this.'

'No, darling. Those things are sent to torment us. If a conversation's worth having it can wait till I get home.'

I take another sip of my perfectly mixed drink, while Phillip tells me about his preparations for the storm, fitting shutters, and carrying furniture inside. I mustn't alarm Phillip in his fragile state, but the most recent attack has shaken me. Sacha Milburn is the third member of Lily's social circle to be targeted, making me afraid she could be next. All the more reason to gather everyone I love close tonight, so no one gets hurt.

37

It's 7p.m. when Nile returns to the police station, still reflecting on Sacha Milburn's attack. Dex Adebayo's behaviour will need checking, and so will Sacha's defensive behaviour towards the doctor. He's determined to find Jose Gomez, before riding down to Britannia beach. The young man can't keep running forever. He's failed to report for duty three days in a row, and his mother has been close-lipped on the phone, but now it's time for answers.

The Gomez family's cabin still looks vulnerable, raised on its flimsy platform beside the beach. Papa Gomez is a fisherman, but his small boat lies stranded on the pink sand. Nile is glad to see that most of the boats have been dragged inland, to protect them from the storm. It looks like someone's at home this time. Luella Gomez is hard at work when he parks the motorbike. She's halfway up a ladder, nailing hardboard to a screen door, as if the thin material could prevent her home from being ripped apart, if the weather turns savage.

Nile is surprised by Luella's reaction when he calls her name. She rushes down the ladder, then launches herself into his arms. The gardener's mother weeps until her tears soak through the fabric of his shirt, and he can only murmur words of comfort. Luella is a thin Creole woman of around fifty, the mother of five children, with a husband who's either at sea, or in the local bar getting drunk, leaving her to cope alone. She juggles two jobs as a cook and a cleaner, just like his mother did, when she was alive.

'Come and sit down, Luella. Tell me what's wrong.'

Mrs Gomez fishes a tissue from the pocket of her house-coat. 'Sorry, I hate being like this, but I'm so worried.'

'What's happened?'

'Jose never came home from work yesterday, and he's been so upset. I'm afraid they'll pull him from the sea, like that boy in Old Plantation Bay.'

'I saw him just now at the Bamboo Church.'

'Thank God he's alive.' Mrs Gomez crosses herself several times, as if Jose's fate will be decided by her faith alone.

'Has he been okay at home? Jose's been following Phillip Everard and Lady Vee around, day and night.'

'Jose's always been restless and he prefers to be outside; he goes walking by the sea at midnight. It's hard to make him sleep indoors.'

'Can you think why he's suddenly following people?'

'My son worships Lady Vee, Lily and Mister Phillip. I think he worries bad things will happen to them. They're the only people on Mustique who've given him a chance, so he wants to keep them safe.'

'He believes they're in danger?'

'That's the only reason I can imagine. He owes his life to them.'

'I don't think so, Luella, that honour's yours. He's lucky you've cared for him so well.' Nile's statement prompts another flurry of tears. 'If I see him, I'll send him straight home.'

Luella's hand settles on Nile's wrist. 'Jose would never cause damage, Solomon. Some people in Lovell fear him because he's mute, but Mama Toulaine says he's a good spirit, on the side of the gods. You believe that, don't you? Please tell me you understand.'

Nile touches her shoulder instead of replying. Luella is one of a small troop of helpers who came to his father's aid after he was widowed. He carries a blurred memory of her singing him to sleep, feeding him meals, and letting him play with her oldest sons on the beach. Mrs Gomez's eyes are still glistening when he leaves. Nile doesn't want to believe that Jose is involved, but his odd behaviour still can't be explained.

38

I LEAVE PHILLIP packing his bags after finishing my drink. My friend still seems thrilled by my invitation, like a child preparing for a sleepover. I often forget how insidious loneliness can be. Jasper keeps me fully entertained, blowing through my life like the whirlwind that's threatening Mustique, causing peril for every ship in the mid-Atlantic. There's a thin line between solitude and despair.

I have just enough time to prepare myself, before picking Lily up from the hospital. My mother taught me how to enjoy parties when I was a child, and I've used her method ever since. Choose good jewellery, apply your make-up with care, but above all, smile. Social events should always be approached in good faith. My smile is twitchy when I apply a layer of fuchsia-pink lipstick tonight, but it's still my best asset. I inspect my appearance closely in the mirror: I'm wearing a lemon-yellow dress from Harvey Nichols, strappy sandals, and a liberal dose of Chanel No. 5. If the killer arrives at the wake tonight, I'm battle ready, behind my shield of make-up. The powers of observation I've honed over the years should help me identify any strange behaviour. I dab a last touch of bronzer onto my cheeks then leave Eden House locked and shuttered, before setting off in my buggy, carrying Lily's favourite red dress and a pair of sandals.

My nerves are on high alert when I head for the medical centre, even though it's early evening. If Sacha Milburn can be attacked in broad daylight, every one of us is vulnerable. When I pass the stables the beautiful Arab mares in the paddock canter away suddenly. The increasing wind is making them skittish, one rearing high into the air before galloping away. The hospital smells of medicine and panic, but there's no escaping it today. I want to know exactly what happened to Sacha Milburn.

Lily is sitting on a bench outside Sacha's room, her bare feet resting on the lino. I can tell how upset she is from the way she jumps up immediately to hug me. The girl has been at her friend's bedside for hours, and I suspect she'd happily spend the night there if I don't drag her away. She looks vibrantly alive, despite the day's ordeals, her skin golden from the tropical summer.

'I thought Sacha had drowned, Vee. She wasn't even breathing.'

'You and Solomon rescued her. That's the important thing.'

Lily's eyes are glossy with tears. 'She seemed fine in the ambulance, talking clearly, but now she's lost consciousness.'

The nurse arrives before I can ask another question. Her expression is full of sympathy when she reports that Sacha remains unconscious, and concussion is unpredictable. A patient can seem fine straight after a head injury, then lapse into a coma due to swelling on the brain. The woman's kind

226

gaze assesses us in turn, before she explains that Sacha should be airlifted to St Vincent for a CT scan, but that can't happen until the storm's passed.

'The doctor's done tests to check her reflexes, and she's still responsive. Her body may just be taking the rest it needs to recover. It's likely she'll regain consciousness, but he can't say when. You're welcome to go in and see her.'

My heart sinks when I catch sight of Sacha in her hospital bed, long auburn hair splayed across the pillow, the sheets pulled tight across her body. The room is a small white box. Instinct makes me yank the window open, so air can circulate, and let her hear the birdsong outside.

Lily is holding her friend's hand, reminding me of her incredible kindness. 'It's weird, Vee. She slipped into a coma straight after Dr Pakefield examined her. I took a break for a few minutes; he was in the room with her alone.'

'The timing's a coincidence. The symptoms of a head injury can be delayed for hours.'

Lily looks unconvinced, and my own thoughts are whirling as I remember Mama Toulaine's warning about the medic. My hopes lift when Sacha's green eyes suddenly fly open, her gaze fixed on something only she can see, before dropping shut again. Her rest no longer looks peaceful, hands twitching with St Vitus' dance.

'Why not get changed, darling? I'll speak to the doctor,' I tell Lily.

There's no sign of Simon Pakefield in the reception area. It's only when I walk further down the corridor that I see the door of his consulting room stands ajar. The doctor is visible through the narrow gap. He's at his desk, head in

227

hands, fingers pressed against his temples. He remains in the same position until I tap on the door, forcing him to scramble to his feet.

'Sorry to disturb you, Simon. Could I have a quick word?'

'I'm afraid we can only wait, if you're here about Sacha,' he mutters. 'My ability to help is limited; she should be on a neurology ward, which is frustrating.'

'You look tired. Are you okay?'

'No doctor enjoys seeing patients suffer.'

When I glance down at his desk my gaze catches on something I've missed until now. Another piece of coral, with a spider's web carved into its surface. When I pick it up, emotions flood the doctor's face for the first time, anxiety mixed with guilt.

'Where did you find this?' I ask.

His neutral expression slips back into place. 'Outside Sacha's room, soon after she arrived.'

'Can I take it with me? Solomon Nile will want to see it.'

'Go ahead.'

'There's one more thing. You were seen taking a speedboat out to the *Aqua Dream* late on Monday night. Can you explain why?'

His eyes blink rapidly. 'That's not true. I'm required to stay here, twenty-four hours a day, unless I give the trustees notice.'

'I place a great deal of trust in the person who told me.'

'They're mistaken.' He picks up a clipboard, attempting to end our conversation. 'Excuse me, but I need to get back to work.'

I can see how badly he wants me off his territory, but my

attitude towards him is shifting. 'I'm concerned about Sacha; the killer's leaving pieces of coral as his calling card, so he may plan to hurt her again. Lily and I must attend the memorial party tonight, but I'll send for a guard, before we leave.'

'She'll be perfectly safe here.'

'Let's not take chances. I don't want another young person's life slipping from our hands.'

The truth is, the killer may be someone I have trusted until now. Dr Pakefield could have used Dr Bunbury's boat to harvest samples of coral, including the one on his desk. But if he's guilty, his violence appears to give him no pleasure. I can see misery in the rigid set of his shoulders when I finally leave his consulting room.

Lily looks striking when she appears in the corridor, in a crimson dress that fits her slim form perfectly. She hasn't bothered with make-up, but her skin seems to glow from the inside. I hate to darken her mood, because she's been through so much lately, but there's no other choice.

'You look stunning, darling, but can you call Solomon? I want one of the Layton brothers here immediately. The killer's left another piece of coral.'

The tension on Lily's face makes an odd contrast with her vivid dress. I feel certain the killer would be overjoyed to see her happiness slipping away.

39

THE BEACH PARTY has begun when Nile receives the call from Lily. Staff from Basil's Bar have already got a bonfire blazing on the sand. Britannia beach looks like it did when he was a boy, its long crescent tinted pink by the powdered coral that forms the island's fabric, but his old sense of safety has vanished, and it would be a mistake to let nostalgia overtake him tonight. It doesn't take long to spot Charlie Layton among a crowd of men from Lovell, enjoying the free beer. When Nile orders him to guard Sacha Milburn at the hospital, he sets off at a heavy jog. The main virtue of the island's smallness is that everything lies within reach. Layton will be at the medical centre in ten minutes, if he keeps up a decent pace.

Nile looks back at the growing crowd. Lady Vee seems to believe that Pakefield is involved, but the killer could be standing metres away, because all murderers are egotists. They believe their own lives matter most, and right now the killer will be overjoyed. He's taken two lives and placed another in jeopardy, leaving three families devastated, but no one would guess that violence hangs over the island. The only sign that the party is actually a wake are two large photos of Tommy and Amanda above a makeshift bar, smiling like they don't have a care in the world. Waiters are circulating with wine glasses balanced on trays, the liquor already flowing. Some of his father's old friends are relaxing in deckchairs, enjoying the atmosphere. The party has drawn some of the island's biggest personalities. Keith Belmont is talking with Dexter Adebayo, the two men's faces serious among the other revellers as they stare at the fire. Speakers have been raised above the sand, blaring out an eclectic range of music, from calypso to Motown and reggae.

The party has tempted the few remaining villa owners down from their villas. There's an actress, a theatre impresario from New York and a British politician. Everyone is starting to unwind, couples dancing together, the volume of laughter rising. There's a round of applause when a Blue Heaven number blares across the beach, with Keith Belmont's rasping voice telling the crowd to dance like the devil, because tomorrow may never come. Nile could watch the island's bone-deep hedonism at play for hours, but that would be a missed opportunity. Lyron's face appears on the far side of the crowd, talking to another staff member from Basil's. His brother looks lighter since their conversation, more like the cheerful schoolboy he remembers. Nile is glad his brother's present tonight, so he can keep him safe.

It's 10.30p.m. and the stars keep slipping behind skeins of cloud, their soft light turning the sea to mercury. When he turns round Jose Gomez is watching him from the dunes, scrambling away once their eyes meet, like he did at the memorial. The young man's shyness is well known, but Nile still believes that facade might be concealing something more sinister. He takes a few paces in his direction, but the gardener has already disappeared. Gomez appears to be keeping tabs on the party guests from a distance. There's nothing else on the beach, except a line of sea grape bushes, sculpted by the wind.

When Nile checks his phone a text has arrived from Charlie Layton. Sacha Milburn's condition is serious but stable. Lady Vee has told him to stay at her bedside, until he's relieved from duty. Nile understands that only the girl can save herself now; she'll have to fight hard to regain consciousness. He scans the crowd again, where over a hundred people are watching the flames leap higher, faces lit by their orange glow. Keith Belmont is surrounded by French tourists from Firefly, flirting with the youngest girl in the group, just like old times. Dexter Adebayo is standing closest to the fire. The man still looks far edgier than the laidback character who taught Nile to dive, staring at the flames while the guests enjoy themselves.

Wesley Gilbert must have been telling the truth about Mama Toulaine, because the couple are side by side, so relaxed in each other's company they don't need to talk. Nile is still on his own when Lily Calder approaches. The young woman is clutching a pair of high heels in one hand, the other holding a cocktail glass. She looks like a typical socialite, gorgeous in a short red dress, but up close she's not so easily categorised. There's too much concern on her face for a bona fide party girl.

'You look thoughtful, Solomon.'

'I've been watching so hard, I'm starting to miss things.'

'Have you seen the girl Keith's chatting up? She doesn't look legal.'

'I checked her ID. She's just turned sixteen; I hope she's drinking lemonade.'

The music rises in volume, Bob Marley and the Wailers' 'Three Little Birds' suddenly so loud Nile can't hear himself think. He points towards the waterline and Lily falls into step. The day's adrenalin is still racing around his system; if he was back in Oxford he'd don his running shoes and pound the streets, but right now he'd like to slip into the water and go for a long swim. Lily Calder appears to feel the same. They walk further down the shoreline, until the party's music becomes a low metallic pulse, the half-moon's bright outline dominating the sky.

'Did you find anything about Sacha's attacker?' Lily asks.

'She could have been followed from the memorial, or someone lay in wait at her villa. I need to dig deeper into people's histories tomorrow, including people we haven't considered. It's a sophisticated campaign for a novice.'

Lily sits on the trunk of a fallen palm tree, waiting for Nile to join her. 'Who's crazy enough to attack my friends, and leave such hateful messages?'

'We'll find out, don't worry. But you need to stay safe.'

'I won't work on Mum's boat alone until this is over.'

'I didn't know the *Revival* belonged to your mother.' Nile avoids looking at her directly. It's been months since a woman attracted him so much, but it's the wrong time to let it overtake him. She seems lost in her own world, head tipped back to admire the night sky. 'How old were you, when she died?'

'Five, how about you?'

'I'd just turned seven. I can hardly picture her now, and maybe that's a blessing. My father remembers her too well. He never remarried.'

Lily's gaze is calmer than the waves as they gain strength. 'Do you ever blame yourself?'

'Nothing I did could have stopped it.'

'I'll never know if caring for me was the final straw after Dad left. She could have followed her career without a kid to look after.' Lily gives a hollow laugh. 'Sorry, I'm getting mawkish. It's a combination of booze and seeing another friend get hurt. I'd better go back.'

Nile rises to his feet at the same time, but Lily loses her footing. When she stumbles against him he puts a hand round her waist to steady her. She rises onto to her toes to kiss his cheek as an old calypso number plays, the guitar music distorting on the breeze. Nile's about to kiss her back when she flits away, back towards the light.

40

THE CARIBBEAN COAST is the best place to admire the night sky, and the party has reached its peak as midnight approaches. The breeze blowing off the sea is intensifying, even though the storm is still a hundred miles north, but none of the guests seem to care. They're still dancing and drinking with gay abandon. The half-moon reminds me of a painting by Atkinson Grimshaw, edged by clouds that soften its silver outline. I can see Phillip in the distance, dressed in a white linen shirt and pale grey trousers. He's chatting to one of the staff from the Cotton House, and looks more relaxed since our chat. The staff from Basil's have managed the evening perfectly, which isn't surprising. Impromptu parties on Mustique happen so often, they can produce food, drink and a sound system in less than an hour. But the gathering has failed to answer my questions. I've spent the last few hours scanning the crowd for signs of guilty behaviour, with Lily and Solomon doing the same. Maybe the simple reason we can't spot the killer is because we've already found him. Dr Pakefield is still at the hospital, with Charlie Layton standing guard, and Keith Belmont disappeared an hour ago, with a young girl from Firefly. I can't imagine why she let a man old enough to be her grandfather take her home, but fame can be seductive when you're young. I can't escape my belief that he's involved in some way. Keith favoured me with a smug smile as he led the girl away, his arm snaking round her shoulder.

Time slips backwards when the bonfire blazes higher, the wind sending showers of orange sparks up into the sky. I wish Jasper was here; his maverick personality comes to the fore at any gathering, ensuring that everyone has fun. Some of the world's biggest celebrities have lost their inhibitions on this beach: all undone by Mustique's freedom. I've seen plenty of famous characters from stage and screen disappear into the dunes for illicit rendez-vous, never mentioned beyond Mustique's shores. But when my eyes blink open, ghosts linger at the edges of my vision. The only light source now is the starlight glinting overhead as the clouds race inland. Tommy and Amanda's deaths stay at the front of my mind. I must keep my wits about me, to find out why they died.

I've attended so many parties in my lifetime, I know the exact moment when the crowd's energy cools. Some party stalwarts have already left, including Dex Adebayo. It's 1a.m. and the dancing is slowing, even though Van Morrison's voice is still calling from the speakers, telling us that it's a marvellous night for a moon dance. Everyone turns to face me when I climb onto a beer crate that's lying on the sand, to give the final eulogy.

'Thank you all for being with us, to remember two special young people. Tommy was still in his twenties, but he had an old soul; kind, serious and loving. Amanda loved to party, but she was bright too, and always loyal, especially to my beloved Lily. Let's never forget them. Please raise a glass with me now, to salute them both, and don't hurry away just yet, will you? There's still plenty of champagne.'

The crowd cheer and clap their hands, Lily beaming up at me, even though the party has failed to deliver answers. I've only seen the usual collection of friends and acquaintances, partying hard to forget the threat we're under. The holidaymakers from Firefly and the Cotton House have danced and knocked back huge quantities of alcohol. I'm still warm in my thin dress, but ready to go home. Wesley's reaction to my request for help fills me with gratitude. When I asked for his protection, he almost saluted me, before rushing home for an overnight bag. I've never felt luckier to have him as my butler, his loyalty unfailing.

Lily is chatting, but I saw her disappear into the dark with Solomon Nile a while back. I hope they've been enjoying each other's company, as well as discussing the investigation. She needs fun after her vigil at Sacha Milburn's bedside, but Solomon looks completely focused. I'm certain that he's stayed sober like me, keeping his wits together. My glass contains clear apple juice mixed with sparkling water, which looks exactly like champagne; I don't want to seem like a killjoy, but it's the wrong time to lower my defences.

Phillip appears out of the crowd suddenly. He takes my drink and deposits it on a table, his hand settling on my wrist. 'Dance with me, Vee. I asked them to play your favourite song. I've waited all night for this.'

The music changes to Bryan Ferry singing 'Smoke Gets

in your Eyes'. Another cheer goes up because Ferry is a much-loved regular visitor to Mustique, then the chatter fades and Phillip is dancing me round the fire in a slow waltz, everyone standing back to watch. I allow myself to imagine being married to Phillip, instead of Jasper, just for a second, before blocking out the thought.

'Getting everyone home safely will be tricky,' Phillip murmurs. 'I've told them to walk in groups.'

'Have you seen anything strange?'

'Dex seemed pretty wired, and Keith Belmont's lured a schoolgirl back to his lair.'

'I hope she's safe.'

'Solomon's going to pay him a call. Let's send people home, then we can have a nightcap on your terrace.'

'Perfect.' He gives my shoulders a squeeze before vanishing into the crowd. I'll call an end to proceedings soon, but my throat's dry from too much talk, so I collect my drink from the table and finish it in a couple of sips.

I spend fifteen minutes chatting with departing guests, then an odd feeling overtakes me when I look at the fire. Flames are burning out of control, people's clothes pulsing so brightly I have to shut my eyes. When I open them again, everything's spinning, my thoughts racing much too fast. I look for Phillip or Lily to help me, but they're too far away. A sudden wave of nausea rises in my throat and instinct makes me escape from the crowd. I rush through the sea grape bushes, before falling on my hands and knees. My head is still whirling, but I'm trying to return to the crowd to get help when something rustles among the leaves. Someone grabs hold of me from behind, gripping my arms so tightly, each fingertip will leave a bruise. Then there's a sudden pain in my back, so raw it leaves me speechless. I can't even call for help, the moon vanishing between trees as my vision fails.

PART THREE

Tropical Weather Outlook

National Hurricane Center, Miami FL

Wednesday, 18 September 2002

Attention all shipping:

The National Hurricane Center is issuing
advisories on Tropical Storm Cristobal, north of Haiti.

Cyclone tracking south towards the Windward Isles at
110 miles per hour, current risk rating: severe

41

Wednesday, 18th September 2002

NILE WATCHES THE guests leave. The storm has finally landed, the wind arriving in gusts that send the guests' clothes billowing, but most are in good spirits, a few drunk enough to lean on friends' shoulders as they say good night. It's after 1a.m. when staff from Basil's Bar gather up ice crates, then fold trestle tables away. Lily is helping to collect empty beer bottles that are scattered across the sand. The fire is dying down already, its flames dancing less wildly in the savage wind. Thick cloud is swirling overhead, snuffing out the stars.

Phillip Everard seems to have coped well with the evening, even though Nile has caught him assessing the crowd, clearly hoping to identify the killer. He looks tired when he approaches Nile.

'Have you seen Vee lately?' he asks.

'She was chatting to a guest from the Cotton House a few minutes ago.'

'I need to find her. She wants to hand out tips before the staff go home.'

The two men scan the beach, then Nile pulls out his

phone and calls Eden House. Panic glitters in Everard's eyes when there's no answer. The man's fondness for Lady Vee has shown from the start, as if she's one of the few people on Mustique the actor really trusts. They're still discussing where she could be when a figure rushes out of the dark. Jose Gomez has chosen a strange time to re-appear, just as the party ends. His hair is dishevelled, clothes covered in sand; there's a wild look on his face when he grabs Lily's wrist. The young man's expression is frantic as he tries to drag her across the beach. Nile can see his lips forming words, but no sound emerges. Lily does her best to reassure him, but he takes no notice. Gomez's behaviour changes when Nile approaches. He cowers, like a child waiting for punishment, but the detect-ive keeps his voice gentle.

'What's wrong, Jose? Your mother's worried about you.'

The gardener transfers his attention to Nile; there's a pleading expression on his face when he beckons him to follow. Gomez crosses the sand at a rapid jog with the detect-ive close behind, their steps guided by moonlight. He comes to a halt by Lady Vee's dune buggy, and Nile's concern increases. She would never walk away before the party ended, leaving her transport behind. Gomez gestures towards the buggy again. When Nile looks more closely a piece of coral lies on the driver's seat. Its surface is incised with crossed arrows.

'Not you too,' Nile mutters under his breath.

Gomez is already running away, but the detective's long stride helps him catch up. The young man is out of breath when he grabs his shoulder.

'Who took her, Jose? What did you see?'

The tears welling in Gomez's eyes spill down his cheeks, but it's his expression that convinces Nile of his innocence. It's full of confusion, as if the adult world is a riddle he can't solve. The detective tells him to run back home. Gomez has proved that Lady Vee's been taken, but can't explain why. Whoever took her has left him terrified. The killer must have been watching from the dunes. Nile has been so busy observing the crowd for unnatural behaviour, he never believed the party's host could be seized right under his nose.

Lily is blank-faced when Nile returns to the buggy; she's clutching Phillip Everard's hand, but her voice is calm.

'Vee's been taken, hasn't she? Jose saw it happen.'

'Go back to Eden House straight away, both of you, please. Lock the doors and wait for me there.'

Everard shakes his head. 'I'll come with you. We have to catch that maniac, before Vee's hurt.'

Nile taps the gun he's carried since collecting his uniform from the police headquarters. 'I'm armed, remember? It's my job to keep you safe.'

Lily protests hard, but Nile waits until Everard helps her into the buggy and they set off for Eden House. Now he's alone on the beach, where the only evidence that a party took place is the fire's dying embers, and the moon's pale face withholding judgement. There's an odd sensation in his gut: he's certain someone's watching. He felt the same in Oxford when another life slipped from his grasp. No one blamed him at the time, but his conscience has needled him ever since.

'You sick bastard!' he yells at the dark.

Nile's only reply comes from the wind shrieking overhead as the storm finally hits, its battle cry condemning him as he hurries inland.

42

MY NIGHTMARES ARE coming thick and fast. I can see Lily swimming out to sea; there's a black ridge of cloud on the horizon, and waves lashing the shore. I call out, but my voice is lost in the storm. She's vanished when my eyes flick open. All I can see is darkness. My mouth is stuffed with cotton, the gag between my lips pulled tight.

I can't make sense of the pain between my shoulders, and there's a dry stench of chemicals whenever I swallow. I'm lying on a wet concrete floor, my cheek resting on the ground, and every muscle hurts. My wrists and ankles are bound so tightly with rope my hands and feet feel numb. I've never felt so exposed, lying in a foetal position, at the killer's mercy.

One minute I was dancing with Phillip, then I spotted him clowning around with Lily on the far side of the crowd and my vision blurred. The truth arrives as I piece the events together. My drink was spiked. That explains why my head's spinning, and the vile taste in my mouth, my limbs still trembling. I should have stayed with people I love, instead of staggering away, desperate for privacy. I have to focus on staying alive, and I must be near someone's property. Whoever dragged me here is afraid I'll cry out, or why bother with the gag? I drag my cheek across the ground, to loosen its grip, but only graze my skin on the floor's rough surface.

I intend to fight for my life with every fibre of my being, but my situation couldn't be much worse. I'm trapped, with a mechanical whir buzzing in my ears, and a tropical bird screaming for morning as it flies overhead.

43

NILE RUNS THROUGH suspects in his head while the dune buggy judders across the sand. He's certain the killer has a personal score to settle with Lady Vee. His strongest suspects are now Keith Belmont and Dexter Adebayo. Knowing which man to pursue first could prevent the murder of a woman he's respected all his life. The wind is suddenly hard enough to make the palm trees sway and bend, when he takes the quickest route to Keith Belmont's villa. The old rock star is the only man on Mustique who Lady Vee actively dislikes, and Nile feels sure he's hiding something. The musician left the party early with a young tourist, but she may only have been his alibi, allowing him to return and complete the abduction.

The detective would never normally approach one of the villas at 2a.m., especially when the owner is seducing a teenage girl, but right now he doesn't care about complaints to head-quarters. He keeps his thumb on the doorbell until a groggy voice on the intercom tells him to stop the bloody row.

Belmont is wearing boxer shorts, a black T-shirt, and a heavy frown when the security door slides open.

'What the hell do you want?'

Nile steps inside, before the musician can banish him. 'Lady Vee's gone missing.'

A shocked look crosses the musician's face, but that could be another sham, like his claim to be a reformed character. The man reeks of booze and cigarettes, his brash body language reflecting his discomfort at being caught in the act. He struts away, then returns in a bathrobe, more relaxed under a fresh layer of camouflage. Belmont fetches two tumblers of water, his scowling still in place when Solomon towers over him at the table.

'Where's the girl from Firefly?'

'I came to my senses just in time, thank God. I walked her back to the hotel and gave her a chaste kiss good night. That deserves a medal, doesn't it?'

'Why's that?'

'I'm trying to change.' Belmont's head drops forward suddenly. 'I only have to try something once to crave it all the time, that's the problem with an addictive personality. People like me don't stop eating when our bellies are full, like the rest of humanity, and it's not just sex. I'm the same with fags, alcohol and drugs. I'm even obsessed with coral now – but I've pushed things too far with Lily's project. I should apologise.'

'You're saying the girl's safe?'

'She'll be tucked up in bed, but I need someone like you to keep me on the straight and narrow. It was so bloody tempting to bring her here, to avoid waking up alone.' Belmont sighs, and Nile wonders if the man's real identity is showing at last. 'I screwed up big style tonight, but tomorrow I'll get back on the wagon.'

'What time did you come home?'

'Over an hour ago, feeling like an idiot. I've screwed up enough women's lives.' Belmont's bloodshot eyes connect with Nile's face at last. 'Do you know what really hurts? My kids stopped talking to me years ago. They don't even answer my calls.'

'That's not relevant. I have to find Lady Vee.'

Belmont ignores his comment. 'Haven't you got any addictions, Solomon?'

'Exercise, maybe. I went to the gym or ran every day in the UK.'

'That doesn't count.' Belmont's mocking laugh sounds like liquid gurgling down a drain. 'Mine were drink and drugs. All I had to do was lift the phone.'

'Who do you call?'

He hesitates before replying. 'Never the same person twice.'

'Dex Adebayo?'

The surprise on Belmont's face proves that Nile's guess is correct. It explains how his brother got involved too; Lyron must see him every day.

'You've never liked Lady Vee, have you, Mr Belmont?'

'We rub along, but most aristocrats despise ordinary people. She thinks she's a cut above, and her husband's the same.'

'That's not my experience.'

'She's had every kind of privilege. I knew she'd put a spanner in the works, with Lily's charity. I could have financed that coral project for years, but she doesn't want me getting my grubby paws on it.' Bitterness resonates through the musician's voice. 'She thinks men like us should stay in the gutter.'

'Lady Vee's the most generous woman on Mustique. The Blakes paid for my education, with no strings attached.'

'You're being naïve.' Belmont places his glass on the table with more force than necessary. 'If you wanted to date her precious goddaughter she'd banish you from Mustique.'

'I disagree,' Nile says, staring back at him. 'Can you prove what time you got home?'

'I've written a few emails. They'll show what time they were sent.'

'Let me see your computer, please.'

'I made a call as well, to Pastor Boakye.'

'Why's that?'

'He lets me ring him whenever I'm tempted. The guy knows I'm battling my demons. Maybe that's because he's got his own too.'

'How do you mean?'

'I like to know who I'm dealing with, so I checked him out on the Internet and made a few phone calls. It turns out there's no record of him training at a seminary in Nigeria, or serving at a church in Lagos, but who cares? The guy's shown me more genuine kindness than anyone here.'

Nile's interest quickens. Many islanders have sung the priest's praises, but it's possible he's a fraud. He should have checked the guy's CV before believing his story about being sent abroad by his bishop.

Belmont is staring at the table's surface. 'The only person I hurt is myself. Lady Vee's a snob, but that's not my problem. Why would I suddenly go on the rampage now, after a lifetime of being patronised?'

'The coral means a lot to you, doesn't it?'

'It's like me, that's why. The original comeback kid. I've overdosed by accident, and had a liver transplant. It's a wonder I'm still here, and the coral's the same. You can regenerate a whole reef with a few well-placed grafts.' The yearning on Belmont's face takes Nile by surprise.

'Show me those emails please.'

'You've got demons too, Solomon. It's written all over your face. Who did you hurt, on your way up?'

'Don't make me arrest you, Mr Belmont.'

The musician rises to his feet at a slow pace. Nile's pulse is racing, even though it's the wrong time to dwell on past mistakes. The storm is gusting over the villa's roof, its cry a high-pitched wail.

THE ROOM IS completely dark, apart from needles of moonlight piercing through holes in the wooden walls. Pictures crowd my mind. My children are small again, running to me as I collect them from boarding school. The two lost ones are flesh and blood in my arms. I want to follow them, and only need to let myself drift, but instinct makes me fight back to the surface. The drug in my body is making me twitch but my mind is alert and ready. I need to get home for Lily's sake. The girl has lost too many loved ones already; I don't want her arranging another funeral.

I can see clearly at last, my vision improving. I catch sight of a lawnmower, buckets and mops. When I strain my eyes again, containers of salt and chlorine are stacked on shelves, and shock overtakes me. The place looks familiar, because it's mine. I'm trapped inside the pool house where Jose keeps cleaning equipment. The building lies a hundred metres from the terrace of Eden House, half-hidden by trees and overgrown hibiscus. Instinct makes me put back my head and yell, but the only sound that escapes my gag is a muffled whisper.

NILE SEES CHARLIE Layton guarding Sacha Milburn's room when he reaches the medical centre. The security guard appears to realise the importance of his role at last; he's sitting bolt upright, eyes fixed on the door, ready to stop any stranger entering. He looks thrilled when Nile thanks him, like a prefect receiving praise from his favourite teacher, but Sacha is still unconscious, her red curls splayed across the pillow. Ten minutes pass before Dr Pakefield rushes through the entrance doors, looking flustered.

'Where have you been, doctor?' Nile asks.

'Outside for a breath of fresh air.'

'In a howling gale? We need to talk in your office please.'

The medic's face is full of suppressed resentment, but he remains silent until they enter his consulting room.

'What's this about? I need to check on Sacha.'

'You took time off recently, without authorisation. I'd call that dereliction of duty.'

'What do you mean?'

'You were seen in a speedboat, visiting the *Aqua Dream*.

Did you really think the whole island was asleep? I've got witnesses, Dr Pakefield. You may as well explain.'

The medic drops into his chair, his energy suddenly fading. 'I got a call, late Monday night, from a crew member on the *Aqua Dream*, saying they needed a doctor urgently.'

'The terms of your contract are to remain on the island, unless you have authority to leave.'

'He was desperate.' The medic's gaze shifts to the door, as if he's planning his escape.

'How much did they pay?'

'It sounded like a genuine emergency. They knew I was breaking my contract, so they compensated me. I never expected a fee.'

Nile's bulk throws a shadow across the desk. 'Keep talking, or do you want to lose your licence?'

'There are only two crewmen on that yacht. One of them had cut his leg, while diving. The wound was infected and needed stitches. I treated him, then left immediately. I was only on board half an hour.'

'How much did you get paid?'

The doctor blinks rapidly. 'The captain gave me an envelope containing three thousand dollars.'

'That's a tidy sum for dressing a cut, if that's all you did. What else did you see on the boat?'

'Just a man in his thirties with a suppurating wound. I got the sense that the crewmen were bored. They want to move on to their next destination, then go home. They've been at sea for months.'

'Why is Sacha Milburn afraid of you? She was terrified, after her attack.'

'I told you, head wounds can cause delirium.'

'Tell me the truth, or I'll have to arrest you.'

Pakefield's shoulders slump even further. 'My marriage is in trouble,' he whispers. 'My wife is back in the UK with the children. I went to Firefly for a drink to drown my sorrows and Sacha was there. We ended up sleeping together, just once. I regretted it immediately, because I want to get back together with my wife. I may not have been kind enough the morning after, but I'd made a stupid mistake.'

'So Sacha's got reason to hate you for rejecting her, and I bet you need money right now for your divorce. You make twice as much cash on Mustique than St Vincent, and your kids' school fees will be crippling.' Nile stares at the doctor again. 'You've got access to a boat, and you've been on board the *Aqua Dream*. How much are they paying you to keep quiet about their operation?'

'I didn't see anything.'

'I think you envy Mustique's residents. Does it make you angry, seeing their huge villas and swimming pools?'

'Why would I work here if it did? It's the physical beauty of the place that draws me.'

'You've lied, Dr Pakefield. How can I trust anything you say? Stay in the corridor, where Charlie Layton can keep an eye, and don't lay a finger on Sacha Milburn. Do you hear me?'

'All I did was help a wounded man.'

'Show me what's in your desk drawer before we go.'

The man's jaw gags open. 'Just private possessions.'

'Open it.'

257

The first thing Nile sees is a bright red notebook with Sacha's name written on the cover.

'Why did you take this?'

'She gave it to me for safekeeping.'

Nile doesn't waste time questioning such an obvious lie. He just jerks his head, signalling him to follow. The detective can feel the fury emanating from Pakefield's skin when he sits in the corridor, arms folded across the starched fabric of his white coat.

Charlie Layton looks gratified to be given an extra responsibility. Nile would prefer to lock Pakefield in a holding cell, but he's the only medic on the island, and Sacha needs his help. He's about to leave when Layton turns towards him.

'The girl's very sick,' he whispers. 'Shall I call Pastor Boakye? He'll save her, if anyone can. The man's a miracle worker.'

'How do you mean?'

'My wife lost a baby in January. Her mind was broken, until he visited us. The guy's got healing powers.'

'I don't believe in miracles, but I need to see him, so I'll send him here soon. Sacha believes in him, so it might help.' Nile is about to leave, but the storm is doing damage already. The wind is hurling rooftiles at the trees, thrashing six-foot-tall pampas grass until it lies flattened. 'You've lived here all your life, Charlie. If you had to pick a local out as a killer who would it be?'

'Dex Adebayo,' Layton says, his reply arriving in a heart-beat. 'There's nothing good about a man who threatens his wife.'

Nile's blood runs cold. 'He's violent towards Cherelle?'

Layton's face is solemn. 'Their cabin is next to ours. We hear them arguing. When I knock on the door she's too afraid to talk.'

46

It's still half dark when I hear a noise. The sound is barely audible behind the screeching wind; it could be my own heart racing, but it's growing clearer all the time. Someone's feet tapping towards me, across the concrete. I can't tell if it's a man or a woman but I keep my eyes open. I have to face whatever's coming without flinching.

There's a burst of light as the door flies open, blinding me after so long in the dark. Someone is shining a flashlight in my face, then a plastic sheet drops over me, my hands still tied behind my back. At least my energy has returned; I won't go down without a fight. I kick out hard, but my punishment is instant. I'm being pulled over the ground outside my pool house, my dress tearing. Plastic material flaps around my face and I catch a glimpse of Eden House. My home is a fairy-tale castle, far out of reach. Now I'm blind again, my body dumped on a hard surface, before an engine throbs into life. They're driving me somewhere. I try to keep my wits about me to quell the panic. We're travelling west, over the island's roughest paths. The killer is trying to stay out of sight.

I can't yet tell who's caught me, but at least the journey is brief. I'm lifted across the ground now, the plastic sheet bound more tightly around my body, making it hard to breathe. This time I understand exactly what's happening. I'm lying in the hold of a speedboat, pain registering as it lists wildly from side to side. Only a madman would put to sea in the face of a huge storm. Waves slap the vessel's sides as it drifts, then the outboard motor judders into life. My shoulders thump against cold fibreglass and I grit my teeth as the engine whines, cold water splashing over me as waves pound the vessel's sides.

47

RAIN IS FALLING in such heavy drops when Nile arrives at Eden House, it feels like buckets of water are being tipped from the trees. The villa is suffering the storm's effects too, window shutters straining on their hinges. Nile has to throw himself against the wind to climb the steps, despite his weight. His clothes are soaked when he reaches the porch and Sacha Milburn's notebook has suffered the same fate; its cover is wet with rain, the pages sticking together. Lily appears to be feeling the stress of Lady Vee's absence when she opens the door, but at least she's followed his instructions to stay safe. She slides the bolt on the door home, then leads him down to the kitchen, where Phillip Everard is sitting at the table. It's a relief to see him; all of Lady Vee's staunchest allies will be needed to bring her home. The actor rises to his feet when he arrives, clearly hungry for news, but Wesley Gilbert marches through the back door before either man can speak.

'I just checked the grounds,' Gilbert says. 'Someone's been in the pool house recently. The lock's been broken, and I found a length of rope. I think this is one of Lady Vee's shoes.'

He places a high-heeled sandal on the table, and Lily gives a solemn nod.

'That's definitely Vee's.'

'We need to work as a team,' Nile says. 'It sounds like they used Lady Vee's own pool house to keep her captive, just to rub our noses in it. We've got three main suspects: Dexter Adebayo, Keith Belmont and Dr Pakefield. Dex and Keith left the party early, and Pakefield went missing from the hospital in time to attack Lady Vee. He's got hold of Sacha's journal, and may have left the medical centre un-attended for long enough to capture Lady Vee and hide her somewhere. It looks like Pastor Boakye's telling lies, but he's not our killer. He couldn't have got from the Bamboo Church to Stargazer so soon after the memorial to attack Sacha, but he could be withholding information. I still think the *Aqua Dream*'s involved in some way, but I don't have authority to search the boat.'

Gilbert replies first. The man's military background has never been more apparent; his back is ramrod straight, like he's received a call to arms.

'We should check out Dexter first. The guy knows everything that goes on here.'

'I think he's been selling drugs on the side,' Nile says. 'It's possible he's violent towards his wife too; he could be unstable enough to carry out the attacks.'

Lily shakes her head. 'He's always seemed like a decent guy.'

'Plenty of killers do, unfortunately.'

Nile glances outside the window, where leaves and branches are being shredded by the wild breeze, debris from the trees

263

covering Lady Vee's lawn. It's too dark to judge the state of the ocean, but waves are crashing on the shore below, another assault on the island's safety. He studies his trio of helpers again. Lily has changed out of her red dress into jeans and a T-shirt, but still looks beautiful, despite her anxiety.

Phillip Everard is hunched over the table, fingers tapping out a rapid rhythm. 'We're losing time. If we don't find her soon, that bastard will pin her to the ocean floor.'

'Someone needs to read Sacha's notebook,' Nile says. 'She's been keeping watch over the island. It may hold useful evidence.'

'Do you want me to do it?' Phillip volunteers. 'I've read enough lousy scripts in my time.'

'That's helpful, thanks. Can you patrol the house, Wesley, in case someone's still sniffing around? Remember, the killer must have a key. Lily, I'd like you to see Dexter and his wife with me. She'll feel safer with you present.'

It's 2a.m. when Nile and Lily run down the path through pouring rain to the Adebayos' cabin. The detective needs to hear Dexter's alibi for this afternoon and evening, because he has everything the killer needs, from the use of a powerful speedboat to intimate knowledge of the victims' habits from his daily visits to Basil's. The man's diving expertise also makes him seem a likely culprit. His character has changed and he's clearly hidden a darker side for a long time.

Nile raps on the door with a heavy fist. Adebayo's wife appears after a minute of constant hammering. Cherelle looks older than he remembers when she stands on the threshold.

'Dex is out,' she says, addressing her comment to Lily. 'He went to someone's cabin after the party, to carry on drinking.'

'Can we talk anyway, Cherelle?' Nile asks. 'It won't take long.'

The place is messy when she leads them inside, with newspapers piled on a bench, beside a stack of ironing. There's no sign here that Dexter is profiting from his side-line – he'd have bought a new refrigerator, instead of the antique in the corner that's emitting such a loud drone it sounds ready to explode.

Cherelle clears the sofa so her visitors can sit down, then perches on a chair opposite, picking at her ruined nail varnish.

'Can you tell us how Dex has been spending his time lately?'

'Working and hanging out at Basil's like always,' the woman says, her tiredness echoing in her voice. 'He doesn't tell me much.'

'I need every detail please, Cherelle.' Nile lounges on the settee like he's got all the time in the world. 'The sooner you talk, the sooner we'll leave, but I have to ask you something first. Has Dex been hurting you?'

Lily reaches out to touch her hand. 'It's okay, you can talk to us. How long's it been going on?'

Cherelle looks set to argue, then her face crumples. 'Something's gone wrong this year. I can hardly recognise him.'

'How do you mean?'

'Whatever's got hold of him, I can't reach him any more. I can't predict what makes him angry. It always used to be something I'd said, or done, but now there doesn't have to be any reason at all.'

Nile feels nausea rising in his throat; he remembers the woman in Oxford all over again.

'No reason's good enough for physical abuse, Cherelle. I'll make sure it doesn't happen again, but right now I need to know when you last saw him. He was at Sacha Milburn's place straight after she was attacked, and he was at the party this evening. Do you know where he is now?'

'Dex makes his own rules these days.'

'Do you know if he ever takes his speedboat out to that big yacht moored outside Britannia Bay?'

'He's delivered beer and cigarettes to the crewmen a few times; they pay him well, but I never see the money.'

Before they leave, Nile checks if Cherelle has someone else she can stay with, and makes arrangements for her to find safety. It's too soon to tell whether Adebayo is helping someone on a vicious killing spree, but Nile's own guilt surfaces before he can suppress it. His head swims with ugly images that bring him to a standstill, until he has to lean on the rail outside the Adebayos' house. He can picture the woman he failed; twenty-five years old, pretty, and terrified.

'She wasn't much older than you,' he mutters.

Lily steps closer. 'Something got to you in there, didn't it?'

'I shouldn't be doing this job.'

'You're working too hard, that's all. Tell me what's wrong.'

Nile lets himself exhale at last. 'Back in Oxford, I got called to see a young married couple. Neighbours heard the girl screaming, but the husband was there both times I visited. She hardly spoke, and I didn't interpret her silence correctly. I could sense the guy was dangerous. I wanted to arrest him, but my senior told me to keep out of it. He said we'd never nail him unless she testified, and pushing her for answers would be contravening the assault law. The husband lost the plot a week later. I found her body in the boot of her car down a country lane, covered in stab wounds. The bloke got eighteen years, but that won't change it.'

He feels the warmth of Lily's hand on his back but can't meet her eye.

'Your boss made a bad call, Solomon. You did what you could.'

'I let her die. It still feels like I should resign from the police force most days; coming here was meant to help me decide.'

Lily's hand is still on his back. 'Forgive yourself. Everyone on Mustique can see your decency and your desire to do good. It's on his conscience, not yours.'

Lily's quiet certainty penetrates his defences at last, his vision slowly clearing.

48

I SUPPRESS MY sea sickness as the boat rocks, panic subsiding as I focus on staying alive. I can't even yell out a protest. The same damp rag is wedged inside my mouth, making it hard to breathe. The killer may have sailed away from Mustique so he can dispose of my body, just like Tommy Rothmore's.

He handles my body like a piece of cargo, hauling me upright, then dumping me in a harness. Pain shoots through my hip from the sudden impact, but the bastard doesn't care about human damage. He pulls me across the surface by my feet, like a piece of furniture, the pain making me black out.

When I come round my situation has changed. I'm sitting on a chair, my eyes blindfolded. I use my other senses to try to understand where I'm being held, while silence presses in on me. I can smell rotting fish, or could it be coral? That salty tang of decay lingered on the air when I found the killer's offering outside Lily's room.

My pulse quickens when footsteps come closer, then a voice grumbling swear words, and suddenly a door creaks open. I'm desperate to see my captor, but can only make out a blur of light round the edges of my mask. Someone removes my gag at last, his calloused hands rough on my skin. Now he's untying my wrists. It's a relief when my arms hang limp at my sides, my hands numb after being bound for hours.

The man's breath reeks of coffee, booze and cigarettes. Maybe he was among the partygoers, drinking at my expense, while he spied on me.

'You won't get away with this. The whole island will be out looking for me,' I say, my voice hoarse.

There's no reply except another physical gesture. He yanks my blindfold away and when my vision clears I'm alone in a small dark storeroom, a door clicking shut behind me, then a key twisting in the lock. My only light source is intermittent starlight shining through a porthole, which gives a foot-wide view of waves, crashing and re-forming, as the boat lists from side to side. There's nothing in the cabin except a bucket, toilet roll, a bottle of water and a sandwich congealing on a plate. He wants me to relieve myself, and it's in my interests to show gratitude, but instinct makes me undo the ties around my ankles and prepare to fight.

When I get to work on the binding, silver light suddenly floods the cabin, confirming where I've been taken. Solomon showed me photos of the *Aqua Dream*'s grey lino and wooden furniture. Did the other victims sit here too, on some mysterious yacht, waiting for their fate? My fingers move faster now, aware that this is my last chance.

49

NILE HAS SO much adrenalin swilling round his system, he wants to rush from house to house looking for the killer, but his phone rings while he decides his next course of action. It's Charlie Layton, saying that Pastor Boakye isn't answering his phone. The information raises Nile's suspicions. Whoever took Lady Vee kept a close eye on the party, creeping out of the darkness to abduct his victim, and Boakye never appeared, so he may be helping the killer in some way.

'We need to visit Pastor Boakye,' he tells Lily. 'It's possible he's been telling lies.'

The detective is led by instinct when they drive downhill to Lovell, where the priest's cabin stands at the edge of the community. Pastor Boakye is fully dressed when he opens the door, even though it's the middle of the night. The man looks tempted to run, but remains rooted to the spot, because there's no escape. There will be no transport off the island while the storm erupts, the wind strong enough to pummel Nile's back as he and Lily wait on the front porch.

'Going somewhere, Father?'

'To see a parishioner,' he mumbles. 'The man's suffering alone.'

'Keith Belmont, you mean?'

'How did you know?'

'You've been accepted here, in such a short time. I bet you know all the villa owners' secrets. Some of them are so famous, you could make a fortune selling information to the media.'

The priest looks horrified. 'I would never do that. Everyone deserves God's protection; it's my job to help whoever needs me.'

Solomon looks him squarely in the eyes. 'You made up your qualifications, didn't you?'

His shoulders drop, like a broken marionette. 'I was hoping for a fresh start.'

'Another woman's missing and you've been telling lies. Maybe you've been helping the killer.'

'I'm just following my vocation, that's why I'm here.'

Nile hisses at him. 'You'd better explain.'

'No one understands poverty, unless they've experienced it.' The man gazes down at his hands. 'Twenty-five million people live in Lagos, many with no running water, or sanitation, like my family. My parents had no money for formal schooling, but religion kept me sane. I almost gave up hope when our priest said I'd need a degree in theology to join the ministry, even though I was born to serve God.' The man's face glows with conviction.

'So you bought a fake degree certificate and made up a CV. How come you know the Bible so well?'

'It's the only book my family owned. I learned many passages by heart.'

271

'You were bound to get found out.'

Boakye's eyes are glossy with tears. 'I thought God would protect me. I've done my best to support the community; no one else would work as hard.'

'Did you hurt Lady Vee tonight?'

'Of course not.' The man bows his head as if to pray.

'Go to the hospital and stay with Sacha Milburn until I call you. She believes in you and needs protection. If I find out you've neglected her, your situation will get a whole lot worse.'

The man presses his hands together like he's found a new deity. 'Don't give away my secret, please. I was born for this job. No other priest would love his community as much.'

'Your cabin's near Dexter Adebayo's. Do you know where he's gone?'

He shakes his head. 'Another man who's struggling to find his way.'

'It's his wife I pity,' Lily mutters.

'He sleeps outside, near to Basil's Bar, some nights, just to be alone.'

Nile is beyond caring about Boakye's fate, but the man's prayers follow him and Lily down the path, his voice low and fervent.

50

I CAN'T TELL how long it takes me to undo the rope around my ankles. I have to flex my feet repeatedly to regain sensation, and I know I may not have long before the killer returns. My left hip is swollen so every movement hurts, but that's the least of my worries. I hunt through the storage cupboards lining the walls but find only marker buoys and life jackets. The only useful item is a speargun, designed for hunting fish in the shallows, the small arrow unlikely to inflict much damage on a human assailant, but it's my only option. I could use the chair and a wooden bench to barricade the door but instinct tells me to leave everything in place. Surprise will be my best weapon, if I keep my wits about me.

The boat is still being attacked by harsh currents. When I peer through the porthole, I can tell exactly where we are, after hundreds of boat trips around Mustique. The *Aqua Dream* is anchored in Honor Bay, which is a poor place to hide in a storm, the yacht drifting towards submerged rocks. Fronds of sea kelp flail from the water's surface like kites on a hard breeze. The rocks' jagged teeth show above the crashing sea, waves hauling the boat closer, while the anchor chain groans. At least I'm free to move around, if the *Aqua Dream* founders, but my chances are slim unless I can open the door. I shut my eyes and picture a searing hot day when I swam out to the royal yacht *Britannia*, after weeks living in a tent on the beach. The princess allowed Jasper and me to shower, then have drinks with her on deck, the afternoon full of laughter, until the time came to swim back to shore. I can feel my body surfacing even now, the sunlit air greeting my face. That moment of remembered happiness provides a burst of energy. I must rescue myself.

The sea's furious motion thumps me against the wall when I hear the footsteps again. It's still pitch dark in the cabin. All I can see is a strand of light under the door, yet I'm oddly calm. Time goes into slow motion when the door finally opens, but I have one advantage: I'm accustomed to the dark. I lash out at his face with the butt of the spear gun. The man swings at me, but I run at him, knocking him backwards. When he falls there's a sickening crunch as his head hits the wall, then silence descends on the cabin.

I'm afraid another crewman will arrive any minute, but there are no sounds outside except the storm's fierce call, the wind plucking the yacht's rigging like harp strings. The man I've attacked is still breathing, which fills me with relief; no matter what happens, I don't want any more deaths. When I peer outside my luck is holding. The key has been left in the cabin door, so I twist it in the lock, leaving the wounded man captive.

Now I'm outside, more dangers lie ahead. I tiptoe down the narrow corridor, trying each cabin door, but they're all locked. When more footsteps sound overhead I duck into the last room, which stands open. I can see the rocks more clearly than before from the porthole, and I need to know who's taken me captive. My hands fumble through the dark until I find a desk, then open the first drawer, rummaging for clues.

51

Nile and Lily return to Eden House straight after their talk with Boakye. There's a chance that Phillip has found useful information in Sacha's journal. Wesley greets them in the hallway, but Phillip is still in the kitchen hunched over the notebook.

'It's a type of parable, set on Mustique,' he says, 'full of local characters and landmarks. It reads like a children's story.'

'What's it about?'

'A dark force trying to steal beauty from the island. It makes people ugly and controls their minds, killing trees and animals, and turning the sky grey.'

'Does she mention names?'

'I can't see any, but her handwriting's so awful, some passages are illegible. She's crossed out whole paragraphs.'

'Let me try,' Lily volunteers. 'Sacha and I wrote each other letters in our teens; I may be able to decipher her scrawl.'

Phillip Everard hesitates before handing the book over, as if he feels bad about finding little hard evidence. He's quick to agree to accompany Nile on his next visit, leaving

276

Lily poring over Sacha Milburn's notes with Wesley at her side. The actor is unusually quiet as they head for Britannia Bay on Lady Vee's buggy, the frown on his face revealing his concern. The man is gazing straight ahead, his eyes unblinking as he watches the sea, observing the thunderous waves.

'Are you okay, Phillip?' Nile asks.

Everard flinches at the sound of his voice. 'I keep thinking of Vee. She and Jasper were wonderful when I bought my place here.'

'We'll find her, don't worry.'

'I hope to God you're right. Lily's seen too much misery already.'

Nile beckons for Phillip to follow him. Dex Adebayo startles awake in the deckchair he's using for a bed when Nile yells his name.

'What the hell are you doing?' he splutters. Adebayo's gaze flicks from Nile's face to Everard's like he's assessing which one is craziest.

'Why didn't you go home tonight, Dex?'

'I can't stand Cherelle's nagging.'

'People are saying you've changed, Dex. You've become strung out, withdrawn, a different man. What are you taking?'

'I don't know what you're talking about.'

'Come on, Dex. I've seen plenty of addicts in the UK,' says Nile.

There's no sign of the island's much-loved local character when he rises to his feet. 'You'd better leave me alone, right now, instead of making accusations.'

'I've only just begun,' Nile says, stepping closer.

'You arrogant piece of shit.'

When Adebayo throws a punch Nile dodges it easily. For the second time in a week, physical force is the best way to close an argument, even though it's not his preferred style. His right hook lands solidly in the man's gut, dropping him to his knees.

'Was that wise?' Everard mutters. 'He could sue for police brutality.'

'That won't save him. I'm arresting you for assault and battery, Dexter. You'd better come with me.'

Nile feels more comfortable as he leads the barman away. He's repaid the violence to Cherelle and begun to wipe the slate clean for the woman he let die. He's never believed in catharsis until now, but the theory might just be true.

'Drive him back to Eden House, please Phillip. Lock him in one of the bedrooms and stand guard, then tell Wesley and Lily to meet me at Old Plantation Bay.'

52

NILE IS ABOUT to jog to the harbour when he decides to make a phone call. He shelters behind the end wall of Basil's Bar to ring DI Black on St Vincent, while the wind shrieks overhead. His boss falls silent at the news of Lady Veronica's abduction, after the party to commemorate the victims' lives, but the peace is short lived. Nile holds the phone away from his ear when his senior's voice rises in volume. Black tells him that he's stupid; he may understand history but he's a lousy detective.

'I need to go out to the *Aqua Dream* tonight, sir. It's the only place I haven't searched.'

DI Black isn't in an obliging mood. 'Don't go near it, Nile. I've told you a hundred times. If you do, you'll land up in jail.'

'Lady Vee must be out there, sir. Do you want her to die?'

'You don't have permission. I forbid it, do you hear?'

Nile steps out from his shelter, feeling the wind's full impact. 'Sorry, I missed that. Can you hear the storm's getting worse?'

'Don't fool with me, Nile.'

'Are you still there, sir? The line's breaking down.'

'Stay on dry land. Do you understand?'

'The connection's gone. I'll try again later, sir.'

Nile has spent enough time following pointless rules; he won't make the same mistake again. He runs south while rain beats the ground around him. It's the worst night for a sea voyage, but there's no other way to learn the truth, even though the storm is hitting the island like a spiteful child. Powerful waves are jostling the small fishing boats in Old Plantation harbour, and Wesley Gilbert and Lily are already on the jetty. Nile shakes his head when Lily suggests they use the *Revival*. The *Aqua Dream* would see the trawler coming and sail out of reach. Their only option is to take the tiny police launch and hope not to get spotted, keeping their front beams switched off. The muscles in Nile's stomach wind tighter as he puts on a life jacket. Instinct makes him call and leave a message on Lyron's phone before they motor off.

The *Aqua Dream* is just a glimmer on the horizon. The half-moon has gone into hiding just when they need it most, the stars obscured by cloud. Wesley Gilbert looks resolute, but there's a glint of excitement in Lily's eyes when he starts the engine, her adventurous spirit rising to the occasion, and the gravity of the situation is inescapable. Nile must pick his moment to set off with perfect accuracy. One mistake and the boat will be flung back onto the pier, shattering into matchsticks. Maybe he should have hung onto the religious faith his father finds so comforting. He'd love a god to pray to right now, but no guardian angel will come to his rescue. Nile manages to steer the police launch away from the jetty, until the vessel is at the sea's mercy, like a cork bobbing towards a waterfall.

When Nile looks across at Lily, she gives him a smile. She's seen plenty of storms, but he's focused on the dangers waiting on the *Aqua Dream*. The two crewmen may have come ashore for a night-time trip and escaped the storm on dry land, but weather conditions could have kept them on board. The engine is grinding at full speed when there's a sudden noise, like cymbals clattering onto a hard floor, and suddenly they're stranded. The next swell rocks the boat by forty-five degrees onto its starboard side. They need to regain power soon, or they'll capsize.

'I'll see if I can fix it,' Lily says, ducking through the doorway below, as another wave hits.

There's still no fear on Wesley's face, and Nile understands at last why he enjoys his role as a butler. He's able to conceal every emotion, even when a storm threatens his life. There's humour in the man's tone when he speaks again.

'The sea plays cruel tricks. This is why I chose the army, Solomon.'

Both men hurry below deck to help Lily work on the engine, but the hold is so cramped, all they can do is watch. The boat is still at the mercy of the waves, being pushed in the wrong direction, into the teeth of the storm. Half an hour passes before she emerges, her hands filthy with oil.

'The drive belt broke,' Lily says. 'Try the engine again; let's see if it works.'

Nile turns the key twice before the engine kicks into life, but the delay has cost them a long time. He can only hope that the crew of the *Aqua Dream* aren't gazing out from the yacht's portholes, their small vessel hidden by the rolling waves. The mega-yacht is growing clearer all the time, at least ten times bigger than the police launch, but suffering the same assault, listing starboard with each tall wave. Nile notices that a speedboat is drifting behind the *Aqua Dream* on a long line. He can't tell when it arrived, but the storm could easily smash it against the bigger vessel's side.

'Want me to steer?' Lily calls out, her voice muted by the wind.

Nile steps back to hand her the wheel. She may not be insured to drive the launch, but she's more experienced, and soon his life will be in her hands. Wesley offers to come with him on deck, but he makes him stay in the wheelhouse with Lily. Nile is alone as he prepares for the transfer. It would only take a small error of judgement to mistime his jump onto the bigger vessel. His heart is in his mouth when a huge wave lifts the police launch higher than the *Aqua Dream*'s deck before smashing it down again. He can hear Lily counting like his father did, when he taught him to sail. Every seventh wave is bigger than the rest. When Lily nods at him, he knows she'll move alongside the bigger vessel after the next cycle.

The detective clings to the handrail. He knows exactly what he's facing; get the timing wrong and he'll land in the water, and his life jacket won't save him. He'll be crushed between the two boats. The water gapes, open-mouthed, ready for him to fall. He glances back at the wheelhouse, waiting for Lily to give her thumbs-up, but she shakes her head. Another huge wave crashes over the prow, leaving him soaked, before he takes his leap.

Nile grabs the bottom rung of the ladder and hauls himself up towards the deck of the *Aqua Dream*, but now he's on his own. Lily must keep the boat close by with Wesley's help, until he's ready to leave. He gestures at her to keep back, but the waves rise again, obscuring the launch from view. He plans to take the captain by surprise, then search the vessel, no matter how much resistance he meets. He may only find a cargo of drugs, but there's an outside chance Lady Vee's still alive.

He makes his way to the *Aqua Dream*'s bow, but when he peers through the window, the wheelhouse is empty. A nautical chart lies open by a panel that's flashing with GPS storm signals. The crew are missing, even though they must be on board. No one would abandon the multi-million-pound yacht to the storm, like the *Mary Celeste*; what has happened?

53

I'VE FOUND A cigarette lighter in the top drawer, so I use it to explore the small office. It's got minimal furniture, with a desk in one corner and a couple of chairs. The place appears to be someone's sanctuary, a bottle of whisky and a tumbler rattling in one of the desk drawers. I need to find a better weapon before another crewman arrives; I remember Solomon telling me there were two men on board. The other could find me at any minute, yet I'm still driven by the need to find out who is carrying out the attacks.

The only weapon I can find is a metal paperweight. I have to use both hands to lift it from the desk, but it's more deadly than the speargun. I ought to wait behind the door and try the same trick. Phillip crosses my mind suddenly, and the look of horror on his face when Solomon Nile found us searching the Rothmores' villa. I kept my courage then, and I need to hang onto it, now more than ever.

I hold the lighter up and see books on a shelf above the desk: classic European novels by Victor Hugo and Thomas Mann. There are plays too, by Ibsen, Chekhov and Pinter, which takes me by surprise. How many vicious murderers have a passion for classic literature and drama?

When I continue rummaging through the drawers, I find an envelope containing photos of Tommy, Amanda, Sacha and Lily as children, and something shifts in my stomach. The images are from my photo albums at Eden House. Someone has wandered round my home, helping themselves to my private possessions. In the next drawer I find a book on the ancient symbols of Obeah. When I open it, a red feather flutters to the floor, like the ones Mama Toulaine weaves into her hair, but I can't believe the artist has anything to do with the violence, even though her spiritual aura puts me on edge. The next thing I find is a small piece of tortoiseshell, shaped in a triangle; a guitar plectrum. The object drops from my hand when I picture Keith Belmont here, playing one of his guitars, and knocking back whisky, but something doesn't add up. Keith may not always be honest, but his newfound love of the marine environment seems genuine.

My gaze drifts upwards to another photo tacked to the wall. It's a close-up of a woman, her features beautiful in the guttering light. The last time we met was twenty years ago. But how did a photo of Lily's mother, Emily Calder, end up on the *Aqua Dream*, two decades after she died?

54

Nile can just make out the police launch from the deck of the *Aqua Dream*. Lily is steering into the oncoming waves, but the vessel looks like a matchbox, tossed upwards by every swell. She and Wesley will have to manage alone, the distance between them too great for signals. He remains in the shadow of the wheelhouse, until he catches sight of the speedboat again, drifting on a tow rope, too far away to read the name on its prow. Nile can't understand why it hasn't been winched aboard, to protect it from storm damage, unless the owner ran out of time before conditions worsened.

The detective's mind brims with theories as he edges towards the boat's living quarters. All of his main suspects are on Mustique right now, yet he's certain one of them is linked to the *Aqua Dream*. The idea slips from Nile's head when he hears a phone ringing. It's coming from the dining room he saw on his last visit, but now the curtains are tightly closed.

He's bending down to peer through a gap in the fabric when someone shoves him forward so hard, his tall form hits the railing. He tries to grab it, but wild laughter sounds in his ears as he plunges overboard. The waves echo like an orchestra playing every note off key, his mouth filled with sea-water as his life jacket bears him to the surface, the water cold enough to numb his mind. He can see the *Aqua Dream*, with light spilling from its portholes, and the tiny outline of the police launch, before everything vanishes. He's trapped inside a giant washing machine, unable to breathe. Memories arrive when the water spits him out again. He recalls losing his virginity to a village girl at fourteen, Lyron running across the beach, his father trapped in his rocking chair. When the water finally leaves him floating on his back, the *Aqua Dream* is further away. He'll have to swim against the waves, but the next breaker is already crashing over his head.

55

I CAN'T HEAR anything except the anchor chain screaming with metal fatigue as the boat faces the storm's assault. I'm still certain another man is on board, but he may not have realised I've escaped from the cabin. When I flick the lighter on again there's a box in the desk. It contains a pack of cigarettes and a palm-sized metal container that clinks when I pick it up. My anxiety rises again when I find half a dozen bullets inside. My hands are trembling when I drop them into my pocket. If the men who brought me here are armed, the odds are stacked against me, and the one I locked inside the cabin is coming round. I can hear him hammering on the locked door, his voice rising to a bellow.

Panic makes me scrabble in the drawer again, but there's nothing useful. The door flies open before I finish, so I hide the paperweight under my arm, covered by the torn fabric of my dress. I can't make out the man's features, light flooding in from the corridor, but his dull laughter reaches me when he flicks on a desk light then flops down on the chair, perfectly at home. His voice is a rough London drawl when he finally speaks, coarsened by a lifetime's cigarettes.

'You're stronger than I thought. I never expected a lady like you to fight tooth and nail.'

'Who are you?'

'Daniel Kellerman; you can call me Dan, if you like.'

'We've met before, haven't we?'

'Only very recently.' His laughter sounds like oil gurgling down a drain. 'You and I don't move in the same circles. We've just been at one party together.'

'Take me back to shore, immediately.'

'That can't happen, I'm afraid.' His face is full of mock-sympathy. 'The boss man only wanted you shaken up, to stop you looking for the killer. You should have stayed in the cabin, then we'd have dumped you back on the beach tomorrow, no harm done. But now it's gone too far.'

'The police are looking for me.'

'Not any more.' He lights a cigarette, then inhales a long drag. His long face and collar-length blond hair still strike me as familiar, but I can't place him. 'Do you want to know what happened to your detective friend?'

'Solomon Nile?'

'It was a case of man overboard. He picked a bad night for a swim, didn't he?'

When I rush to the porthole, waves are swirling like a rollercoaster, and the yacht is perilously close to the rocks, but the sight of Mustique so close by gives me strength. I have to play for time, until I can find my way back.

56

NILE'S ANGER PROPELS him forward. The waves dash in one direction, then the next; he will only beat them by being single-minded. His goal is to reach the *Aqua Dream* by any means possible. He waits for a lull between waves, then swims at a steady crawl until the next surge knocks him back. His progress is slow, but the yacht grows bigger with each attempt, lit up like a beacon.

Nile's mind is playing tricks, the past calling to him again as he kicks through the water. The woman who died appears in his mind again, giving her brittle smile, willing him to stay alive. Her expression tells him that one pointless death is better than two, and he realises she'll stay in his memory forever, because he cares about his job. He's not prepared to give up.

Another surge knocks Nile off course, his mind clicking back to the duty he has to fulfil. He can drown in memories, or go on fighting. He sucks in a long breath, then swims at his fastest crawl. It takes forever to reach that metal rung again and he's almost too weak to climb aboard. He hides behind the *Aqua Dream*'s wheelhouse until his breathing steadies, but the ocean's chill has seeped into his bones, making him shiver, despite the warm night air. The yacht is still rocking from side to side, making every movement a challenge. Instinct makes him reach for his gun, but when he pulls it out, water gushes from the barrel. His training course never explained if it can be fired wet, but it's a useful prop. If the crewmen are unarmed the sight of it might panic them enough to drop their guard.

Nile is about to stand up when a shadow passes his hiding place. It's a man with back turned, dressed in dark clothes. He pauses by the handrail with his hood raised, watching the storm. The figure stands there for a long time. Nile sees him disappear down a stairwell, so he follows, without making a sound. His heart is in his mouth when he finds himself in a narrow corridor.

The hooded man waits outside a door at the end of the passageway, his body language strained as voices drift towards him. He seems transfixed by the sound. His head is cocked towards the door like he can't bear to miss a single word.

57

I'M STANDING WITH my back against the wall, still clutching the paperweight against my side. It still feels like my only chance of staying alive is to keep him talking long enough to weaken his defences.

'The boss won't like this,' he says. 'He hates getting his hands dirty.'

'Tell me who it is, please. If you plan to kill me, I'll take it to my grave.'

The man grins. 'Maybe you can guess. He keeps saying he wants to turn over a new leaf; he's staying off the booze and party drugs, but seeing is believing. The guy's an addict. He's still got a thing for pretty girls, and boys for that matter.'

'Why are you working for him?'

'We're old friends. I met him years ago, when life was easier.' The man grins widely. 'I've enjoyed our chat, but orders are orders. Killing a mature lady or a child is never fun, so I want to get it over.'

'Haven't you noticed we're drifting close to shore? We'll soon hit the rocks by Honor Bay. You chose the most dangerous place to drop anchor.'

The man glances out of the porthole and panic crosses his face, but his body language is changing. He intends to kill me before steering the yacht to safety. When he straightens up, something shiny sticks out of his pocket – the silver handle of a gun. Words spill from my mouth as I buy myself another minute.

'Tell me about the coral first, please. It's fascinated me from the start. Why did he leave those pieces in the victim's properties?'

'The boss hates the coral regeneration and those involved in it. The signs he carved are Obeah symbols; that voodoo shit fascinates him.' Kellerman smiles again, a gold tooth glinting in the dim light. 'He's got a chip on his shoulder like the Grand Canyon. By the time he's finished on Mustique there'll be no one left.'

A face suddenly appears in my mind, making me gasp out loud. Kellerman's face blanks as he pulls the gun from his pocket, but a sudden swell makes the boat roll; I grab the paperweight and heft it against the underside of his jaw, leaving him stunned. His grip weakens for a moment, allowing me to grab the gun.

'Sit in that chair, you fool. Give me your keys.'

He still looks shocked when I train the gun between his eyes, even though I've never fired a pistol in my life. There are voices in the corridor, but the weapon has restored my confidence. It only takes me a minute to back away, then lock up my second assailant. The corridor is empty when I get outside, and I can't help smiling when I hear my first attacker, still howling to be set free.

58

NILE HOLDS THE man by his throat as he drags him on deck, his other hand pressed over his mouth. It takes effort to keep the guy down after his long swim; he's twisting away, forcing him to draw his gun.

'Stay there, or I'll use this,' Nile says. 'I've had plenty of training.'

The man is just a shape in the dark; there's no glimmer of starlight to help identify his enemy. Nile's tempted to pull the trigger after his own brush with death, but his sense of justice prevents it. The man's features are obscured by his hooded top, and the guy seems determined not to speak.

'What made you do it?' Nile asks. 'Enjoy your freedom, you'll never leave jail.'

The man lashes out, but Nile hits him with the butt of his gun, ignoring the boat's rocking. Sea-water floods the deck, and the wind's scream sounds furious as it whistles through the rigging. He couldn't care less if the bastard's washed overboard because new footsteps are running across the deck, then there's a sudden report of gunfire. Shock makes Nile lurch forward, trying to dodge the next bullet, but the blood spattering at his feet isn't his own. The man he was fighting lies face down, moaning, as more red liquid splashes onto the deck.

59

THE BULLET'S REPORT is still ringing in my ears, but the
fight continues, ten metres away. The man I shot has staggered to his feet, with blood dripping from his arm. Solomon
Nile is wrestling with him, but I can't help him yet. The
two men's bodies are locked so close, I'm terrified my next
bullet might hit Solomon by mistake. There's another deafening sound as a bullet fires, but this time the weapon isn't
mine. Solomon's tall form collapses onto his assailant, and
his attacker's strength finally expires. When his arm goes
limp I pluck the gun from his hand, then hurl it overboard
along with my own, before either can do more damage.

I can't see the man's face, but I know who he is. The
office downstairs gave me enough clues, leaving me shocked
to my core.

Solomon is already staggering to his feet, but the other
man stays prone on deck, even though high waves keep
crashing overboard. I grab a piece of rope and tie his hands
behind his back, leaving him face down. Solomon's welfare
matters far more now.

Solomon is slumped against the wheelhouse, arms at his

sides. There's so little light I can't see the full extent of his injury, but panic hits me when I see blood welling from his right side.

'Are you in pain?'

His eyes are out of focus. 'Let's get back to Mustique, Lady Vee. Those men should be in cells.'

'They soon will be. Help's on its way.'

I can see two boats edging closer. Lily is waving frantically from the police launch, with Wesley at her side, and there's an old trawler from Mustique's fishing fleet, but it may be too late. Solomon's bleeding so heavily I can tell he's slipping away, his face vacant with shock.

'I'm going to put pressure on your wound, Solomon. It'll hurt, so feel free to swear.'

He gasps for breath when I cover the opening with my hands. The pressure must be agonising, but he's gazing at the middle distance, glassy-eyed.

'Talk to me, please. Don't go to sleep.'

His lips curve into a smile. 'Lily kissed me earlier, on the beach.'

'Sensible girl, she'll do that again, if we ever get back to shore.'

'Don't worry, Lady Vee. The storm's over. Can't you tell?'

The young man's face blanks before he slips out of reach.

60

NILE FIGHTS TO stay awake, but there's a lead weight on his chest. Lady Vee is leaning over him, whispering words he can't follow. He can only feel the sea's cold in his bones. It's a shock when Lyron looms into view, his face tense as he drags him to his feet.

'Try and walk, Sol. You're too big to carry.'

Nile manages to reach the rail, where the sea is smoother than before. His father's old trawler waits below, proving that Lyron set out straight after he got his phone message. Someone helps him down to the boat, but next time he's conscious, Lyron is pressing a wad of cloth against his side and shock has been replaced by pain. It feels like a branding iron is buried inside his ribcage, and his brother looks terrified.

'You'll be okay, Ly.'

'Don't waste your strength, just breathe, slow and steady.'

'Look after Dad for me. Make sure he's comfortable.'

'Stop it, Sol. We'll get you patched up.'

Nile hears his brother and Winston Layton agreeing to leave the two members of the gang locked up on board until tomorrow, as he drifts into unconsciousness. If the storm finishes them, it's no great loss.

His eyes open again when Lady Vee is lowered on board. The look on her face is triumphant, even though her tattered dress is stained with blood. Next he sees the shadowy figure who shot him. Nile's curiosity cuts through his pain. The killer looks anonymous, dressed in dark jeans, his hooded top still hiding his face.

'Isn't it time you revealed yourself, Phillip?' Lady Vee hisses. 'I guessed it was you ages ago.'

When the moon shines overhead she pulls back the man's hood, exposing features that were once judged perfect by Hollywood. Starlight has bleached every scrap of colour from his face and Phillip Everard no longer looks like a film star. He's just an old man, with eyes full of rage.

61

I ONLY NOTICE my ragged state when Lily helps me off the boat as the storm continues to howl. Last night's party dress is in tatters, oil smeared down my forearm, my bare feet covered in grime. Laughter escapes from my lips when I think of Princess Margaret. She set a high standard for her ladies-in-waiting, expecting us to be perfectly attired. I look like a castaway as the dawn light rises, desperate for the first sight of home. Lily's eyes are brimming; the last twenty-four hours must have been hell for her too. It's only when my feet are on dry land that she throws her arms around me.

'Thank God you're alive, Vee. We're going to the medical centre right now.'

'No need, darling. It can wait until tomorrow.'

'Don't be ridiculous, you're covered in bruises. What did those bastards do to you?'

'Nothing serious.' I don't want to share details yet, she's dealt with enough misery.

'Tell me who the killer is, Vee. He was on the boat just now, wasn't he?'

Lily looks stunned when she hears the truth, and anger hits me for the first time. The man was a charlatan, he deceived every one of us for years, but what was his intention? I push the thought aside, as my hip throbs, glad to grip Lily's hand. Soon someone arrives with a buggy and we're carried to the medical centre, then Lily finds a wheelchair and pushes me towards the entrance, where Wesley Gilbert is emerging. My butler looks dishevelled, just as he did when he chased into the Fortinis' villa looking for his sister, but this time he risked his life for my sake. His voice is unusually gentle when he crouches beside me.

'I'm glad you survived your adventure, Lady Vee. You had me worried.'

I touch his shoulder. 'Have I told you how incredibly lucky I am to have you taking care of me?'

'Not long ago,' he replies, his stern face softening. 'It's always good to hear.'

'How's Solomon?' I ask.

'Alive, but he's lost some blood. That bullet went straight through his side. The doctor's working on him right now.'

Wesley hurries away to speak to Nile's brother before I can ask another question. There's no point in going indoors while Dr Pakefield is busy, so we sit outside, allowing me to catch my breath. I could be imagining it, but the storm's ferocity seems to have faded by a fraction. Mustique has been caught in a whirlwind for almost an entire week, ever since Amanda Fortini went missing, even though Storm Cristobal only made land last night. Trees have been torn apart, a corrugated-iron roof panel dumped in a flowerbed, the sound of birdsong muted. The creatures must be afraid

301

that the dreadful wind may return, and I too am struggling to believe the violence has ended. Lily sits on a bench beside me, shading her eyes from the early morning sun.

'Go and find Solomon, darling. He needs someone holding his hand.'

She argues for a moment, then rushes inside. Exhaustion floods over me like a tsunami. I fall asleep bolt upright in the chair, lulled by the storm's parting song, as it spins back out to sea.

62

NILE CAN'T GUESS how long he's been asleep. When his eyes blink open, a drip is feeding colourless liquid into his arm. There's pressure in his side, but hardly any pain. His mind is a vacuum until Dr Pakefield walks through the door. The medic still looks deathly pale, as if the sunlight filtering through the blind is slowly killing him. Pakefield studies his watch as he presses two fingers to Nile's neck.

'You've got the constitution of an ox, Detective Nile, but you caused me problems last night. Your blood group's quite rare. Lyron donated two units and so did Keith Belmont; you owe those men your life.'

Nile stifles a laugh – he'll be blood brothers with the lead singer of Blue Heaven until the end of his days – but Lyron's gift doesn't surprise him. He feels a moment's guilt for all the people he suspected during the case, while the true culprit lay right under his nose.

'I'm sorry, doctor. All you did was break a rule to try and help someone out. I shouldn't have been so accusatory.'

'Apology accepted,' the doctor says, with a narrow smile. 'A team of officers is coming over from St Vincent tomorrow, to take your suspects to Belle Isle Correctional Facility. Your boss has agreed you should take a week or two to recover from such a serious wound. He'll interview Phillip Everard in the morning.'

Nile struggles to sit upright, a blast of pain making his head spin, until the doctor's cold hand settles on his shoulder.

'Rest now, or you won't heal properly. Press the buzzer if you need anything.'

'How's Sacha?'

'She regained consciousness last night, and I apologised for my actions. I'll let her recuperate at home from tomorrow if she carries on improving.'

'I should be at the station. Can someone drive me there?'

'Don't be stupid.' The doctor fixes him with a hard stare. 'You're staying in bed for the next forty-eight hours. Sleep now, I'll come and check on you later.'

Nile lets his eyes close again. Mama Toulaine may just be part of his dream when she appears at his bedside, carrying a bunch of orchids. She looks like an African queen, her vivid blue dress covered in yellow brocade. Her expression's tender when her fingertips caress his face.

'How are you doing, young man?'

'Better, Mama. I'll soon be fit again.'

'Gede's still at the crossroads, Solomon. There will be one more death before he leaves the island in peace; don't let it be yours.'

When Toulaine kisses his cheek, Solomon falls into the deepest sleep of his life. The quality of light has changed when he wakes up. It's softer than before, turning the room a dull ochre. It hurts to sit up, but he doesn't care; there's a jolt of eye-watering pain in his ribs every time he moves, yet he can't stay in bed. He makes a phone call to Lily, then drags himself upright, just as Lady Vee appears in the doorway. She's dressed in her usual pale attire, elegant as ever, with only a few bruises on show.

'I hear you saved my life, Lady Vee. You're the bravest woman on Mustique.'

She gives a gentle smile. 'You saved mine too. I'm glad I learned first aid in the Girl Guides. No matter how big the wound, you have to staunch the flow of blood.'

'If I'd lost much more, I wouldn't be here now.'

'That would be a pity, for all of us,' she says, coming closer. 'This is a dreadful mess, isn't it?'

'At least we found our killer.'

'What's our next course of action?'

'My boss plans to interview him tomorrow, then he'll be held in jail until his trial.'

Lady Vee's face hardens. 'He can't take all the credit, when you and I have done all the work. You deserve a promotion on the back of this, and I need to hear Phillip's confession from the horse's mouth.'

Nile manages to grin. 'I knew you'd see it that way. Lily will be here soon, in your buggy. Let's go to the station together.'

'Perfect. Your brother brought you clean clothes. Why don't I help you into that shirt? You can rest here again after we've seen Phillip.'

'The doctor won't like us leaving the building.'

'Who cares?' She leans closer, her clear gaze assessing his face. 'After last night, nothing can stop us.'

A fresh wave of pain cuts through Nile's core as he dresses, but Lady Vee's triumphant tone lifts him. He's so focused on the task ahead, it barely registers.

63

STORM CRISTOBAL HAS attacked the police station with full force. The roof over the reception area has torn away, the yard littered with dead branches, an old bicycle dangling from a tree, but Solomon appears too focused to notice. DI Black will take over tomorrow, but today he's still in charge, and we both need to know why Phillip committed such unspeakable crimes. We limp through the door together, leaving Lily waiting in the buggy.

I'm not prepared for the emotional pain of seeing Phillip again. I have known him for thirty years, believing he was sensitive enough to require my support, but he must be the finest actor on record. He fooled me so completely, my emotions are in freefall.

'Are you ready, Lady Vee?' Solomon asks.

'I've had better days, but he can't harm either of us now, thank God.'

'We need a complete confession; he may give us more if you pretend to feel sympathy. I'll record everything he says.'

'I shall do my best.'

When Solomon and I walk through the door, Phillip is

sitting cross-legged on the floor of his cell, gazing up at the skylight. He doesn't acknowledge either of us when we position ourselves on the bench opposite, giving me time to look at him. Fragments from the stories he's told me over the years drift through my head, from the poverty of his childhood, to painful relationship break ups that he never fully explained. Phillip's temper cost him acting jobs too, over his tendency to start vendettas with his co-stars, in case they stole his limelight. Why didn't I notice that his violence had never truly gone away? A few minutes of silence pass before he speaks at last.

'Not a cloud in sight. That shade of blue is called cerulean, isn't it?'

'Azure, I'd say,' Solomon replies. 'Turquoise, with a hint of yellow.'

'You could be right.' A relaxed smile crosses Phillip's face. 'I'm sorry you got hurt last night, Solomon. Collateral damage is always a pity.'

The detective keeps his mouth shut. He seems to understand that silence is the best route to information; very few people can handle its yawning emptiness.

'I'm glad you're here, Vee. I was going to ask for you, because our conversations always comfort me.' He turns his head by a fraction, but still doesn't meet my eye. 'I don't care about anyone else's opinion. You were the only one to work it all out.'

'The things in your desk drawers gave you away. They showed how much you've kept hidden; not just occasional cigarettes, but your yearning for theatrical roles. You started out on stage, with Ibsen and Chekhov, didn't you?'

'Hollywood typecast me. They put me in rom coms, and nothing else.'

'Very few people have enough talent to win an Oscar, like you.'

'You've always been so kind. Can I speak to Vee alone, one last time, Solomon?'

'I'm afraid not. Everything has to be on record.'

Phillip carries on gazing at the patch of sky above his head. It seems that I'm his desired audience, so I drop my voice to a whisper, mimicking past intimacy.

'You poor darling, you must have been in so much pain.'

'It was unbearable, Vee, I hate myself for all of it.' He swings round to face me at last. 'But I knew you'd understand.'

I muster a smile. 'It explains why Jose's been so upset, doesn't it? He must have seen you do something frightening, or following Lily home. The boy was only trying to protect me.'

When I catch a glimpse of Solomon from the corner of my eye, his pain is obvious; his handsome face is sheened with sweat, like last night, when I believed he was dying. I want to help him get the confession, after all his bravery, but it's difficult to meet Phillip's eye, while I carry so much anger. He's seated himself on a hard plastic chair in his cell, directly opposite me, only a few metres away. It looks like a film set for a new blockbuster, where a veteran movie star is framed for crimes he didn't commit, and I wish the truth was that simple. There's so much misery on his face, instinct makes me put my hand through the bars, and he reaches for it instantly.

'I'm sorry, Vee. I guessed you were close to finding the truth, because you're always so perceptive. I only wanted to throw you off course for long enough to escape on my boat, but now everything's lost.'

'I have to understand why you did it. Was it something in your past?'

He looks on the verge of tears. 'My family tore itself apart, but I can't blame them for all my troubles. I was born with too much darkness in me. I tried to strangle one of my brothers when I was fifteen, until my father pulled me away. They never listened to me. It made me so angry that I physically hurt whoever stood in my way. When I attacked one of my sisters, they sent me to live with an uncle of mine. I got beaten almost every day. I started skipping school, getting involved in drugs and petty crime.'

'It sounds terrible.'

'Something switched off in me. I was driven to escape, and acting allowed me to become someone else, but the damage was done. I could tell people were scared of me and the power was intoxicating. I didn't care how many people I stamped on along the way. The hurt and violence in me was out of my control.'

'I only got to see your light side, didn't I?' I pause. 'Were you planning to sail somewhere in particular on the *Aqua Dream*?'

'Venezuela or Ecuador. I could have disappeared into the mountains . . .' His voice trails into silence.

'Tell me how it happened, Phillip. It might make you feel better.'

He withdraws his hand suddenly, sitting taller in his chair, head tipped back, like he's under a spotlight. 'I loved it here at first. I was a big noise then, getting huge roles, invited to every party. That all changed when Emily Calder arrived. She was New York royalty; utterly mesmerising and I fell for her completely. But to her I was that dirt-poor farm boy all over again. She looked down her nose at me, from day one.'

'You're mistaken, Emily was very fond of you.'

'People talked about her reef project, like nothing else mattered. She was everyone's blue-eyed girl.'

'You killed her for what?'

'I loved her and she rejected me. I've swallowed a lifetime of feeling second-best. People overlooked me for lack of class, always cutting me down to size, never giving me roles I wanted. That's why I adore you and Jasper. You're aristocrats, yet you treat me with respect.'

Phillip carries on; his feeling of exclusion chimed with his childhood suffering, triggering his campaign. Emily Calder spurned his advances, so he waited outside her villa, then strangled her in the gardens. He waited until the island slept, then dragged her body down to the sea, leaving her dress folded on the sand.

'Lily and her friends invited me everywhere, until she began working on Emily's coral project full-time. Lily knows I can't dive, but she went on regardless. The young, beautiful ones chose to spend their time on that damned boat, leaving me alone. They turned away from me, one by one.'

'Starting with Amanda Fortini?'

'She fell for me after two French lessons, then rejected me just as fast as Emily had all those years ago. All she really wanted was to hang out with her younger buddies and dive down to that bloody reef. It was like history repeating itself, and my rage came roaring back.'

'What about Tommy Rothmore?'

'I thought he'd guessed the truth about me and Amanda, so I told him about leaving her body underwater. I tried to finish him in the Fortinis' summerhouse, but he got away. I didn't catch him again until the night I torched the Fortinis' villa. That got rid of Amanda's phone, camera, and the idiotic love letters she gave me at the start. I also planted the photos of her on his wall.'

'You had no need to attack Sacha Milburn or break into Keith Belmont's house.'

His eyes glitter with fury. 'Sacha was always spying on people and scribbling in that stupid notebook so I tore out the sections about me. I gave the notebook to the doctor, because she'd written about their one-night stand. I told him I'd copied each page, to keep him quiet. I couldn't risk him blabbing about seeing me on the *Aqua Dream*. My friendship with Keith fell apart when he became obsessed by saving the coral, just like the rest. I wanted to give him a warning.'

'You tried to frame Dex Adebayo, didn't you? The Obeah symbols made us suspect anyone who followed the religion.'

'Dex and I are old friends; we've had a little side business running for years now. But everyone's disposable. He lost his way when he got hooked.'

'Why are you still so full of hate, after all your success? Your childhood was a long time ago.'

'Don't you understand, Vee? No one's ever cared for me unconditionally, from childhood until now. Sacha, Amanda and Tommy were all born millionaires, and they looked down on me, like Emily Calder, because I scraped my way up from the gutter.'

'That doesn't explain why you targeted Lily.'

His expression sours again. 'She becomes more like her mother every year – beautiful and thoughtless, obsessed with coral. I left those messages on her boat.'

'She loved you like an uncle and trusted you completely.' I can hardly bear to look at him. 'How did you get a key to leave the coral outside Lily's room?'

'Don't you remember giving one to Emily Calder, all those years ago? It was so she could stay at Eden House, when you were away. You never changed the locks after she died.'

I can only just remember handing a key to Emily, at a lunch party with Jasper and Phillip, while Lily played in the pool. 'Why did you carve those symbols into the coral?'

'Obeah's full of gods and demons that reflect human nature. We're all a blend of good and evil, aren't we?'

Solomon asks quietly: 'Did your boat hit Amanda then? And how did you persuade the men on the *Aqua Dream* to leave the victims' bodies on the reef?'

He releases a slow laugh. 'Those fools would do anything for money, but they're not bright. The fools chose the worst place to drop anchor in the storm last night, without consulting me. I did the work on land, in the villas and stealing what we needed from the medical centre; and they did the work at sea. They made the firecracker for the police station. I found them both in Hollywood. Tinseltown's full of failed stuntmen, has-beens, and fantasists. You'll see their faces in the background of old soap operas and cop shows.

313

I let them both choose new names then gave them fake passports. For a time it was just moving shipments around, but the last few weeks have been more of an adventure.'

'Is that how you made enough cash to keep the *Aqua Dream*?'

'I spent my Hollywood wages on the purchase, but kept it secret. I needed funds to keep it going, so I did whatever it took. Why accept a minor part when I could make ten times more from a drugs pick-up at sea?'

'Ironic for someone who hates the water.'

Phillip laughs as if I've told a first-class joke. 'My sea legs were always a little sturdier than I let on. That's how I managed to reach the boat last night ahead of you.'

'How did you get diplomatic immunity?' Solomon asks.

'It didn't cost much, my friend. I bought a favour from your boss; he oversaw the whole thing for me, no questions asked.'

'That explains why he was so keen to keep me off the *Aqua Dream*.'

Phillip turns to face me. 'None of that matters now. Tell me I'm forgiven, please, Vee. That's all I care about.'

Our years of friendship pass before my eyes, through all the good times on Mustique, to now. Reality wipes my memories away, like chalk from a blackboard. Tears form in my eyes.

'Do you really believe I'd forgive you? Lily lost her mother when she was five years old. Then you killed two more innocent young people. Solomon and Sacha almost died, and you spiked my drink at the beach party. You'd have let those men kill me, without a second thought.'

The look of hatred on his face when I refuse to pardon him makes me glad that iron bars separate us. How did I miss the psychotic glitter in Phillip's eye, or his abject narcissism? My old friend is crying and shouting my name when I walk away. Solomon murmurs encouragement in my ear, supporting me to the exit. Old loyalties pull at me, but I won't allow myself to look back.

64

Monday, 23rd September 2002

SOLOMON NILE IS sitting in a deckchair on the porch while his father takes his afternoon nap. The island looks as it did before Storm Cristobal arrived, apart from a few damaged roofs, which his neighbours are busy repairing. He'd like to help out, but his wound is still healing, after three days at home. Mustique appears to have returned to normal, the sea a vivid blue, not a cloud in the sky, but things are already changing. Lyron is growing up at last; he plans to labour as a handyman for a higher wage, then follow his dream of becoming a pilot.

Nile watches a small fishing boat drifting back to harbour, content to observe the island's beauty until his wound heals. He sips his iced tea while the inhabitants of Lovell go about their business. It's a surprise to see Lily Calder walking up the path, dressed in shorts and a white top, a canvas bag hanging from her shoulder. She still looks like a dancer, with her long-legged stride. He assumed their paths wouldn't cross again after Phillip Everard was flown to St Vincent to await trial, Mustique free to breathe easily again, yet she's heading straight for his cabin.

Lily slips into the deckchair beside him without saying hello, as if visits to his home happened every day.

'I bring news from the outside world, Solomon.'

'Is any of it good?'

'Quite a bit, actually.'

'Hit me with it then.'

'Your boss has been fired, for taking backhanders from Phillip. Vee says the police force want to promote you to his job instead, with a big pay rise. Some senior officers are at the station now, sorting out the problems you identified. Dex Adebayo's been arrested for drug dealing. He'll be charged with assault too – Cherelle decided to press charges after all. The guys from the boat will be prosecuted for manslaughter.'

'What else? I can see you're not finished.'

'Dr Pakefield's been allowed to keep his job until Dr Bunbury comes back; the only thing he did wrong was take a boat ride out to the *Aqua Dream*, late at night, and accept money to help his children. It looks like Pastor Boakye could be pardoned too.'

'I don't believe it. He invented his entire CV.'

Lily smiles at him. 'The whole island knows what he did, to free his family from poverty, and follow his mission. He's been sending almost his whole wage home to Lagos, and he's got big fans here like Keith Belmont. They're standing by him. He'll spend a year at seminary college on St Vincent, then see where he can be posted after that.'

'Let's hope the guy's sincere.'

'There's one more thing, I'm afraid.' She takes off her sunglasses, her eyes matching the sea's calm turquoise. 'Phillip killed himself last night, in his prison cell.'

Nile remembers Mama Toulaine saying there would be one more death, then releases a stream of curses. 'What the hell happened? Weren't those idiots keeping watch?'

'They checked his cell every fifteen minutes. He must have been pretty motivated; he used his clothes to hang himself.'

Nile's thoughts buzz with anger. Everard found a way to steal the limelight again after all. 'Is that why you dropped by, Lily?'

'I'd have come sooner, but I thought you needed time to rest.'

'Sorry, I didn't mean to snap.'

'It's okay. I'm still processing it all too; I can still hardly believe two people I spent every summer with, since I was small, are no longer here. It's weird that I feel better about Mum. She never meant to leave me behind, and it wasn't my fault. She was just in the wrong place at the wrong time.'

There's so much sadness on her face that Nile reaches out to touch her wrist. 'I'm glad you're here.'

Lily's smile slowly revives. 'I borrowed Vee's buggy for the afternoon. If you feel well enough, we could find an empty beach somewhere, and lie on a blanket. I even brought a picnic. I thought it might stop you brooding.'

'I don't brood.'

A stream of laughter slips from her mouth. 'That's rubbish, and I've got witnesses.'

'I could handle a trip to the beach.'

'Call it a chauffeur-driven deluxe picnic by the sea.'

'That works for me.'

Nile slides his feet into some old flip-flops. His hand settles on her shoulder as they head for the ocean that unfolds in front of them, like a magic carpet, glittering with late afternoon sun.

65

Saturday, 28th September 2002

THE MOON BALL will begin in an hour's time. I'm putting the finishing touches to my make-up, a few dashes of glitter on my cheekbones, applying a little more spray paint to my hair. Jasper and I considered cancelling the party and replacing it with a far smaller celebration of Lily's birthday, but it felt right to proceed. The Rothmores are on Mustique and the Fortinis are our guests, both families insisting we go ahead. The ball will celebrate the lives of Lily's lost friends, as well as her coming of age. Tommy and Amanda will be in all our minds tonight, but her life matters too. I want her to progress confidently as she comes of age, aware that she's central to our family. I am so grateful to be here.

When I stand up from my dressing table, my costume fulfils my design perfectly. It's made of diaphanous grey silk, my hair swept into a chignon. I may not look precisely like a moonbeam, but I feel elegant, and ready for the evening. When I go downstairs, there's no sign of Jasper, but things appear to be ready. The marquee on our lawn glows like a spaceship preparing to ascend into the heavens, the tables inside loaded with delectable food and wines from all over the world.

I stand on the terrace, watching Jose Gomez testing strings of star-shaped fairy lights that adorn the trees, even though the sun still hangs above the horizon. His movements are slow and graceful as he completes the task, and I'm thrilled he's happy again. Jasper and I have rewarded his brave attempts to prove that Phillip was dangerous, to keep watch over us all. I hope that a much bigger wage will help his family. All our guests have made it in time for our moon dance to begin. I can hear distant music, as some of the world's biggest rock stars prepare to serenade Lily on Britannia beach. The ball will be just like the old days, a wave of glamorous guests flowing from one villa to the next, until our musical finale on the shore with a huge firework display.

When rapid footsteps sound behind me, I can't help jumping. My nerves are still on edge after my adventure at sea, even though my injuries have healed and a week has elapsed. It's Wesley, with a tray that bears a single drink. He's dressed in a gold jacket, glittering with sequins, the rest of his clothes in subdued black.

'Vodka tonic for you, Lady Vee, to get your evening started.'

'Thank you, that's so thoughtful. You look very handsome by the way, Wesley.'

My butler gives a narrow smile. 'Lord Blake suggested I should dress up as a shooting star, but I refused, point blank.'

Wesley marches away, in command of the situation as usual, his dignity intact. People are beginning to gather. There's no sign of Jasper but I can hear his laughter in the distance and feel relieved that he's happy tonight, prepared to live up to his nickname, the Lord of the Dance. On the far side of the lawn I clap eyes on Lily at last. She's not yet wearing her costume, which doesn't surprise me, because she and Solomon Nile have spent every spare minute together since the case ended. They've been out on her boat, checking that all her coral grafts survived the storm, and repairing any damage. He's helping her recover from her losses. I think he seems lighter too, as if he's cast aside some burden he was carrying. My own grief is harder to define. Why do I care so much about losing something that never really existed? Phillip's kindness was just another pretence, in a lifetime of play-acting. The space he left behind will fill, as time passes.

I take a sip of my drink and hear Jasper's voice again in the crowd, closer now, calling for me – I'm quite tempted to stay here but I should join the party and see what chaos he's creating now. The sun is sinking behind the horizon and I almost think I catch a flash of emerald green on the sea's surface – but no. Mustique looks absolutely beautiful, a home from home, and my heart is full of gratitude as I hurry down the steps to greet my friends.

PROLOGUE

One morning at the beginning of 2019, when I was in my London flat, the telephone rang.

'Hello?'

'Lady Glenconner? It's Helena Bonham Carter.'

It's not every day a Hollywood film star rings me up, although I had been expecting her call. When the producers of the popular Netflix series *The Crown* contacted me, saying that I was going to be portrayed by Nancy Carroll in the third series, and that Helena Bonham Carter had been cast as Princess Margaret, I was delighted. Asked whether I minded meeting them so they could get a better idea of my friendship with Princess Margaret, I said I didn't mind in the least.

Nancy Carroll came to tea, and we sat in armchairs in my sitting room and talked. The conversation was surreal as I became extremely self-aware, realising that Nancy must be absorbing what *I* was like.

A few days later when Helena was on the telephone, I invited her for tea too. Not only do I admire her as an actress but, as it happens, she is a cousin of my late husband Colin

Tennant, and her father helped me when one of my sons had a motorbike accident in the eighties.

As Helena walked through the door, I noticed a resemblance between her and Princess Margaret: she is just the right height and figure, and although her eyes aren't blue, there is a similar glint of mischievous intelligence in her gaze.

We sat down in the sitting room, and I poured her some tea. Out came her notebook, where she had written down masses of questions in order to get the measure of the Princess, 'to do her justice', she explained.

A lot of her questions were about mannerisms. When she asked how the Princess had smoked, I described it as rather like a Chinese tea ceremony: from taking her long cigarette holder out of her bag and carefully putting the cigarette in, to always lighting it herself with one of her beautiful lighters. She hated it when others offered to light it for her, and when any man eagerly advanced, she would make a small but definite gesture with her hand to make it quite clear.

I noticed that Helena moved her hand in the tiniest of reflexes, as if to test the movement I'd just described, before going on to discuss Princess Margaret's character. I tried to capture her quick wit – how she always saw the humorous side of things, not one to dwell, her attitude positive and matter-of-fact. As we talked, the descriptions felt so vivid, it was as though Princess Margaret was in the room with us. Helena listened to everything very carefully, making lots of notes. We talked for three hours, and when she left, I felt certain that she was perfectly cast for the role.

Both actors sent me letters thanking me for my help,

Helena Bonham Carter expressing the hope that Princess Margaret would be as good a friend to her as she was to me. I felt very touched by this and the thought of Princess Margaret and I being reunited on screen was something I looked forward to. I found myself reflecting back on our childhood spent together in Norfolk, the thirty years I'd been her Lady in Waiting, all the times we had found ourselves in hysterics, and the ups and downs of both our lives.

I've always loved telling stories, but it never occurred to me to write a book until these two visits stirred up all those memories. From a generation where we were taught not to over-think, not to look back or question, only now do I see how extraordinary the nine decades of my life have really been, full of extreme contrasts. I have found myself in a great many odd circumstances, both hilarious and awful, many of which seem, even to me, unbelievable. But I feel very fortunate that I have my wonderful family and for the life I have led.

CHAPTER ONE

The Greatest Disappointment

HOLKHAM HALL COMMANDS the land of North Norfolk with a hint of disdain. It is an austere house and looks its best in the depths of summer when the grass turns the colour of Demerara sugar so the park seems to merge into the house. The coast nearby is a place of harsh winds and big skies, of miles of salt marsh and dark pine forests that hem the dunes, giving way to the vast stretch of the grey-golden sand of Holkham beach: a landscape my ancestors changed from open marshes to the birthplace of agriculture. Here, in the flight path of the geese and the peewits, the Coke (pronounced 'cook') family was established in the last days of the Tudors by Sir Edward Coke, who was considered the greatest jurist of the Elizabethan and Jacobean eras, successfully prosecuting Sir Walter Raleigh and the Gunpowder

Plot conspirators. My family crest is an ostrich swallowing an iron horseshoe to symbolise our ability to digest anything.

There is a photograph of me, taken at my christening in the summer of 1932. I am held by my father, the future 5th Earl of Leicester, and surrounded by male relations wearing solemn faces. I had tried awfully hard to be a boy, even weighing eleven pounds at birth, but I was a girl and there was nothing to be done about it.

My female status meant that I would not inherit the earldom, or Holkham, the fifth largest estate in England with its 27,000 acres of top-grade agricultural land, neither the furniture, the books, the paintings, nor the silver. My parents went on to have two more children, but they were also daughters: Carey two years later and Sarah twelve years later. The line was broken, and my father must have felt the weight of almost four centuries of disapproval on his conscience.

My mother had awarded her father, the 8th Lord Hardwicke, the same fate, and maybe in solidarity, and because she thought I needed to have a strong character, she named me Anne Veronica, after H. G. Wells's book about a hardy feminist heroine. Born Elizabeth Yorke, my mother was capable, charismatic and absolutely the right sort of girl my grandfather would have expected his son to marry. She herself was the daughter of an earl, whose ancestral seat was Wimpole Hall in Cambridgeshire.

My father was handsome, popular, passionate about country pursuits, and eligible as the heir to the Leicester earldom. They met when she was fifteen and he was seventeen, during a skiing trip in St Moritz, becoming unofficially engaged immediately, he apparently having said to her, 'I just know I want to marry you.' He was also spurred on by being rather frightened of another girl who lived in Norfolk and had taken a fancy to him, so he was relieved to be able to stop her advances by declaring himself already engaged.

My mother was very attractive and very confident, and I think that's what drew my father to her. He was more reserved so she brought out the fun in him and they balanced each other well.

Together, they were one of the golden couples of high society and were great friends of the Duke and Duchess of York, who later, because of the abdication of the Duke's brother, King Edward VIII, unexpectedly became King and Queen. They were also friends with Prince Philip's sisters, Princesses Theodora, Margarita, Cecilie and Sophie, who used to come for holidays at Holkham. Rather strangely, Prince Philip, who was much younger, still only a small child, used to stay with his nanny at the Victoria, a pub right next to the beach, instead of at Holkham. Recently I asked him why he had stayed at the pub instead of the house, but he didn't know for certain, so we joked about him wanting to be as near to the beach as possible.

My parents were married in October 1931 and I was a honeymoon baby, arriving on their first wedding anniversary.

Up until I was nine, my great-grandfather was the Earl of Leicester and lived at Holkham with my grandfather, who occupied one of the four wings. The house felt enormous, especially seen through the eyes of a child. So vast, the footmen would put raw eggs in a bain-marie and take them from the kitchen to the nursery: by the time they arrived, the eggs would be perfectly boiled. We visited regularly and I adored my grandfather, who made an effort to spend time with me: we would sit in the long gallery, listening to classical music on the gramophone together, and when I was a bit older, he introduced me to photography, a passion he successfully transferred to me.

With my father in the Scots Guards, we moved all over the country, and I was brought up by nannies, who were in charge of the ins and outs of daily life. My mother didn't wash or dress me or my sister Carey; nor did she feed us or put us to bed. Instead, she would interject daily life with treats and days out.

My father found fatherhood difficult: he was strait-laced and fastidious and he was always nagging us to leave our bedroom windows open and checking to make sure we had been to the lavatory properly. I used to struggle to sit on his knee but because I was too big he would push me away in favour of Carey, whom he called 'my little dolly daydreams'.

Having grown up with Victorian parents, his childhood was typical of a boy in his position. He was brought up by nannies and governesses, sent to Eton and then on to Sandhurst, his father making sure his son knew what was expected of him as heir. He was loving, but from afar: he was not affectionate or sentimental, and did not share his emotions. No one did, not even my mother, who would give us hugs and show her affection but rarely talked about her feelings or mine – there were no heart-to-hearts. As I got older she would give me pep talks instead. It was a generation and a class who were not brought up to express emotions.

But in many other ways my mother was the complete opposite of my father. Only nineteen years older than me, she was more like a big sister, full of mischief and fun. Carey and I used to shin up trees with her and a soup ladle tied to a walking stick. With it, we would scoop up jackdaws' eggs, which were delicious to eat, rather like plovers'. Those early childhood days were filled with my mother making camps with us on the beach or taking us on trips in her little Austin, getting terribly excited as we came across ice-cream sellers on bicycles calling, 'Stop me and buy one.'

The epitome of grace and elegance when she needed to be, she also had the gumption to pursue her own hobbies, which were often rather hands-on: she was a fearless horse-woman and rode a Harley-Davidson. She passed on her love of sailing to me. I was five when I started navigating the nearby magical creeks of Burnham Overy Staithe in dinghies, and eighty when I stopped. I used to go in for local races, but I was quite often last, and would arrive only to find everyone had gone home.

Holkham was a completely male-oriented estate and the whole set-up was undeniably old-fashioned. My great-great-grandfather, the 2nd Earl, who had inherited his father's title in 1842 and was the earl when my father was a boy, was a curmudgeon and so set in his ways that even his wife had to call him 'Leicester'. When he was younger, he apparently passed a nurse with a baby in the corridor and asked, 'Whose child is that?'

The nurse had replied, 'Yours, my lord!'

A crusty old thing, he had spent his last years lying in a truckle bed in the state rooms. He wore tin-framed spectacles, and when he went outside, he would go around the park in a horse-drawn carriage, with his long-suffering second wife, who sat on a cushion strapped to a mudguard.

Influenced by the line of traditional earls, Holkham was slow to modernise, keeping distinctly separate roles for the men and women. In the summer, the ladies would go and stay in Meales House, the old manor down by the beach, for a holiday known as 'no-stays week' when they quite literally let their hair down and took off their corsets.

From when I was very little, my grandfather started to teach me about my ancestors: about how Thomas Coke, 1st Earl of Leicester in its fifth creation (the line had been broken many times, only adding to the disappointment of my father at having no sons), had gone off to Europe on a grand tour – the equivalent of an extremely lavish gap year – and shipped back dozens of paintings and marble statues from Italy that came wrapped in *Quercus ilex* leaves and acorns, the eighteenth-century answer to bubble wrap.

He told me all about when the *ilex* acorns were planted, becoming the first avenue of *ilex* trees (also called holm oak, a Mediterranean evergreen) in England. My grandfather's father had sculpted the landscape, pushing the marshes away from the house by planting the pine forests that now line Holkham beach. Before him, the 1st Earl in its seventh creation became known as 'Coke of Norfolk' because he had such a huge impact on the county through his influence on farming – he was the man credited with British agricultural reform.

Life at Holkham continued to revolve around farming the land, all elements of which were taken seriously. As well as dozens of tenant farmers, there were a great many gardeners to look after the huge kitchen garden. The brick walls were heated with fires all along, stoked through the night by the garden boys, so nectarines and peaches would ripen sooner. On hot summer days I loved riding my bike up to the kitchen gardens, being handed a peach, then cycling as fast as I could to the fountain at the front of the house and jumping into the water to cool down.

Shooting was also a huge part of Holkham life, and really what my father and all his friends lived for. It was the main bond between the Cokes and the Royal Family, especially with Sandringham only ten miles away – a mere half an hour's drive. Queen Mary had once rung my great-grandmother, suggesting she come over with the King, only for my great-grandfather to be heard bellowing, 'Come over? Good God, no! We don't want to encourage them!'

My father shot with the present Queen's father, King George VI, and my great-grandfather and grandfather with King George V on both estates, but it was Holkham that was particularly famous for shooting: it held the record for wild partridges for years and it's where covert shooting was invented (where a copse is planted in a round so that it shelters the game, the gun dogs flushing out the birds gradually, allowing for maximum control, making the shoot more efficient).

It was also where the bowler hat was invented: one of my ancestors had got so fed up with the top hat being so impractical that he went off to London and ordered a new type of hat, checking how durable it was by stamping and jumping on it until he was content. From then on game-keepers wore the 'billy coke', as it was called then.

There were other royal connections in the family too. It is well documented that Edward, Prince of Wales, later King Edward VIII, had many love affairs with married, often older glamorous aristocrats, the first being my paternal grand-mother, Marion.

My father was Equerry to the Duke of York and his sister, my aunt Lady Mary Harvey, was Lady in Waiting to the Duchess of York after she became Queen. When the Duke of York was crowned King George VI in 1937, my father became his Extra Equerry; and in 1953 my mother became a Lady of the Bedchamber, a high-ranking Lady in Waiting, to Queen Elizabeth II on her Coronation.

My father especially was a great admirer of the Royal Family and was always very attentive when they came to visit. My earliest memories of Princess Elizabeth and Princess Margaret come from when I was two or three years old. Princess Elizabeth was five years older, which was quite a lot – she was rather grown-up – but Princess Margaret was only two years older and we became firm friends. She was naughty, fun and imaginative – the very best sort of friend to have. We used to rush around Holkham, past the grand pictures, whirling through the labyrinth of corridors on our trikes or jumping out at the nursery footmen as they carried huge silver trays from the kitchen. Princess Elizabeth was much better behaved. 'Please don't do that, Margaret,' or 'You shouldn't do that, Anne,' she would scold us.

In one photograph we are all standing in a line. Princess

Elizabeth is frowning at Princess Margaret, suspecting she is up to no good, while Princess Margaret is staring down at my shoes. Years afterwards, I showed Princess Margaret the photo and asked, 'Ma'am, why were you looking at my feet?'

And she replied, 'Well, I was so jealous because you had silver shoes and I had brown ones.'

In the summer the Princesses would come down to Holkham beach where we would spend whole days making sandcastles, clad in the most unattractive and prickly black bathing suits with black rubber caps and shoes. The nannies would bundle us all into the beach bus, along with wicker picnic baskets full of sandwiches, and set up in the beach hut every day, whatever the weather – the grown-ups had a separate hut among the trees at the back. We had wonderful times, digging holes in the sand, hoping people would fall into them.

Every Christmas, my family would go to a party at Buckingham Palace, and Carey and I would be dressed up in frilly frocks and the coveted silver shoes. At the end of the parties, the children would be invited to take a present each from the big table in the hall near the Christmas tree. Behind the table stood the formidable Queen Mary, who was quite frightening. She was tall and imposing, and Princess Margaret never warmed to her because every time she saw her, Queen Mary would say, 'I can see you haven't grown.' Princess Margaret minded frightfully about being small all her life, so never liked her grandmother.

Queen Mary did teach me a valuable life lesson, however. One year Carey rushed up to the table and clasped a huge teddy bear, which was sitting upright among the other presents. Before I chose mine, Queen Mary leant down towards me. 'Anne,' she said quietly, 'quite often rather nice, rather valuable things come in little boxes.' I froze. I'd had my eye on another teddy bear but now I was far too frightened to choose anything other than a little box. Inside it was a beautiful necklace of pearl and coral. Queen Mary was quite right. My little box contained something that is still appreciated to this day.

Our connection to the Royal Family was close. When I was in my late teens, Prince Charles became like a younger brother to me, spending weeks with us all at Holkham. He would come to stay whenever he had any of the contagious childhood diseases, like chickenpox, because the Queen, having never gone to school, had not been exposed to them. Sixteen years younger than me, Prince Charles was nearer in age to my youngest sister Sarah, but all of us would go off to the beach together.

My father taught him how to fish for eel in the lake, and when he got a bit older, my mother let him drive the Jaguar and the Mini Minor around the park, something he loved doing, sending great long thank-you letters telling her he couldn't wait to return. He was such a kind and loving little boy and I've loved him ever since – the whole family have always been deeply fond of him.

As soon as I was old enough to ride, I made the park at Holkham my own, riding past the great barn, making little jumps for Kitty, my pony. When we were a bit older, Carey and I would follow one of the very good-looking tenant farmers, Gary Maufe, on our ponies. Many years later I became a great friend of his wife, Marit. He used to gallop across the park on a great big black stallion, and after him we would go on our hopeless ponies, giddying them up, desperately trying to keep up.

It wasn't just my family who were part of Holkham but everybody who worked on the estate, some of whom had very distinctive characters. Mr Patterson, the head gardener, would enthusiastically play his bagpipes in the mornings whenever my parents had friends to stay, until my mother would shout, 'That's quite enough, Mr Patterson, thank you!'

My early childhood was idyllic, but the outbreak of war in 1939 changed everything. I was seven, Carey was five. My father was posted to Egypt with the Scots Guards so my mother followed to support him, as many wives did. Holkham Hall was partly occupied by the army, and the temple in the park was used to house the Home Guard, while the gardeners and footmen were called up, and the maids and cooks went off to work in factories to help with the war effort.

Everybody thought the Germans would choose to invade Britain from the Norfolk coast, so before my mother left for Egypt, she moved Carey and me up to Scotland, to stay with my Great-aunt Bridget, away from Mr Hitler's U-boats.

When she said goodbye, she told me, 'Anne, you're in charge. You've got to look after Carey.' If we had known how long she was going to be away, it would have been even harder, but no one had any idea how long the war would last and that, in fact, she and my father would be gone for three years.